LAD
A DOG

LAD
A DOG

ALBERT PAYSON TERHUNE

GRAMERCY BOOKS
New York • Avenel

Foreword copyright © 1995 by Random House Value Publishing, Inc.
All rights reserved.

This edition is published by Random House Value Publishing, Inc.,
40 Engelhard Avenue, Avenel, New Jersey 07001.

Printed and bound in the United States of America

Library of Congress Cataloging-in-Publication Data
Terhune, Albert Payson, 1872-1942.
Lad, a dog / Albert Payson Terhune.
p.   cm.
Summary: Recounts the heroic and adventurous life of a thoroughbred
collie that was particularly devoted to his owners.
ISBN 0-517-12286-3
1. Dogs—Juvenile fiction. [1. Dogs—Fiction.] I. Title.
PZ10.3.T273Lae   1994
[Fic]—dc20   94-40309
                                                            CIP
                                                            AC

8 7 6 5 4 3 2 1

Publisher's Note: This is a complete and unabridged edition of
Lad: A Dog, edited for today's young readers.

MY BOOK IS DEDICATED
TO THE MEMORY OF

LAD

THOROUGHBRED IN BODY AND SOUL

CONTENTS

FOREWORD ix
1. HIS MATE 1
2. "QUIET" 19
3. A MIRACLE OF TWO 35
4. HIS LITTLE SON 53
5. FOR A BIT OF RIBBON 69
6. LOST! 89
7. THE THROWBACK 109
8. THE GOLD HAT 125
9. SPEAKING OF UTILITY 151
10. THE KILLER 173
11. WOLF 203
12. IN THE DAY OF BATTLE 219
AFTERWORD 237

FOREWORD

When Albert Payson Terhune wrote *Lad: A Dog,* he set out to immortalize in print the great four-legged love of his life, a thoroughbred collie named Lad At that he certainly succeeded. But in addition he created one of the greatest dog stories of all time.

Since the book was first published early in this century, countless readers have breathlessly followed the saga of the indomitable Lad, laughing at his antics, crying at his misfortunes, and cheering him on through edge-of-the-seat adventures.

Among the many dogs Terhune bred and raised, Lad was his favorite and the one he most admired. For Terhune, Lad was not only the finest, most sensitive dog that ever lived, but he was also a kind of "everydog," the supreme example of bravery, nobility, and superb instinct that was the result of thousands of years of evolution from wolf to man's best friend.

As Terhune explains in the moving Afterword to the book—in response to the many queries he had received from readers of earlier stories—Lad was indeed a real dog, and his adventures were recounted as they had really happened. It is apparent from the separate stories that became the chapters of *Lad* that Terhune was a keen observer of his canine friends—and of his fellow humans. And obviously he often admired and appreciated those four-legged creatures far more than the two-legged ones who called themselves their masters. This theme he repeated time and again, not only in *Lad: A Dog,* but also in the many other dog stories he wrote.

It was Terhune's opinion that any "man with the money to make the purchase may become a dog's *owner.* But no man—spend he ever so much coin and food and tact in the effort—may become a dog's *master* without the consent of the dog." And dogs, according to Terhune, always know from the start which humans might be sufficiently worthy of their respect to become their masters.

Terhune did believe, despite his occasional negative comments about his fellow men, that dogs embody the best instincts of both their own kind and of humankind, that they are part human, and that the "*human* side of the dog" can be seen in its "brain, fidelity, devotion."

In his dog books Terhune was not only telling marvelous yarns, but he was also acting as a passionate advocate and champion of all dogs everywhere. In the stories, he had a tendency to editorialize, sometimes not very subtly, against the mistreatment of these animals. He asked for understanding and kind treatment of strays, and he campaigned against the miserable conditions that in those days were the norm at the big national dog shows—conditions that, as he described them, constituted a form of torture and subjugation of a dog's good and noble nature.

There were several themes that Terhune touched on in *Lad* and returned to many times in his other stories. He often wrote, for example, about episodes of a dog's instinctual return to its wolf ancestry in such situations as when attacked by an enemy, be it another dog or some other, undomesticated creature. In one case, Lad is bitten by a poisonous snake and somehow knows to go to a nearby lake and bury himself in the mud until the poison passes from his system. That knowledge, Terhune felt, was most certainly a throwback to earliest times, when dogs were still wolves.

Terhune also wrote tirelessly and with endless variety about canine bravery and loyalty. Lad and other dogs who star in the books are always vigilant, sometimes to the death, in guarding the master's home and in protecting the master and his family. In one chapter in *Lad: A Dog,* Lad not only saves his mistress from drowning in an icy lake but also stands guard at her door, to the neglect of his own needs, until he knows she will survive the illness that results from her misadventure.

Terhune wrote frequently about dog families and the interesting relationships between canine mates and dog parents and children. In one touching and humorous story, Lad woos a newcomer to his master's home—the aptly named Lady, who eventually becomes his mate. As Lady plays hard to get, Terhune sympathetically observes Lad's efforts to win her affections, comparing them to courtships between men and women: "Humans—sighing swains, vow-laden suitors—can any of *you* match it . . ."

Lad: A Dog is also generously peppered with tidbits of dog lore, information, and advice about dog training and care, as well as with perceptive observations and descriptions of the people and places of a world now long gone.

What remains after the last page is turned is the love and admiration Albert Payson Terhune felt for his great collie, Lad, "who always understood," and who, from "his earliest days . . . had never forgotten he was an aristocrat among inferiors." Terhune felt this love and admiration for Lad's brother and sister dogs, as well. No reader can remain untouched by the tremendous awe he experienced in the company of these animals. And this, above all, was Terhune's great purpose—and his great accomplishment.

NAOMI KLEINBERG

New York
1995

LAD
A DOG

CHAPTER 1

HIS MATE

LADY was as much a part of Lad's everyday happiness as the sunshine itself. She seemed to him quite as perfect, and as gloriously indispensable. He could no more have imagined a Ladyless life than a sunless life. It had never occurred to him to suspect that Lady could be any less devoted than he—until Knave came to the Place.

Lad was an eighty-pound collie, thoroughbred in spirit as well as in blood. He had the benign dignity that was a heritage from endless generations of high-strain ancestors. He had, too, the gay courage of a d'Artagnan, and an uncanny wisdom. Also—who could doubt it, after a look into his mournful brown eyes—he had a soul.

His shaggy coat, set off by the snowy ruff and chest, was like orange-flecked mahogany. His absurdly tiny forepaws—in which he took inordinate pride—were silver white.

Three years earlier, when Lad was in his first prime (before the mighty chest and shoulders had filled out and the tawny coat had waxed so shaggy), Lady had been brought to the Place. She had been brought in the master's overcoat pocket, rolled up into a fuzzy gold-gray ball of softness no bigger than a half-grown kitten.

1

The master had fished the month-old puppy out of the cavern of his pocket and set her down, asprawl and shivering and squealing, on the veranda floor. Lad had walked cautiously across the veranda, sniffed inquiry at the blinking pygmy who gallantly essayed to growl defiance up at the huge welcomer—and from that first moment he had taken her under his protection.

First it had been the natural impulse of the thoroughbred—brute or human—to guard the helpless. Then, as the shapeless yellow baby grew into a slenderly graceful collie, his guardianship changed to stark adoration. He was Lady's life slave.

And she bullied him unmercifully—bossed the gentle giant in a shameful manner, crowding him from the warmest spot by the fire, brazenly yet daintily snatching from between his jaws the choicest bone of their joint dinner, hectoring her dignified victim into lawn romps in hot weather when he would far rather have drowsed under the lakeside trees.

Her vagaries, her teasing, her occasional little flurries of temper, were borne by Lad not meekly, but joyously. All she did was, in his eyes, perfect. And Lady graciously allowed herself to be idolized, for she was marvelously human in some ways. Lad, a thoroughbred descended from a hundred generations of thoroughbreds, was less human and more disinterested.

Life at the Place was wondrous pleasant for both the dogs. There were thick woods to roam in, side by side; there were squirrels to chase and rabbits to trail. (Yes, and if the squirrels had played fair and had not resorted to unsportsmanly tactics by climbing trees when close pressed, there would doubtless have been squirrels to catch as well as to chase. As for the rabbits, they were easier to overtake. And Lady got the lion's share of all such morsels.)

There was the ice-cool lake to plunge into for a swim or a wallow, after a run in the dust and July heat. There was a deliciously comfortable old rug in front of the living room's open fire whereon to lie, shoulder to shoulder, on the nights when the wind screamed through bare trees and the snow scratched hungrily at the panes.

Best of all, to them both, there were the master and the mistress; especially the mistress.

Any man with money to make the purchase may become a dog's *owner*. But no man—spend he ever so much coin and food and tact in the effort—may become a dog's *master* without the consent of the dog. Do you get the difference? And he whom a dog once unreservedly accepts as master is forever that dog's God.

To both Lad and Lady, from the first, the man who bought them was not the mere owner but the absolute master. To them he was the unquestioned lord of life and death, the hearer and answerer, the Eternal Law; his the voice that must be obeyed, whatever the command.

From earliest puppyhood, both Lad and Lady had been brought up within the Law. As far back as they could remember, they had known and obeyed the Place's simple code.

For example: All animals of the woods might lawfully be chased; but the mistress's prize chickens and the other little folk of the Place must be ignored no matter how hungry or how playful a collie might chance to be. A human, walking openly or riding down the drive into the Place by daylight, must not be barked at except by way of friendly announcement. But anyone entering the grounds from other ingress than the drive, or anyone walking furtively or with a thief's slouch, must be attacked at sight.

Also, the interior of the house was sacrosanct. It was a place for perfect behavior. No rug must be scratched, nothing gnawed or played with. In fact, Lady's one whipping had followed a puppy frolic effort of hers to "worry" the huge stuffed bald eagle that stood on a papier-maché stump in the master's study, just off the big living room where the fireplace was.

That eagle, shot by himself as it raided the flock of prize chickens, was the delight of the master's heart. And at Lady's attempt on it, he had taught her a lesson that made her cringe for weeks thereafter at bare sight of the dogwhip. To this day, she would never walk past the eagle without making the widest possible detour around it.

But that punishment had been suffered while she was still in the idiotic days of puppyhood. After she was grown, Lady would no more have thought of tampering with the eagle or with anything else in the house than it would occur to a human to stand on his head in church.

Then, early one spring, came Knave—a showy, magnificent collie, red-gold of coat save for a black "saddle," and with alert topaz eyes.

Knave did not belong to the master, but to a man who, going to Europe for a month, asked him to care for the dog in his absence. The master, glad to have so beautiful an ornament to the Place, had willingly consented. He was rewarded when, on the train from town, an admiring crowd of commuters flocked to the baggage car to stare at the splendid-looking collie.

The only dissenting note in the praise chorus was the grouchy old baggage man's.

"Maybe he's a thoroughbred, like you say," drawled the old fellow to the master, "but I never yet saw a yellow-eyed, prick-eared dog I'd give hell-room to."

Knave showed his scorn for such silly criticism by a cavernous yawn.

"Thoroughbred?" grunted the baggage man. "With them streaks of pinkish-yeller on the roof of his mouth? Ever see a thoroughbred that didn't have a black mouth-roof?"

But the old man's slighting words were ignored with disdain by the crowd of volunteer dog experts in the baggage car. In time the master alighted at his station, with Knave straining joyously at the leash. As the master reached the Place and turned into the drive, both Lad and Lady, at sound of his far-off footsteps, came tearing around the side of the house to greet him.

On simultaneous sight and scent of the strange dog frisking along at his side, the two collies paused in their madly joyous onrush. Up went their ruffs. Down went their heads.

Lady flashed forward to do battle with the stranger who was monopolizing so much of the master's attention. Knave, not at all averse to battle (especially with a smaller dog), braced himself and then moved forward, stiff-legged, fangs bare.

But of a sudden his head went up; his stiff-poised brush broke into swift wagging; his lips curled down. He had recognized that his prospective foe was not of his own sex. (And nowhere, except among humans, does a full-grown male ill-treat or even defend himself against the female of his species.)

Lady, noting the stranger's sudden friendliness, paused irresolute in her charge. And at that instant Lad darted past her. Full at Knave's throat he launched himself.

The master rasped out, "Down, Lad! *Down!*"

Almost in midair the collie arrested his onset—coming to earth bristling, furious and yet with no thought but to obey. Knave, seeing his foe was not going to fight, turned once more toward Lady.

"Lad," ordered the master, pointing toward Knave and speaking with quiet intentness, "let him alone. Understand? Let him *alone.*"

And Lad understood—even as years of training and centuries of ancestry had taught him to understand every spoken wish of the master's. He must give up his impulse to make war on this intruder whom at sight he hated. It was the Law; and from the Law there was no appeal.

With yearningly helpless rage he looked on while the newcomer was installed on the Place. With a wondering sorrow he found himself forced to share the master's and mistress's caresses with this interloper. With growing pain he submitted to Knave's gay attentions to Lady, and to Lady's evident relish of the guest's companionship. Gone were the peaceful old days of utter contentment.

Lady had always regarded Lad as her own special property—to tease and to boss and to despoil of choice food bits. But her attitude toward Knave was far different. She coquetted, human fashion, with the gold-and-black dog—at one moment affecting to scorn him, at another meeting his advances with a delighted friendliness.

She never presumed to boss him as she had always bossed Lad. He fascinated her. Without seeming to follow him about, she was forever at his heels. Lad, cut to the heart at her sudden indifference toward his loyal self, tried in every way his simple soul could devise to win back her interest. He essayed clumsily to romp with her as the lithely graceful Knave romped, to drive rabbits for her on their woodland rambles, to thrust himself, in a dozen gentle ways, upon her attention.

But it was no use. Lady scarcely noticed him. When his overtures of friendship chanced to annoy her, she rewarded them with a snap or with an impatient growl. And ever she turned to the all-conquering Knave in a keenness of attraction that was all but hypnotic.

As his divinity's total loss of interest in himself grew too apparent to be doubted, Lad's big heart broke. Being only a dog, and a Grail knight in thought, he did not realize that Knave's newness and his difference from anything she had known, formed a large part of Lady's desire for the visitor's favor; nor did he understand that such interest must wane when the novelty should wear off.

All Lad knew was that he loved her, and that for the sake of a flashy stranger she was snubbing him.

As the Law forbade him to avenge himself in true dog fashion by fighting for his Lady's love, Lad sadly withdrew from the unequal contest, too proud to compete for a fickle sweetheart. No longer did he try to join in the others' lawn romps, but lay at a distance, his splendid head between his snowy little forepaws, his brown eyes sick with sorrow, watching their gambols.

Nor did he thrust his undesired presence on them during their woodland rambles. He took to moping, solitary, infinitely miserable. Perhaps there is on earth something unhappier than a bitterly aggrieved dog. But no one has ever discovered that elusive something.

Knave from the first had shown and felt for Lad a scornful indifference. Not understanding the Law, he had set down the older collie's refusal to fight as a sign of exemplary, if timorous prudence, and he looked down upon him accordingly. One day Knave came home from the morning run through the forest without Lady. Neither the master's calls nor the ear-ripping blasts of his dog whistle could bring her back to the Place. Whereat Lad arose heavily from his favorite resting place under the living room piano and cantered off to the woods. Nor did he return.

Several hours later the master went to the woods to investigate, followed by the rollicking Knave. At the forest edge the master shouted. A far-off bark from Lad answered. And the master made his way through shoulder-deep underbrush in the direction of the sound.

In a clearing he found Lady, her left forepaw caught in the steel jaws of a fox trap. Lad was standing protectingly above her, stooping now and then to lick her cruelly pinched foot or to whine consolation to her; then snarling in fierce hate at a score of crows that flapped hopefully in the treetops above the victim.

The master set Lady free, and Knave frisked forward right joyously to greet his released inamorata. But Lady was in no condition to play—then nor for many a day thereafter. Her forefoot was so lacerated and swollen that she was fain to hobble awkwardly on three legs for the next fortnight.

It was on one pantingly hot August morning, a little later, that Lady limped into the house in search of a cool spot where she might lie and lick her throbbing forefoot. Lad was lying, as usual, under the piano in the living room. His tail thumped shy welcome on the hardwood floor as she passed, but she would not stay or so much as notice him.

On she limped, into the master's study, where an open window sent a faint breeze through the house. Giving the stuffed eagle a wide berth, Lady hobbled to the window and made as though to lie down just beneath it. As she did so, two things happened: she leaned too much weight on the sore foot, and the pressure wrung from her an involuntary yelp of pain; at the same moment a crosscurrent of air from the other side of the house swept through the living room and blew shut the door of the adjoining study. Lady was a prisoner.

Ordinarily this would have caused her no ill ease, for the open window was only thirty inches above the floor, and the drop to the veranda outside was a bare three feet. It would have been the simplest matter in the world for her to jump out, had she wearied of her chance captivity.

But to undertake the jump with the prospect of landing her full weight and impetus on a forepaw that was horribly sensitive to the lightest touch—this was an exploit beyond the sufferer's willpower. So Lady resigned herself to imprisonment. She curled herself up on the floor as far as possible from the eagle, moaned softly and lay still.

At sound of her first yelp, Lad had run forward, whining eager sympathy. But the closed door blocked his way. He crouched, wretched and anxious, before it, helpless to go to his loved one's assistance.

Knave, too, loping back from a solitary prowl of the woods, seeking Lady, heard the yelp. His prick-ears located the sound at once. Along the veranda he trotted, to the open study window. With a bound he had cleared the sill and alighted inside the room.

It chanced to be his first visit to the study. The door was usually kept shut, that drafts might not blow the master's desk papers about. And Knave felt, at best, little interest in exploring the interior of houses. He was an outdoor dog, by choice.

He advanced now toward Lady, his tail awag, his head on one side, with his most irresistible air. Then, as he came forward into the room, he saw the eagle. He halted in wonder at sight of the enormous white-crested bird with its six-foot sweep of pinion. It was a wholly novel spectacle to Knave, and he greeted it with a gruff bark, half of fear, half of bravado. Quickly, however, his sense of smell told him this wide-winged apparition was no living thing. And ashamed of his momentary cowardice, he went over to investigate it.

As he went, Knave cast over his shoulder a look of invitation to Lady to join him in his inspection. She understood the invitation, but memory of that puppyhood beating made her recoil from accepting it. Knave saw her shrink back, and he realized with a thrill that she was actually afraid of this lifeless thing which could harm no one. With due pride in showing off his own heroism before her, and with the scamp dog's innate craving to destroy, he sprang growling upon the eagle.

Down tumbled the papier-maché stump. Down crashed the huge stuffed bird with it; Knave's white teeth buried deep in the soft feathers of its breast.

Lady, horror-struck at this sacrilege, whimpered in terror. But her plaint served only to increase Knave's zest for destruction.

He hurled the bird to the floor, pinned it down with his feet and at one jerk tore the right wing from the body. Coughing out the mouthful of dusty pinions, he dug his teeth into the eagle's throat. Again bracing himself with his forelegs on the carcass, he gave a sharp tug. Head and neck came away in his mouth. And then before he could drop the mouthful and return to the work of demolition, he heard the master's step.

All at once, now, Knave proved he was less ignorant of the Law —or, at least, of its penalties—than might have been supposed from his act of vandalism. In sudden panic he bolted for the window, the silvery head of the eagle still, unheeded, between his jaws. With a vaulting spring, he shot out through the open casement, in his reckless eagerness to escape, knocking against Lady's injured leg as he passed.

He did not pause at Lady's scream of pain, nor did he stop until he reached the chicken house. Crawling under this, he deposited the incriminating eagle head in the dark recess. Finding no pursuer, he emerged and jogged innocently back toward the veranda.

The master, entering the house and walking across the living room toward the stairs, heard Lady's cry. He looked around for her, recognizing from the sound that she must be in distress. His eye fell on Lad, crouching tense and eager in front of the shut study door.

The master opened the door and went into the study.

At the first step inside the room he stopped, aghast. There lay the chewed and battered fragments of his beloved eagle. And there, in one corner, frightened, with guilt writ plain all over her, cowered Lady. Men have been "legally" done to death on far lighter evidence than encompassed her.

The master was thunderstruck. For more than two years Lady

had had the free run of the house. And this was her first sin—at that, a sin unworthy any well-bred dog that has graduated from puppyhood and from milk teeth. He would not have believed it. He *could* not have believed it. Yet here was the hideous evidence, scattered all over the floor.

The door was shut, but the window stood wide. Through the window, doubtless, she had gotten into the room. And he had surprised her at her vandal-work before she could escape by the same opening.

The master was a just man—as humans go; but this was a crime the most maudlin dog spoiler could not have condoned. The eagle, moreover, had been the pride of his heart—as perhaps I have said. Without a word, he walked to the wall and took down a braided dogwhip, dust-covered from long disuse.

Lady knew what was coming. Being a thoroughbred, she did not try to run, nor did she roll for mercy. She cowered, moveless, nose to floor, awaiting her doom.

Back swished the lash. Down it came, whistling as a man whistles whose teeth are broken. Across Lady's slender flanks it smote, with the full force of a strong driving arm. Lady quivered all over. But she made no sound. She who would whimper at a chance touch to her sore foot, was mute under human punishment.

But Lad was not mute. As the master's arm swung back for a second blow, he heard, just behind, a low, throaty growl that held all the menace of ten thousand wordy threats.

He wheeled about. Lad was close at his heels, fangs bared, eyes red, head lowered, tawny body taut in every sinew.

The master blinked at him, incredulous. Here was something infinitely more unbelievable than Lady's supposed destruction of the eagle. The impossible had come to pass.

For, know well, a dog does not growl at its master. At its owner, perhaps; at its master, never. As soon would a devout priest blaspheme his deity.

Nor does a dog approach anything or anybody, growling and with lowered head, unless intent on battle. Have no fear when a dog barks or even growls at you, so long as his head is erect. But when he growls and lowers his head—then look out. It means but one thing.

The master had been the master—the sublime, blindly revered and worshiped master—for all the blameless years of Lad's life. And now, growling, head down, the dog was threatening him.

It was the supreme misery, the crowning hell, of Lad's career. For the first time, two overpowering loves fought with each other in his Galahad soul. And the love for poor, unjustly blamed, Lady hurled down the superlove for the master.

In baring teeth upon his lord, the collie well knew what he was incurring. But he did not flinch. Understanding that swift death might well be his portion, he stood his ground.

(Is there greater love? Humans—sighing swains, vow-laden suitors—can any of *you* match it? I think not. Not even the much-lauded Antonys. They throw away only the mere world of earthly credit, for love.)

The master's jaw set. He was well-nigh as unhappy as the dog. For he grasped the situation, and he was man enough to honor Lad's proffered sacrifice. Yet it must be punished, and punished instantly—as any dog master will testify. Let a dog once growl or show his teeth in menace at his master, and if the rebellion be not put down in drastic fashion, the master ceases forever to be master and degenerates to mere owner. His mysterious power over his dog is gone for all time.

Turning his back on Lady, the master whirled his dogwhip in air. Lad saw the lash coming down. He did not flinch. He did not cower. The growl ceased. The orange-tawny collie stood erect. Down came the braided whiplash on Lad's shoulders—again over his loins, and yet again and again.

Without moving—head up, dark tender eyes unwinking—the hero-dog took the scourging. When it was over, he waited only to see the master throw the dogwhip fiercely into a corner of the study. Then, knowing Lady was safe, Lad walked majestically back to his "cave" under the piano, and with a long, quivering sigh he lay down.

His spirit was sick and crushed within him. For the first time in his thoroughbred life he had been struck. For he was one of those not wholly rare dogs to whom a sharp word of reproof is more effective than a beating—to whom a blow is not a pain, but a damning and overwhelming ignominy. Had a human, other than the master, presumed to strike him, the assailant must have fought for life.

Through the numbness of Lad's grief, bit by bit, began to smolder and glow a deathless hate for Knave, the cause of Lady's humiliation. Lad had known what passed behind that closed study door as well as though he had seen. For ears and scent serve a true collie quite as usefully as do mere eyes.

The master was little happier than was his favorite dog. For he loved Lad as he would have loved a human son. Though Lad did not realize it, the master had let off Lady from the rest of her beating, in order not to increase her champion's grief. He simply ordered her out of the study.

And as she limped away, the master tried to rekindle his own indignation and deaden his sense of remorse by gathering together the strewn fragments of the eagle. It occurred to him that though the bird was destroyed, he might yet have its fierce-eyed silvery head mounted on a board, as a minor trophy.

But he could not find the head.

Search the study as he would, he could not find it. He remembered distinctly that Lady had been panting as she slunk out of the room. And dogs that are carrying things in their mouths cannot pant. She had not taken the head away with her. The absence of the head only deepened the whole annoying domestic mystery. He gave up trying to solve any of the puzzle—from Lady's incredible vandalism to this newest turn of the affair.

Not until two days later could Lad bring himself to risk a meeting with Lady, the cause and the witness of his beating. Then, yearning for a sight of her and for even her grudged recognition of his presence, after his forty-eight hours of isolation, he sallied forth from the house in search of her.

He traced her to the cool shade of a lilac clump near the outbuildings. There, having with one paw dug a little pit in the cool earth, she was curled up asleep under the bushes. Stretched out beside her was Knave.

Lad's spine bristled at sight of his foe. But ignoring him, he moved over to Lady and touched her nose with his own in timid caress. She opened one eye, blinked drowsily and went to sleep again.

But Lad's coming had awakened Knave. Much refreshed by his nap, he woke in playful mood. He tried to induce Lady to romp with him, but she preferred to doze. So, casting about in his shallow mind for something to play with, Knave chanced to remember the prize he had hidden beneath the chicken house.

Away he ambled, returning presently with the eagle's head between his teeth. As he ran, he tossed it aloft, catching it as it fell—a pretty trick he had long since learned with a tennis ball.

Lad, who had lain down as near to sleepily scornful Lady as he dared, looked up and saw him approach. He saw, too, with what Knave was playing; and as he saw, he went quite mad. Here was the thing that had caused Lady's interrupted punishment and his own black disgrace. Knave was exploiting it with manifest and brazen delight.

For the second time in his life—and for the second time in three days—Lad broke the Law. He forgot, in a trice, the command "Let him alone!" And noiseless, terrible, he flew at the gamboling Knave.

Knave was aware of the attack, barely in time to drop the eagle's head and spring forward to meet his antagonist. He was three years Lad's junior and was perhaps five pounds heavier. Moreover, constant exercise had kept him in steel-and-whalebone condition; while lonely brooding at home had begun of late to soften Lad's tough sinews.

Knave was mildly surprised that the dog he had looked on as a dullard and a poltroon should have developed a flash of spirit. But he was not at all unwilling to wage a combat whose victory must make him shine with redoubled glory in Lady's eyes.

Like two furry whirlwinds the collies spun forward toward

each other. They met, upreared and snarled, slashing wolf-like for the throat, clawing madly to retain balance. Then down they went, rolling in a right unloving embrace, snapping, tearing, growling.

Lad drove straight for the throat. A half-handful of Knave's golden ruff came away in his jaws. For except at the exact center, a collie's throat is protected by a tangle of hair as effective against assault as were Andrew Jackson's cotton-bale breastworks at New Orleans. And Lad had missed the exact center.

Over and over they rolled. They regained their footing and reared again. Lad's saber-shaped tusk ripped a furrow in Knave's satiny forehead; and Knave's half deflected slash in return set bleeding the big vein at the top of Lad's left ear.

Lady was wide awake long before this. Standing immovable, yet wildly excited—after the age-old fashion of the female brute for whom males battle and who knows she is to be the winner's prize— she watched every turn of the fight.

Up once more, the dogs clashed, chest to chest. Knave, with an instinctive throwback to his wolf forebears of five hundred years earlier, dived for Lad's forelegs with the hope of breaking one of them between his foaming jaws.

He missed the hold by a fraction of an inch. The skin alone was torn. And down over the little white forepaw—one of the forepaws that Lad was wont to lick for an hour a day to keep them snowy— ran a trickle of blood.

That miss was a costly error for Knave. For Lad's teeth sought and found his left shoulder, and sank deep therein. Knave twisted and wheeled with lightning speed and with all his strength. Yet had not his gold-hued ruff choked Lad and pressed stranglingly against his nostrils, all the heavier dog's struggles would not have set him free.

As it was, Lad, gasping for breath enough to fill his lungs, relaxed his grip ever so slightly. And in that fraction of a second Knave tore free, leaving a mouthful of hair and skin in his enemy's jaws.

In the same wrench that liberated him—and as the relieved tension sent Lad stumbling forward—Knave instinctively saw his chance and took it. Again heredity came to his aid, for he tried a maneuver known only to wolves and to collies. Flashing above his stumbling foe's head, Knave seized Lad from behind, just below the base of the skull. And holding him thus helpless, he proceeded to grit and grind his tight-clenched teeth in the slow, relentless motion that must soon or late eat down to and sever the spinal cord.

Lad, even as he thrashed frantically about, felt there was no escape. He was well-nigh as powerless against a strong opponent in this position as is a puppy that is held up by the scruff of the neck.

Without a sound, but still struggling as best he might, he awaited his fate. No longer was he growling or snarling.

His patient, bloodshot eyes sought wistfully for Lady. And they did not find her.

For even as they sought her, a novel element entered into the battle. Lady, hitherto awaiting with meekness the outcome of the scrimmage, saw her old flame's terrible plight, under the grinding jaws. And, proving herself false to all canons of ancestry—moved by some impulse she did not try to resist—she jumped forward. Forgetting the pain in her swollen foot, she nipped Knave sharply in the hind leg. Then, as if abashed by her behavior, she drew back, in shame.

But the work was done.

Through the red war lust Knave dimly realized that he was attacked from behind—perhaps that his new opponent stood an excellent chance of gaining upon him such a death hold as he himself now held.

He loosed his grip and whizzed about, frothing and snapping, to face the danger. Before Knave had half completed his lightning whirl, Lad had him by the side of the throat.

It was no death grip, this. Yet it was not only acutely painful, but it held its victim quite as powerless as he had just now held

Lad. Bearing down with all his weight and setting his white little front teeth and his yellowing tusks firmly in their hold, Lad gradually shoved Knave's head sideways to the ground and held it there.

The result on Knave's activities was much the same as is obtained by sitting on the head of a kicking horse that has fallen. Unable to wrench loose, helpless to counter, in keen agony from the pinching of the tender throat skin beneath the masses of ruff, Knave lost his nerve. And he forthwith justified those yellowish streaks in his mouth roof whereof the baggage man had spoken.

He made the air vibrate with his abject howls of pain and fear. He was caught. He could not get away. Lad was hurting him horribly. Wherefore he ki-yi-ed as might any gutter cur whose tail is stepped upon.

Presently, beyond the fight haze, Lad saw a shadow in front of him—a shadow that resolved itself in the settling dust, as the master. And Lad came to himself.

He loosed his hold on Knave's throat, and stood up, groggily. Knave, still yelping, tucked his tail between his legs and fled for his life—out of the Place, out of your story.

Slowly, stumblingly, but without a waver of hesitation, Lad went up to the master. He was gasping for breath, and he was weak from fearful exertion and from loss of blood. Up to the master he went—straight up to him.

And not until he was a scant two yards away did he see that the master held something in his hand—that abominable, mischief-making eagle's head, which he had just picked up! Probably the dogwhip was in the other hand. It did not matter much. Lad was ready for this final degradation. He would not try to dodge it, he the double breaker of laws.

Then—the master was kneeling beside him. The kind hand was caressing the dog's dizzy head, the dear voice—a queer break in it —was saying remorsefully, "Oh Lad! Laddie! I'm so sorry. So sorry! You're—you're more of a man than I am, old friend. I'll make it up to you, somehow!"

And now besides the loved hand, there was another touch, even more precious—a warmly caressing little pink tongue that licked his bleeding foreleg.

Lady—timidly, adoringly—was trying to stanch her hero's wounds.

"Lady, I apologize to you too," went on the foolish master. "I'm sorry, girl."

Lady was too busy soothing the hurts of her newly discovered mate to understand. But Lad understood. Lad always understood.

CHAPTER 2

"QUIET"

To Lad the real world was bounded by the Place. Outside, there were a certain number of miles of land and there were an uncertain number of people. But the miles were uninspiring, except for a cross-country tramp with the master. And the people were foolish and strange folk who either stared at him—which always annoyed Lad—or else tried to pat him; which he hated. But the Place was— the Place.

Always, he had lived on the Place. He felt he owned it. It was assuredly his to enjoy, to guard, to patrol from high road to lake. It was his world.

The denizens of every world must have at least one deity to worship. Lad had one: the master. Indeed, he had two: the master and the mistress. And because the dog was strong of soul and chivalric, withal, and because the mistress was altogether lovable, Lad placed her altar even above the master's. Which was wholly as it should have been.

There were other people at the Place—people to whom a dog must be courteous, as becomes a thoroughbred, and whose caresses he must accept. Very often, there were guests, too. And from

19

puppyhood, Lad had been taught the sacredness of the Guest Law. Civilly, he would endure the pettings of these visiting outlanders. Gravely, he would shake hands with them, on request. He would even permit them to paw him or haul him about, if they were of the obnoxious, dog-mauling breed. But the moment politeness would permit, he always withdrew, very quietly, from their reach and, if possible, from their sight as well.

Of all the dogs on the Place, big Lad alone had free run of the house, by day and by night.

He slept in a "cave" under the piano. He even had access to the sacred dining room, at mealtimes—where always he lay to the left of the master's chair.

With the master, he would willingly unbend for a romp at any or all times. At the mistress's behest he would play with all the silly abandon of a puppy; rolling on the ground at her feet, making as though to seize and crush one of her little shoes in his mighty jaws; wriggling and waving his legs in air when she buried her hand in the masses of his chest-ruff; and otherwise comporting himself with complete loss of dignity.

But to all except these two, he was calmly unapproachable. From his earliest days he had never forgotten he was an aristocrat among inferiors. And, calmly aloof, he moved among his subjects.

Then, all at once, into the sweet routine of the house of peace, came horror.

It began on a blustery, sour October day. The mistress had crossed the lake to the village, in her canoe, with Lad curled up in a furry heap in the prow. On the return trip, about fifty yards from shore, the canoe struck sharply and obliquely against a half-submerged log that a fall freshet had swept down from the river above the lake. At the same moment a flaw of wind caught the canoe's quarter. And, after the manner of such eccentric craft, the canvas shell proceeded to turn turtle.

Into the ice-chill waters splashed its two occupants. Lad bobbed to the top, and glanced around at the mistress to learn if this were a new practical joke. But, instantly, he saw it was no joke at all, so far as she was concerned.

Swathed and cramped by the folds of her heavy outing skirt, the mistress was making no progress shoreward. And the dog flung himself through the water toward her with a rush that left his shoulders and half his back above the surface. In a second he had reached her and had caught her sweater-shoulder in his teeth.

She had the presence of mind to lie out straight, as though she were floating, and to fill her lungs with a swift intake of breath. The dog's burden was thus made infinitely lighter than if she had struggled or had lain in a posture less easy for towing. Yet he made scant headway, until she wound one hand in his mane, and, still lying motionless and stiff, bade him loose his hold on her shoulder.

In this way, by sustained effort that wrenched every giant muscle in the collie's body, they came at last to land.

Vastly rejoiced was Lad, and inordinately proud of himself. And the plaudits of the master and the mistress were music to him. Indefinably, he understood he had done a very wonderful thing and that everybody on the Place was talking about him, and that all were trying to pet him at once.

This promiscuous handling he began to find unwelcome. And he retired at last to his "cave" under the piano to escape from it. Matters soon quieted down, and the incident seemed at an end.

Instead, it had just begun.

For, within an hour, the mistress—who, for days had been half-sick with a cold—was stricken with a chill, and by night she was in the first stages of pneumonia.

Then over the Place descended gloom—a gloom Lad could not understand until he went upstairs at dinnertime to escort the mistress, as usual, to the dining room. But to his light scratch at her door there was no reply. He scratched again and presently master came out of the room and ordered him downstairs again.

Then from the master's voice and look, Lad understood that something was terribly amiss. Also, as she did not appear at dinner and as he was for the first time in his life forbidden to go into her room, he knew the mistress was the victim of whatever mishap had befallen.

A strange man, with a black bag, came to the house early in the evening; and he and the master were closeted for an interminable time in the mistress's room. Lad had crept dejectedly upstairs behind them, and sought to crowd into the room at their heels. The master ordered him back and shut the door in his face.

Lad lay down on the threshold, his nose to the crack at the bottom of the door, and waited. He heard the murmur of speech.

Once he caught the mistress's voice—changed and muffled and with a puzzling new note in it—but undeniably the mistress's. And his tail thumped hopefully on the hall floor. But no one came to let him in. And, after the mandate to keep out, he dared not scratch for admittance.

The doctor almost stumbled across the couchant body of the dog as he left the room with the master. Being a dog owner himself, the doctor understood and his narrow escape from a fall over the living obstacle did not irritate him. But it reminded him of something.

"Those other dogs of yours outside there," he said to the master, as they went down the stairs, "raised a fearful racket when my car came down the drive, just now. Better send them all away somewhere till she is better. The house must be kept perfectly quiet."

The master looked back, up the stairway; at its top, pressed close against the mistress's door, crouched Lad. Something in the dog's heartbroken attitude touched him.

"I'll send them over to the boarding kennels in the morning," he answered. "All except Lad. He and I are going to see this through, together. He'll be quiet, if I tell him to."

All through the endless night, while the October wind howled and yelled around the house, Lad lay outside the sickroom door, his nose between his absurdly small white paws, his sorrowful eyes wide open, his ears alert for the faintest sound from the room beyond.

Sometimes, when the wind screamed its loudest, Lad would lift his head—his ruff abristle, his teeth glinting from under his upcurled lip. And he would growl a throaty menace. It was as though he heard, in the tempest's racket, the strife of evil gale spirits to burst in through the rattling windows and attack the stricken mistress. Perhaps—well, perhaps there are things visible and audible to dogs, to which humans are deaf and blind. Or perhaps they are not.

Lad was there when day broke and when the master, heavy-eyed from sleeplessness, came out. He was there when the other dogs were herded into the car and carried away to the boarding kennels.

Lad was there when the car came back from the station, bringing to the Place an angular, wooden-faced woman with yellow hair and a yellower suitcase—a horrible woman who vaguely smelt of disinfectants and of rigid efficiency, and who presently approached the sickroom, clad and capped in stiff white. Lad hated her.

He was there when the doctor came for his morning visit to the invalid. And again he tried to edge his own way into the room, only to be rebuffed once more.

"This is the third time I've nearly broken my neck over that miserable dog," chidingly announced the nurse, later in the day, as she came out of the room and chanced to meet the master on the landing. "Do please drive him away. I've tried to do it, but he only snarls at me. And in a dangerous case like this—"

"Leave him alone," briefly ordered the master.

But when the nurse, sniffing, passed on, he called Lad over to him. Reluctantly, the dog quitted the door and obeyed the summons.

"Quiet!" ordered the master, speaking very slowly and distinctly. "You must keep quiet. Quiet! Understand?"

Lad understood. Lad always understood. He must not bark. He must move silently. He must make no unnecessary sound. But, at least, the master had not forbidden him to snarl softly and loathingly at that detestable white-clad woman every time she stepped over him.

So there was one grain of comfort.

Gently, the master called him downstairs and across the living room, and put him out of the house. For, after all, a shaggy eighty-pound dog is an inconvenience stretched across a sickroom doorsill.

Three minutes later, Lad had made his way through an open window into the cellar and thence upstairs; and was stretched out, head between paws, at the threshold of the mistress's room.

On his thrice-a-day visits, the doctor was forced to step over him, and was man enough to forbear to curse. Twenty times a day, the nurse stumbled over his massive, inert body, and fumed in impotent rage. The master, too, came back and forth from the sickroom, with now and then a kindly word for the suffering collie, and again and again put him out of the house.

But always Lad managed, by hook or crook, to be back on guard within a minute or two. And never once did the door of the mistress's room open that he did not make a strenuous attempt to enter.

Servants, nurse, doctor, and master repeatedly forgot he was there, and stubbed their toes across his body. Sometimes their feet drove agonizingly into his tender flesh. But never a whimper or growl did the pain wring from him. *"Quiet!"* had been the command, and he was obeying.

And so it went on, through the awful days and the infinitely worse nights. Except when he was ordered away by the master, Lad would not stir from his place at the door. And not even the master's authority could keep him away from it for five minutes a day.

The dog ate nothing, drank practically nothing, took no exercise; moved not one inch, of his own will, from the doorway. In vain did the glories of autumn woods call to him. The rabbits would be thick, out yonder in the forest, just now. So would the squirrels—against which Lad had long since sworn a blood feud (and one of which it had ever been his futile life ambition to catch).

For him, these things no longer existed. Nothing existed; except his mortal hatred of the unseen Something in that forbidden room—the something that was seeking to take the mistress away with it. He yearned unspeakably to be in that room to guard her from her nameless peril. And they would not let him in—these humans.

Wherefore he lay there, crushing his body close against the door and—waiting.

And, inside the room, death and the Napoleonic man with the black bag fought their no-quarter duel for the life of the still, little white figure in the great white bed.

One night, the doctor did not go home at all. Toward dawn the master lurched out of the room and sat down for a moment on the stairs, his face in his hands. Then and then only, during all that time of watching, did Lad leave the doorsill of his own accord.

Shaky with famine and weariness, he got to his feet, moaning softly, and crept over to the master; he lay down beside him, his huge head athwart the man's knees, his muzzle reaching timidly toward the tight-clenched hands.

Presently the master went back into the sickroom. And Lad was left alone in the darkness—to wonder and to listen and to wait. With a tired sigh he returned to the door and once more took up his heartsick vigil.

Then—on a golden morning, days later, the doctor came and went with the look of a conqueror. Even the wooden-faced nurse forgot to grunt in disgust when she stumbled across the dog's body. She almost smiled. And presently the master came out through the doorway. He stopped at sight of Lad, and turned back into the room. Lad could hear him speak. And he heard a dear, *dear* voice make answer; very weakly, but no longer in that muffled and foreign tone which had so frightened him. Then came a sentence the dog could understand.

"Come in, old friend," said the master, opening the door and standing aside for Lad to enter.

At a bound, the collie was in the room. There lay the mistress. She was very thin, very white, very feeble. But she was there. The dread something had lost the battle.

Lad wanted to break forth into a peal of ecstatic barking that would have deafened everyone in the room. The master read the wish and interposed, *"Quiet!"*

Lad heard. He controlled the yearning. But it cost him a world of willpower to do it. As sedately as he could force himself to move, he crossed to the bed.

The mistress was smiling at him. One hand was stretched weakly forth to stroke him. And she was saying almost in a whisper, "Lad! Laddie!"

That was all. But her hand was petting him in the dear way he loved so well. And the master was telling her all over again how the dog had watched outside her door. Lad listened—not to the man's praise, but to the woman's caressing whisper—and he quivered from head to tail. He fought furiously with himself once again, to choke back the rapturous barking that clamored for utterance. He knew this was no time for noise. Even without the word of warning, he would have known it. For the mistress was whispering. Even the master was speaking scarce louder.

But one thing Lad realized: the black danger was past. The mistress was alive! And the whole house was smiling. That was enough. And the yearning to show, in noise, his own wild relief, was all but irresistible. Then the master said, "Run on, Lad. You can come back by-and-by."

And the dog gravely made his way out of the room and out of the house.

The minute he was out-of-doors, he proceeded to go crazy. Nothing but sheer mania could excuse his actions during the rest of that day. They were unworthy of a mongrel puppy. And never before in all his blameless, stately life had Lad so grossly misbehaved as he now proceeded to do. The mistress was alive. The horror was past. Reaction set in with a rush. As I have said, Lad went crazy.

Peter Grimm, the mistress's cynical and temperamental gray cat, was picking its dainty way across the lawn as Lad emerged from the house.

Ordinarily, Lad regarded Peter Grimm with a cold tolerance. But now, he dashed at the cat with a semblance of stark wrath. Like a furry whirlwind he bore down upon the amazed feline. The cat, in dire offense, scratched his nose with a quite unnecessary virulence and fled up a tree, spitting and yowling, tail fluffed out as thick as a man's wrist.

Seeing that Peter Grimm had resorted to unsportsmanly tactics by scrambling whither he could not follow, Lad remembered the need for silence and forbore to bark threats at his escaped victim. Instead, he galloped to the rear of the house where stood the dairy.

The dairy door was on the latch. With his head Lad butted it open and ran into the stone-floored room. A line of full milk pans were ranged side by side on a shelf. Rising on his hind legs and bracing his forepaws on the shelf, Lad seized edges of the deep pans, one after another, between his teeth, and, with a succession of sharp jerks brought them one and all clattering to the floor.

Scampering out of the dairy, ankle deep in a river of spilled milk, and paying no heed to the cries of the scandalized cook, he charged forth in the open again. His eye fell on a red cow, tethered by a long chain in a pasture patch beyond the stables.

She was an old acquaintance of his, this cow. She had been on the Place since before he was born. Yet, today Lad's spear knew no brother. He tore across the lawn and past the stables, straight at the astonished bovine. In terror, the cow threw up her tail and sought to lumber away at top speed. Being controlled by her tether she could run only in a wide circle. And around and around this circle Lad drove the bellowing brute as fast as he could make her run, until the gardener came panting to her relief.

But neither the gardener nor any other living creature could stay Lad's rampage that day. He fled merrily up to the lodge at the gate, burst into its kitchen and through to the refrigerator. There, in a pan, he found a raw leg of mutton. Seizing this twelve-pound morsel in his teeth and dodging the indignant housewife, he careered out into the highway with his prize, dug a hole in the roadside ditch and was gleefully preparing to bury the mutton therein, when its outraged owner rescued it.

A farmer was jogging along the road behind a half-dozing horse. A painful nip on the rear hind leg turned the nag's drowsy jog into a really industrious effort at a runaway. Already, Lad had sprung clear of the front wheel. As the wagon bumped past him, he leaped upward, deftly caught a hanging corner of the lap robe and hauled it free of the seat.

Robe in mouth, he capered off into a field, playfully keeping just out of the reach of the pursuing agrarian; and at last he deposited the stolen treasure in the heart of a bramble patch a full half-mile from the road.

Lad made his way back to the Place by a wide detour that brought him through the grounds of a neighbor of the master's.

This neighbor owned a dog—a mean-eyed, rangy and mangy pest of a brute that Lad would ordinarily have scorned to notice. But, most decidedly, he noticed the dog now. He routed it out of its kennel and bestowed upon it a thrashing that brought its possessor's entire family shrieking to the scene of conflict.

Courteously refusing to carry the matter further, in face of a half-dozen shouting humans, Lad cantered homeward.

From the clothesline, on the drying ground at the Place, fluttered a large white object. It was palpably a nurse's uniform—palpably *the* nurse's uniform. And Lad greeted its presence there with a grin of pure bliss.

In less than two seconds the uniform was off the line, with three huge rents marring its stiff surface. In less than thirty seconds, it was reposing in the rich black mud on the verge of the lake, and Lad was rolling playfully on it.

Then he chanced to remember his long-neglected enemies, the squirrels, and his equally neglected prey, the rabbits. And he loped off to the forest to wage gay warfare upon them. He was gloriously, idiotically, criminally happy. And, for the time, he was a fool.

All day long, complaints came pouring in to the master. Lad had destroyed the whole set of cream. Lad had chased the red cow till it would be a miracle if she didn't fall sick of it. Lad had scared poor dear little Peter Grimm so badly that the cat seemed likely to spend all the rest of its nine lives squalling in the treetop and crossly refusing to come down.

Lad had spoiled a Sunday leg of mutton, up at the lodge. Lad had made a perfectly respectable horse run madly away for nearly twenty-five feet, and had given the horse's owner a blasphemous half-mile run over a plowed field after a cherished and ravished lap robe. Lad had well-nigh killed a neighbor's particularly killable dog. Lad had wantonly destroyed the nurse's very newest and most expensive uniform. All day it was Lad—Lad—Lad!

Lad, it seemed, was a storm center, whence radiated complaints that ran the whole gamut from tears to lurid profanity; and, to each and every complainant, the master made the same answer, "Leave him alone. We're just out of hell—Lad and I! He's doing the things I'd do myself, if I had the nerve."

Which, of course, was a manifestly asinine way for a grown man to talk.

Long after dusk, Lad pattered meekly home, very tired and quite sane. His spell of imbecility had worn itself out. He was once more his calmly dignified self, though not a little ashamed of his babyish pranks, and mildly wondering how he had come to behave so.

Still, he could not grieve over what he had done. He could not grieve over anything just yet. The mistress was alive! And while the craziness had passed, the happiness had not. Tired, drowsily at peace with all the world, he curled up under the piano and went to sleep.

He slept so soundly that the locking of the house for the night did not rouse him. But something else did. Something that occurred long after everyone on the Place was sound asleep. Lad was joyously pursuing, through the forest aisles of dreamland, a whole army of squirrels that had not sense enough to climb trees—when in a moment, he was wide awake and on guard. Far off, very far off, he heard a man walking.

Now, to a trained dog there is as much difference in the sound of human footfalls as, to humans, there is a difference in the aspect of human faces. A belated countryman walking along the highway, a furlong distant, would not have awakened Lad from sleep. Also, he knew and could classify, at any distance, the footsteps of everyone who lived on the Place. But the steps that had brought him wide awake and on the alert tonight, did not belong to one of the Place's people; nor were they the steps of anybody who had a right to be on the premises.

Someone had climbed the fence, at a distance from the drive, and was crossing the grounds, obliquely, toward the house. It was a man, and he was still nearly two hundred yards away. Moreover, he was walking stealthily, and pausing every now and then as if to reconnoiter.

No human, at that distance, could have heard the steps. No dog could have helped hearing them. Had the other dogs been at home instead of at the boarding kennels, the Place would by this time have been re-echoing with barks. Both scent and sound would have given them ample warning of the stranger's presence.

To Lad, on the lower floor of the house, where every window was shut, the aid of scent was denied. Yet his sense of hearing was enough. Plainly, he heard the softly advancing steps—heard and read them. He read them for an intruder's—read them for the steps of a man who was afraid to be heard or seen, and who was employing all the caution in his power.

A booming, trumpeting bark of warning sprang into Lad's throat —and died there. The sharp command *"Quiet!"* was still in force. Even in his madness, that day, he had uttered no sound. He strangled back the tumultuous bark and listened in silence. He had risen to his feet and had come out from under the piano. In the middle of the living room he stood, head lowered, ears pricked. His ruff was abristle. A ridge of hair rose grotesquely from the shaggy mass of coat along his spine. His lips had slipped back from his teeth. And so he stood and waited.

The shuffling, soft steps were nearer now. Down through the trees they came, and then onto the springy grass of the lawn. Now they crunched lightly on the gravel of the drive. Lad moved forward a little and again stood at attention.

The man was climbing to the veranda. The vines rustled ever so slightly as he brushed past them. His footfall sounded lightly on the veranda itself.

Next there was a faint clicking noise at the old-fashioned lock of one of the bay windows. Presently, by half inches, the window began to rise. Before it had risen an inch, Lad knew the trespasser was no one with whose scent he was familiar.

Another pause, followed by the very faintest scratching, as the man ran a knife blade along the crack of the inner wooden blinds in search of the catch.

The blinds parted slowly. Over the windowsill the man threw a leg. Then he stepped down, noiselessly into the room.

He stood there a second, evidently listening.

And, before he could stir or breathe, something in the darkness hurled itself upon him.

Without so much as a growl of warning, eighty pounds of muscular, hairy energy smote the man full in the chest. A set of hot-breathing jaws flashed for his jugular vein, missed it by a half-inch, and the graze left a red-hot searing pain along his throat. In the merest fraction of a moment, the murderously snapping jaws sank into the thief's shoulder. It is collie custom to fight with a running accompaniment of snarling growls. But Lad did not give voice. In total silence he made his onslaught. In silence, he sought and gained his hold.

The thief was less considerate of the mistress's comfort. With a screech that would have waked every mummy in Egypt, he reeled back, under that first unseen impact, lost his balance and crashed to the hardwood floor, overturning a table and a lamp in his fall. Certain that a devil had attacked him there in the black darkness, the man gave forth yell after yell of mortal terror. Frantically, he strove to push away his assailant and his clammy hand encountered a mass of fur.

The intruder had heard that all the dogs on the Place had been sent away because of the mistress's illness. Hence his attempt at burglary. Hence also, his panic fear when Lad had sprung on him.

But with the feel of the thick warm fur, the man's superstitious terror died. He knew he had roused the house; but there was still time to escape if he could rid himself of this silent, terrible creature. He staggered to his feet. And, with the knife he still clutched, he smote viciously at his assailant.

Because Lad was a collie, Lad was not killed then and there. A bulldog or a bull terrier, attacking a man, seeks for some convenient hold. Having secured that hold—be it good or bad—he locks his jaws and hangs on. You can well-nigh cut his head from his body before he will let go. Thus, he is at the mercy of any armed man who can keep cool long enough to kill him.

But a collie has a strain of wolf in his queer brain. He seeks a hold, it is true. But at an instant's notice, he is ready to shift that hold for a better. He may bite or slash a dozen times in as many seconds and in as many parts of the body. He is everywhere at once —he is nowhere in particular. He is not a pleasant opponent.

Lad did not wait for the thief's knife to find his heart. As the man lunged, the dog transferred his profitless shoulderhold to a grip on the stabbing arm. The knife blade plowed an ugly furrow along his side. And the dog's curved eye-tooth slashed the man's arm from elbow to wrist, clean through to the bone.

The knife clattered to the floor. The intruder wheeled and made a leap for the open window; he had not cleared half the space when Lad bounded for the back of his neck. The dog's upper set of teeth raked the man's hard skull, carrying away a handful of hair and flesh; and his weight threw the thief forward on hands and knees again. Twisting, the man found the dog's furry throat; and with both hands sought to strangle him; at the same time backing out through the window. But it is not easy to strangle a collie. The piles of tumbled ruff hair form a protection no other breed of dog can boast. Scarcely had the hands found their grip when one of them was crushed between the dog's viselike jaws.

The man flung off his enemy and turned to clear the veranda at a single jump. But before he had half made the turn, Lad was at his throat again, and the two crashed through the vines together and down onto the driveway below. The entire combat had not lasted for more than thirty seconds.

The master, pistol and flashlight in hand, ran down to find the living room amuck with blood and with smashed furniture, and one of the windows open. He flashed the electric ray through the window. On the ground below, stunned by striking against a stone jardinière in his fall, the thief sprawled senseless upon his back. Above him was Lad, his searching teeth at last having found their coveted throat-hold. Steadily, the great dog was grinding his way through toward the jugular.

There was a deal of noise and excitement and light after that.

The intruder was trussed up and the local constable was summoned by telephone. Everybody seemed to be doing much loud talking.

Lad took advantage of the turmoil to slip back into the house and to his "cave" under the piano; where he proceeded to lick solicitously the flesh wound on his left side.

He was very tired; and he was very unhappy and he was very much worried. In spite of all his own precautions as to silence, the intruder had made a most ungodly lot of noise. The commandment *"Quiet!"* had been fractured past repair. And, somehow, Lad felt blame for it all. It was really his fault—and he realized it now—that the man had made such a racket. Would the master punish him? Perhaps. Humans have such odd ideas of justice. He—

Then it was that the master found him and called him forth from his place of refuge. Head adroop, tail low, Lad crept out to meet his scolding. He looked very much like a puppy caught tearing a new rug.

But suddenly, the master and everyone else in the room was patting him and telling him how splendid he was. And the master had found the deep scratch on his side and was dressing it, and stopping every minute or so, to praise him again. And then, as a crowning reward, he was taken upstairs for the mistress to stroke and make much of.

When at last he was sent downstairs again, Lad did not return to his piano lair. Instead, he went out-of-doors and away from the Place. And, when he thought he was far enough from the house, he solemnly sat down and began to bark.

It was good—*passing* good—to be able to make a noise again. He had never before known how needful to canine happiness a bark really is. He had long and pressing arrears of barks in his system. And thunderously he proceeded to divest himself of them for nearly half an hour.

Then, feeling much, *much* better, he ambled homeward, to take up normal life again after a whole fortnight of martyrdom.

CHAPTER 3

A MIRACLE OF TWO

The connecting points between the inner and outer Lad were a pair of the wisest and darkest and most sorrowful eyes in all dogdom— eyes that gave the lie to folk who say no dog has a soul. There are such dogs once in a human generation.

Lad had but one tyrant in all the world. That was his dainty gold-and-white collie-mate, Lady; Lady, whose affections he had won in fair life-and-death battle with a younger and stronger dog; Lady, who bullied him unmercifully and teased him and did fearful things to his stately dignity; and to whom he allowed liberties that would have brought any other aggressor painfully near to death.

Lady was high-strung and capricious; a collie de luxe. Lad and she were as oddly contrasted a couple, in body and mind, as one could find in a day's journey through their North Jersey hinterland. To the Place (at intervals far too few between to suit Lad), came human guests; people, for the most part, who did not understand dogs and who either drew away in causeless fear from them or else insisted on patting or hauling them about.

Lad detested guests. He met their advances with cold courtesy, and, as soon as possible, got himself out of their way. He knew the

Law far too well to snap or to growl at a guest. But the Law did not compel him to stay within patting distance of one.

The careless caress of the mistress or the master—especially of the mistress—was a delight to him. He would sport like an overgrown puppy with either of these deities, throwing dignity to the four winds. But to them alone did he unbend—to them and to his adored tyrant, Lady.

To the Place, of a cold spring morning, came a guest; or two guests. Lad at first was not certain which. The visible guest was a woman. And, in her arms she carried a long bundle that might have been anything at all.

Long as was the bundle, it was ridiculously light. Or, rather, pathetically light. For its folds contained a child, five years old; a child that ought to have weighed more than forty pounds and weighed barely twenty. A child with a wizened little old face, and with a skeleton body which was powerless from the waist down.

Six months earlier, the Baby had been as vigorous and jolly as a collie pup. Until an invisible something prowled through the land, laying its fingertips on thousands of such jolly and vigorous youngsters, as frost's fingers are laid on autumn flowers—and with the same hideous effect.

This particular baby had not died of the plague, as had so many of her fellows. At least, her brain and the upper half of her body had not died.

Her mother had been counseled to try mountain air for the hopeless little invalid. She had written to her distant relative, the mistress, asking leave to spend a month at the Place.

Lad viewed the arrival of the adult guest with no interest and with less pleasure. He stood, aloof, at one side of the veranda, as the newcomer alighted from the car.

But, when the master took the long bundle from her arms and carried it up the steps, Lad waxed curious. Not only because the master handled his burden so carefully, but because the collie's uncanny scent power told him all at once that it was human.

Lad had never seen a human carried in this manner. It did not make sense to him. And he stepped, hesitantly, forward to investigate.

The master laid the bundle tenderly on the veranda hammock swing, and loosed the blanket folds that swathed it. Lad came over to him, and looked down into the pitiful little face.

There had been no baby at the Place for many a year. Lad had seldom seen one at such close quarters. But now the sight did something queer to his heart—the big heart that ever went out to the weak and defenseless, the heart that made a playfully snapping puppy or a cranky little lapdog as safe from his terrible jaws as was Lady herself.

He sniffed in friendly fashion at the child's pathetically upturned face. Into the dull baby eyes, at sight of him, came a look of pleased interest—the first that had crossed their blankness for many a long day. Two feeble little hands reached out and buried themselves lovingly in the mass of soft ruff that circled Lad's neck.

The dog quivered all over, from nose to brush, with joy at the touch. He laid his great head down beside the drawn cheek, and positively reveled in the pain the tugging fingers were inflicting on his sensitive throat.

In one instant, Lad had widened his narrow and hard-established circle of loved ones, to include this half-dead wisp of humanity.

The child's mother came up the steps in the master's wake. At sight of the huge dog, she halted in quick alarm.

"Look out!" she shrilled. "He may attack her! Oh, *do* drive him away!"

"Who? Lad?" queried the mistress. "Why, Lad wouldn't harm a hair of her head if his life depended on it! See, he adores her already. I never knew him to take to a stranger before. And she looks brighter and happier, too, than she has looked in months. Don't make her cry by sending him away from her."

"But," insisted the woman, "dogs are full of germs. I've read so. He might give her some terrible—"

"Lad is just as clean and as germless as I am," declared the mistress, with some warmth. "There isn't a day he doesn't swim in the lake, and there isn't a day I don't brush him. He's—"

"He's a collie, though," protested the guest, looking on in uneasy distaste, while Baby secured a tighter and more painful grip on the delighted dog's ruff. "And I've always heard collies are awfully treacherous. Don't you find them so?"

"If we did," put in the master, who had heard that same asinine question until it sickened him, "if we found collies were treacherous, we wouldn't keep them. A collie is either the best dog or the worst dog on earth. Lad is the best. We don't keep the other kind. I'll call him away, though, if it bothers you to have him so close to Baby. Come, Lad!"

Reluctantly, the dog turned to obey the Law; glancing back, as he went, at the adorable new idol he had acquired; then crossing obediently to where the master stood.

The Baby's face puckered unhappily. Her pipestem arms went out toward the collie. In a tired little voice she called after him:

"Dog! *Doggie!* Come back here, right away! I love you, Dog!"

Lad, vibrating with eagerness, glanced up at the master for leave to answer the call. The master, in turn, looked inquiringly at his nervous guest. Lad translated the look. And, instantly, he felt an unreasoning hate for the fussy woman.

The guest walked over to her weakly gesticulating daughter and explained, "Dogs aren't nice pets for sick little girls, dear. They're rough; and besides, they bite. I'll find Dolly for you as soon as I unpack."

"Don't want Dolly," fretted the child. "Want the dog! He isn't rough. He won't bite. Doggie! I love you! Come *here!*"

Lad looked up longingly at the master, his plumed tail awag, his ears up, his eyes dancing. One hand of the master's stirred toward the hammock in a motion so imperceptible that none but a sharply watchful dog could have observed it.

Lad waited for no second bidding. Quietly, unobtrusively, he crossed behind the guest, and stood beside his idol. The Baby fairly squealed with rapture, and drew his silken head down to her face.

"Oh, well!" surrendered the guest, sulkily. "If she won't be happy any other way, let him go to her. I suppose it's safe, if you people say so. And it's the first thing she's been interested in, since—*No, darling*," she broke off, sternly. "You shall *not* kiss him! I draw the line at that. Here! Let Mamma rub your lips with her handkerchief."

"Dogs aren't made to be kissed," said the master, sharing, however, Lad's disgust at the lip-scrubbing process. "But she'll come to less harm from kissing the head of a clean dog than from kissing the mouths of most humans. I'm glad she likes Lad. And I'm still gladder that he likes her. It's almost the first time he ever went to an outsider of his own accord."

That was how Lad's idolatry began. And that, too, was how a miserably sick child found a new interest in life.

Every day, from morning to dusk, Lad was with the Baby. Forsaking his immemorial "cave" under the music-room piano, he lay all night outside the door of her bedroom. In preference even to a romp through the forest with Lady, he would pace majestically alongside the invalid's wheelchair as it was trundled along the walks or up and down the veranda.

Forsaking his post on the floor at the left of the master's seat, at meals—a place that had been his alone since puppyhood—he lay always behind the Baby's table couch. This to the vast discomfort of the maid who had to step over him in circumnavigating the board, and to the open annoyance of the child's mother.

Baby, as the days went on, lost none of her first pleasure in her shaggy playmate. To her, the dog was a ceaseless novelty. She loved to twist and braid the great white ruff on his chest, to toy with his sensitive ears, to make him "speak" or shake hands or lie down or stand up at her bidding. She loved to play a myriad of intricate games with him—games ranging from *Beauty and the Beast* to *Fairy Princess and Dragon.*

Whether as Beast (to her Beauty) or in the more complex and exacting role of Dragon, Lad entered wholesouledly into every such game. Of course, he always played his part wrong. Equally, of course, Baby always lost her temper at his stupidity, and pummeled him, by way of chastisement, with her nerveless fists—a punishment Lad accepted with a grin of idiotic bliss.

Whether because of the keenly bracing mountain air or because of her outdoor days with a chum who awoke her dormant interest in life, Baby was growing stronger and less like a sallow ghostling. And, in the relief of noting this steady improvement, her mother continued to tolerate Lad's chumship with the child, although she had never lost her own first unreasoning fear of the big dog.

Two or three things happened to revive this foolish dread. One of them occurred about a week after the invalid's arrival at the Place.

Lady, being no fonder of guests than was Lad, had given the veranda and the house itself a wide berth. But one day, as Baby lay in the hammock (trying in a wordy irritation to teach Lad the alphabet), and as the guest sat with her back to them, writing letters, Lady trotted around the corner of the porch.

At sight of the hammock's queer occupant, she paused, and stood blinking inquisitively. Baby spied the graceful gold-and-white creature. Pushing Lad to one side, she called, imperiously, "Come here, new Doggie. You pretty, *pretty* Doggie!"

Lady, her vanity thus appealed to, strolled mincingly forward. Just within arm's reach, she halted again. Baby thrust out one hand, and seized her by the ruff to draw her into petting distance.

The sudden tug on Lady's fur was as nothing to the haulings and maulings in which Lad so meekly reveled. But Lad and Lady were by no means alike, as I think I have said. Boundless patience and a chivalrous love for the weak, were not numbered among Lady's erratic virtues. She liked liberties as little as did Lad; and she had a far more drastic way of resenting them.

At the first pinch of her sensitive skin there was an instant flash of gleaming teeth, accompanied by a nasty growl and a lightning-quick forward lunge of the dainty gold-white head. As the wolf slashes at a foe—and as no animals but wolf and collie know how to—Lady slashed murderously at the thin little arm that sought to pull her along.

And Lad, in the same breath, hurled his great bulk between his mate and his idol. It was a move unbelievably swift for so large a dog. And it served its turn.

The eye-tooth slash that would have cut the little girl's arm to the bone, sent a red furrow athwart Lad's massive shoulder.

Before Lady could snap again, or, indeed, could get over her surprise at her mate's intervention, Lad was shouldering her off the edge of the veranda steps. Very gently he did this, and with no show of teeth. But he did it with much firmness.

In angry amazement at such rudeness on the part of her usually subservient mate, Lady snarled ferociously, and bit at him.

Just then, the child's mother, roused from her letter writing by the turmoil, came rushing to her endangered offspring's rescue.

"He growled at Baby," she reported hysterically, as the noise brought the master out of his study and to the veranda on the run. "He *growled* at her, and then he and that other horrid brute got to fighting, and—"

"Pardon me," interposed the master, calling both dogs to him, "but man is the only animal to maltreat the female of his kind. No male dog would fight with Lady. Much less would Lad—Hello!" he broke off. "Look at his shoulder, though! That was meant for Baby. Instead of scolding Lad, you may thank him for saving her from an ugly slash. I'll keep Lady chained up, after this."

"But—"

"But, with Lad beside her, Baby is in just about as much danger as she would be with a guard of forty U.S. Regulars," went on the master. "Take my word for it. Come along, Lady. It's the kennel for you for the next few weeks, old girl. Lad, when I get back, I'll wash that shoulder for you."

With a sigh, Lad went over to the hammock and lay down, heavily. For the first time since Baby's advent at the Place, he was unhappy—very, *very* unhappy. He had had to jostle and fend off Lady, whom he worshipped. And he knew it would be many a long day before his sensitively temperamental mate would forgive or forget. Meantime, so far as Lady was concerned, he was in Coventry.

And just because he had saved from injury a baby who had meant no harm and who could not help herself! Life, all at once, seemed dismayingly complex to Lad's simple soul.

He whimpered a little, under his breath, and lifted his head toward Baby's dangling hand for a caress that might help make things easier. But Baby had been bitterly chagrined at Lady's reception of her friendly advances. Lady could not be punished for this. But Lad could.

She slapped the lovingly upthrust muzzle with all her feeble force. For once, Lad was not amused by the castigation. He sighed, a second time, and curled up on the floor beside the hammock, in a right miserable heap; his head between his tiny forepaws, his great sorrowful eyes abrim with bewildered grief.

Spring drowsed into early summer. And, with the passing days, Baby continued to look less and less like an atrophied mummy, and more like a thin, but normal, child of five. She ate and slept, as she had not done for many a month.

The lower half of her body was still dead. But there was a faint glow of pink in the flat cheeks, and the eyes were alive once more. The hands that pulled at Lad, in impulsive friendliness or in punishment, were stronger, too. Their fur tugs hurt worse than at first. But the hurt always gave Lad that same twinge of pleasure—a twinge that helped to ease his heart's ache over the defection of Lady.

On a hot morning in early June, when the mistress and the master had driven over to the village for the mail, the child's mother wheeled the invalid chair to a tree-roofed nook down by the lake— a spot whose deep shade and lush long grass promised more coolness than did the veranda.

It was just the spot a city dweller would have chosen for a nap— and just the spot through which no countryman would have cared to venture, at that dry season, without wearing high boots.

Here, not three days earlier, the master had killed a copperhead snake. Here, every summer, during the late June mowing, the Place's scythe-wielders moved with glum caution. And seldom did their progress go unmarked by the scythe-severed body of at least one snake.

The Place, for the most part, lay on hillside and plateau, free from poisonous snakes of all kinds, and usually free from mosquitoes as well. The lawn, close-shaven, sloped down to the lake. To one side of it, in a narrow stretch of bottomland, a row of weeping willows pierced the loose stone lake wall.

Here, the ground was seldom bone-dry. Here, the grass grew rankest. Here, also, driven to water by the drought, abode eft, lizard and an occasional snake, finding coolness and moisture in the long grass, and a thousand hiding places amid the stone crannies or the lake wall.

If either the mistress or the master had been at home on this morning, the guest would have been warned against taking Baby there at all. She would have been doubly warned against the folly which she now proceeded to commit—of lifting the child from the wheelchair, and placing her on a spread rug in the grass, with her back to the low wall.

The rug, on its mattress of lush grasses, was soft. The lake breeze stirred the lower boughs of the willows. The air was pleasantly cool here, and had lost the dead hotness that brooded over the higher ground.

The guest was well pleased with her choice of a resting place. Lad was not.

The big dog had been growingly uneasy from the time the wheelchair approached the lake wall. Twice he put himself in front of it; only to be ordered aside. Once the wheels hit his ribs with jarring impact. As Baby was laid upon her grassy bed, Lad barked loudly and pulled at one end of the rug with his teeth.

The guest shook her parasol at him and ordered him back to the house. Lad obeyed no orders, save those of his two deities. Instead of slinking away, he sat down beside the child, so close to her that his ruff pressed against her shoulder. He did not lie down as usual, but sat—tulip ears erect, dark eyes cloudy with trouble, head turning slowly from side to side, nostrils pulsing.

To a human, there was nothing to see or hear or smell—other than the cool beauty of the nook, the soughing of the breeze in the willows, the soft fragrance of a June morning. To a dog, there were faint rustling sounds that were not made by the breeze. There were equally faint and elusive scents that the human nose could not register. Notably, a subtle odor as of crushed cucumbers. (If ever you have killed a pit viper, you know that smell.)

The dog was worried. He was uneasy. His uneasiness would not let him sit still. It made him fidget and shift his position; and, once or twice, growl a little under his breath.

Presently, his eyes brightened, and his brush began to thud gently on the rug edge. For, a quarter mile above, the Place's car was turning in from the highway. In it were the mistress and the master, coming home with the mail. Now everything would be all right. And the onerous duties of guardianship would pass to more capable hands.

As the car rounded the corner of the house and came to a stop at the front door, the guest caught sight of it. Jumping up from her seat on the rug, she started toward it in quest of mail. So hastily did she rise that she dislodged one of the wall's small stones and sent it rattling down into a wide crevice between two larger rocks.

She did not heed the tinkle of stone on stone, nor a sharp little hiss that followed, as the falling missile smote the coils of a sleeping copperhead snake in one of the wall's lowest cavities. But Lad heard it. And he heard the slithering of scales against rocksides, as the snake angrily sought new sleeping quarters.

The guest walked away, all ignorant of what she had done. And, before she had taken three steps, a triangular grayish-ruddy head was pushed out from the bottom of the wall.

Twistingly, the copperhead glided out onto the grass at the very edge of the rug. The snake was short, and thick, and dirty, with a distinct and intricate pattern interwoven on its rough upper body. The head was short, flat, wedge-shaped. Between eye and nostril, on either side, was the sinister "pinhole," that is the infallible mark of the poison-sac serpent.

(The rattlesnake swarms among some of the stony mountains of the North Jersey hinterland; though seldom, nowadays, does it venture into the valleys. But the copperhead—twin brother in murder to the rattler—still infests meadow and lakeside. Smaller, fatter, deadlier than the diamondback, it gives none of the warning which redeems the latter from complete abhorrence. It is a creature as evil as its own aspect—and name. Copperhead and rattlesnake are the only pit-vipers left now between Canada and Virginia.)

Out from its wall cranny oozed the reptile. Along the fringe of the rug it moved for a foot or two; then paused uncertain—perhaps momentarily dazzled by the light. It stopped within a yard of the child's wizened little hand that rested idle on the rug. Baby's other arm was around Lad, and her body was between him and the snake.

Lad, with a shiver, freed himself from the frail embrace and got nervously to his feet.

There are two things—and perhaps *only* two things—of which the best type of thoroughbred collie is abjectly afraid and from which he will run for his life. One is a mad dog. The other is a poisonous snake. Instinct, and the horror of death, warn him violently away from both.

At stronger scent, and then at sight of the copperhead, Lad's stout heart failed him. Gallantly had he attacked human marauders who had invaded the Place. More than once, in dashing fearlessness, he had fought with dogs larger than himself. With a d'Artagnan-like gaiety of zest, he had tackled and deflected a bull that had charged head down at the mistress.

Commonly speaking, he knew no fear. Yet now he was afraid; tremulously, quakingly, *sickly* afraid. Afraid of the deadly thing that was halting within three feet of him, with only the Baby's fragile body as a barrier between.

Left to himself, he would have taken, incontinently, to his heels. With the lower animal's instinctive appeal to a human in moments of danger, he even pressed closer to the helpless child at his side, as if seeking the protection of her humanness. A great wave of cowardice shook the dog from foot to head.

The master had alighted from the car, and was coming down the hill, toward his guest, with several letters in his hand. Lad cast a yearning look at him. But the master, he knew, was too far away to be summoned in time by even the most imperious bark.

And it was then that the child's straying gaze fell on the snake.

With a gasp and a shudder, Baby shrank back against Lad. At least, the upper half of her body moved away from the peril. Her legs and feet lay inert. The motion jerked the rug's fringe an inch or two, disturbing the copperhead. The snake coiled, and drew back its three-cornered head, the forklike maroon tongue playing fitfully.

With a cry of panic-fright at her own impotence to escape, the child caught up a picture book from the rug beside her, and flung it at the serpent. The fluttering book missed its mark. But it served its purpose by giving the copperhead reason to believe itself attacked.

Back went the triangular head, farther than ever; and then flashed forward. The double move was made in the minutest fraction of a second.

A full third of the squat reddish body going with the blow, the copperhead struck. It struck for the thin knee, not ten inches away from its own coiled body. The child screamed again in mortal terror.

Before the scream could leave the fear-chalked lips, Baby was knocked flat by a mighty and hairy shape that lunged across her toward her foe.

And the copperhead's fangs sank deep in Lad's nose.

He gave no sign of pain; but leaped back. As he sprang his jaws caught Baby by the shoulder. The keen teeth did not so much as bruise her soft flesh as he half-dragged, half-threw her into the grass behind him.

Athwart the rug again, Lad launched himself bodily upon the coiled snake.

As he charged, the swift-striking fangs found a second mark— this time in the side of his jaw.

An instant later the copperhead lay twisting and writhing and thrashing impotently among the grassroots; its back broken, and its body seared almost in two by a slash of the dog's saberlike tusk.

The fight was over. The menace was past. The child was safe.

And, in her rescuer's muzzle and jaw were two deposits of mortal poison.

Lad stood panting above the prostrate and crying Baby. His work was done; and instinct told him at what cost. But his idol was unhurt and he was happy. He bent down to lick the convulsed little face in mute plea for pardon for his needful roughness toward her.

But he was denied even this tiny consolation. Even as he leaned downward he was knocked prone to earth by a blow that all but fractured his skull.

At the child's first terrified cry, her mother had turned back. Nearsighted and easily confused, she had seen only that the dog had knocked her sick baby flat, and was plunging across her body. Next, she had seen him grip Baby's shoulder with his teeth and drag her, shrieking, along the ground.

That was enough. The primal mother instinct (that is, sometimes, almost as strong in woman as in lioness—or cow) was aroused. Fearless of danger to herself, the guest rushed to her child's rescue. As she ran she caught her thick parasol by the ferule and swung it aloft.

Down came the agate handle of the sunshade on the head of the dog. The handle was as large as a woman's fist, and was composed of a single stone, set in four silver claws.

As Lad staggered to his feet after the terrific blow felled him, the impromptu weapon arose once more in air, descending this time on his broad shoulders.

Lad did not cringe—did not seek to dodge or run—did not show his teeth. This mad assailant was a woman. Moreover, she was a guest, and as such, sacred under the Guest Law which he had mastered from puppyhood.

Had a man raised his hand against Lad—a man other than the

master or a guest—there would right speedily have been a case for a hospital, if not for the undertaker. But, as things now were, he could not resent the beating.

His head and shoulders quivered under the force and the pain of the blows. But his splendid body did not cower. And the woman, wild with fear and mother love, continued to smite with all her random strength.

Then came the rescue.

At the first blow the child had cried out in fierce protest at her pet's ill-treatment. Her cry went unheard.

"Mother!" she shrieked, her high treble cracked with anguish. "Mother! Don't! *Don't!* He kept the snake from eating me! He—!"

The frantic woman still did not heed. Each successive blow seemed to fall upon the little onlooker's own bare heart. And Baby, under the stress, went quite mad.

Scrambling to her feet, in crazy zeal to protect her beloved playmate, she tottered forward three steps, and seized her mother by the skirt.

At the touch the woman looked down. Then her face went yellow-white; and the parasol clattered unnoticed to the ground.

For a long instant the mother stood thus; her eyes wide and glazed, her mouth open, her cheeks ashy—staring at the swaying child who clutched her dress for support and who was sobbing forth incoherent pleas for the dog.

The master had broken into a run and into a flood of wordless profanity at sight of his dog's punishment. Now he came to an abrupt halt and was glaring dazedly at the miracle before him.

The child had risen and had walked.

The child had *walked*—she whose lower motive-centers, the wise doctors had declared, were hopelessly paralyzed—she who could never hope to twitch so much as a single toe or feel any sensation from the hips downward!

Small wonder that both guest and master seemed to have caught, for the moment, some of the paralysis that so magically departed from the invalid!

And yet—as a corps of learned physicians later agreed—there was no miracle—no magic—about it. Baby's was not the first, nor the thousandth case in pathologic history, in which paralyzed sensory powers had been restored to their normal functions by means of a shock.

The child had had no malformation, no accident, to injure the spine or the coordination between limbs and brain. A long illness had left her powerless. Country air and new interest in life had gradually built up wasted tissues. A shock had reestablished communication between brain and lower body—a communication that had been suspended, not broken.

When, at last, there was room in any of the human minds for aught but blank wonder and gratitude, the joyously weeping mother was made to listen to the child's story of the fight with the snake—a story corroborated by the master's find of the copperhead's half-severed body.

"I'll—I'll get down on my knees to that heaven-sent dog," sobbed the guest, "and apologize to him. Oh, I wish some of you would beat me as I beat him! I'd feel so much better! Where is he?"

The question brought no answer. Lad had vanished. Nor could eager callings and searchings bring him to view. The master, returning from a shout-punctuated hunt through the forest, made Baby tell her story all over again. Then he nodded.

"I understand," he said, feeling a ludicrously unmanly desire to cry. "I see how it was. The snake must have bitten him, at least once. Probably oftener, and he knew what that meant. Lad knows everything—*knew* everything, I mean. If he had known a little less he'd have been human. But—if he'd been human, he probably wouldn't have thrown away his life for Baby."

"Thrown away his life," repeated the guest. "I—I don't understand. Surely I didn't strike him hard enough to—"

"No," returned the master, "but the snake did."

"You mean, he has—?"

"I mean it is the nature of all animals to crawl away, alone, into the forest to die. They are more considerate than we. They try to cause no further trouble to those they have loved. Lad got his death from the copperhead's fangs. He knew it. And while we were all taken up with the wonder of Baby's cure, he quietly went away—to die."

The mistress got up hurriedly, and left the room. She loved the great dog, as she loved few humans. The guest dissolved into a flood of sloppy tears.

"And I beat him," she wailed. "I beat him—horribly! And all the time he was dying from the poison he had saved my child from! Oh, I'll never forgive myself for this, the longest day I live."

"The longest day is a long day," dryly commented the master. "And self-forgiveness is the easiest of all lessons to learn. After all, Lad was only a dog. That's why he is dead."

The Place's atmosphere tingled with jubilation over the child's cure. Her uncertain, but always successful, efforts at walking were an hourly delight.

But, through the general joy, the mistress and the master could not always keep their faces bright. Even the guest mourned frequently, and loudly, and eloquently the passing of Lad. And Baby was openly inconsolable at the loss of her chum.

At dawn on the morning of the fourth day, the master let himself silently out of the house, for his usual before-breakfast cross-country tramp—a tramp on which, for years, Lad had always been his companion. Heavy-hearted, the master prepared to set forth alone.

As he swung shut the veranda door behind him, something arose stiffly from a porch rug—something the master looked at in a daze of unbelief.

It was a dog—yet no such dog as had ever before sullied the cleanness of the Place's well-scoured veranda.

The animal's body was lean to emaciation. The head was swollen —though, apparently, the swelling had begun to recede. The fur, from spine to toe, from nose to tail tip, was one solid and shapeless mass of caked mud.

The master sat down very suddenly on the veranda floor beside the dirt-encrusted brute, and caught it in his arms, sputtering disjointedly, "Lad!—*Laddie*—Old *friend!* You're alive again! You're—you're—*alive!*"

Yes, Lad had known enough to creep away to the woods to die. But, thanks to the wolf strain in his collie blood, he had also known how to do something far wiser than die.

Three days of self-burial, to the very nostrils, in the mysteriously healing ooze of the marshes, behind the forest, had done for him what such mud baths have done for a million wild creatures. It had drawn out the viper poison and had left him whole again—thin, shaky on the legs, slightly swollen of head—but *whole.*

"He's—he's awfully dirty, though! Isn't he?" commented the guest, when an idiotic triumph-yell from the master had summoned the whole family, in sketchy attire, to the veranda. "Awfully dirty and—"

"Yes," curtly assented the master, Lad's head between his caressing hands. " 'Awfully dirty.' That's why he's still alive."

CHAPTER 4

HIS LITTLE SON

Lad's mate Lady was the only one of the Little People about the
Place who refused to look on Lad with due reverence. In her frolic
moods she teased him unmercifully; in a prettily imperious way she
bossed and bullied him—for all of which Lad adored her. He had
other reasons, too, for loving Lady—not only because she was dainty
and beautiful, and was caressingly fond of him, but because he had
won her in fair mortal combat with the younger and showier Knave.

For a time after Knave's routing, Lad was blissfully happy in
Lady's undivided comradeship. Together they ranged the forests beyond the Place in search of rabbits. Together they sprawled shoulder to shoulder on the disreputable old fur rug in front of the living
room fire. Together they did joyous homage to their gods, the mistress and the master.

Then in the late summer a new rival appeared—to be accurate,
three rivals. And they took up all of Lady's time and thought and
love. Poor old Lad was made to feel terribly out in the cold. The
trio of rivals that had so suddenly claimed Lady's care were fuzzy
and roly-poly, and about the size of month-old kittens. In brief,
they were three thoroughbred collie puppies.

Two of them were tawny brown, with white forepaws and chests. The third was not like Lad in color, but like the mother—at least, all of him not white was of the indeterminate yellowish mouse-gray which, at three months or earlier, turns to pale gold.

When they were barely a fortnight old—almost as soon as their big mournful eyes opened—the two brown puppies died. There seemed no particular reason for their death, except the fact that a collie is always the easiest or else the most impossible breed of dog to raise.

The fuzzy grayish baby alone was left—the puppy which was soon to turn to white and gold. The mistress named him Wolf.

Upon baby Wolf the mother dog lavished a ridiculous lot of attention—so much that Lad was miserably lonely. The great collie would try with pathetic eagerness, a dozen times a day, to lure his mate into a woodland ramble or into a romp on the lawn, but Lady met his wistful advances with absorbed indifference or with a snarl. Indeed when Lad ventured overnear the fuzzy baby, he was warned off by a querulous growl from the mother or by a slash of her shiny white teeth.

Lad could not at all understand it. He felt no particular interest —only a mild and disapproving curiosity—in the shapeless little whimpering ball of fur that nestled so helplessly against his beloved mate's side. He could not understand the mother love that kept Lady with Wolf all day and all night. It was an impulse that meant nothing to Lad.

After a week or two of fruitless effort to win back Lady's interest, Lad coldly and wretchedly gave up the attempt. He took long solitary walks by himself in the forest, retired for hours at a time to sad brooding in his favorite "cave" under the living room piano, and tried to console himself by spending all the rest of his day in the company of the mistress and the master. And he came thoroughly to disapprove of Wolf. Recognizing the baby intruder as the cause of Lady's estrangement from himself, he held aloof from the puppy.

The latter was beginning to emerge from his newborn shapelessness. His coat's texture was changing from fuzz to silk. Its color was turning from gray into yellow. His blunt little nose was lengthening and growing thin and pointed. His butterball body was elongating, and his huge feet and legs were beginning to shape up. He looked more like a dog now, and less like an animated muff. Also within Wolf's youthful heart awoke the devil of mischief, the keen urge of play. He found Lady a pleasant enough playfellow up to a certain point. But a painfully sharp pinch from her teeth or a reproving and breathtaking slap from one of her forepaws was likely to break up every game that she thought had gone far enough; when Wolf's clownish roughness at length got on her hair-trigger nerves.

So, in search of an additional playmate, the frolicsome puppy turned to Lad, only to find that Lad would not play with him at all. Lad made it very, very clear to everyone—except to the fool puppy himself—that he had no desire to romp or to associate in any way with this creature which had ousted him from Lady's heart! Being cursed with a soul too big and gentle to let him harm anything so helpless as Wolf, he did not snap or growl, as did Lady, when the puppy teased. He merely walked away in hurt dignity.

Wolf had a positive genius for tormenting Lad. The huge collie, for instance, would be snoozing away a hot hour on the veranda or under the wisteria vines. Down upon him, from nowhere in particular, would pounce Wolf.

The puppy would seize his sleeping father by the ear, and drive his sharp little milkteeth fiercely into the flesh. Then he would brace himself and pull backward, possibly with the idea of dragging Lad along the ground.

Lad would wake in pain, would rise in dignified unhappiness to his feet and start to walk off—the puppy still hanging to his ear. As Wolf was a collie and not a bulldog, he would lose his grip as his fat little body left the ground. Then, at a clumsy gallop, he would pursue Lad, throwing himself against his father's forelegs and nipping the slender ankles. All this was torture to Lad, and dire mortification too—especially if humans chanced to witness the scene. Yet never did he retaliate; he simply got out of the way.

Lad, nowadays, used to leave half his dinner uneaten, and he took to moping in a way that is not good for dog or man. For the moping had in it no ill temper—nothing but heartache at his mate's desertion, and a weary distaste for the puppy's annoying antics. It was bad enough for Wolf to have supplanted him in Lady's affection, without also making his life a burden and humiliating him in the eyes of his gods.

Therefore Lad moped. Lady remained nervously fussy over her one child. And Wolf continued to be a lovable, but unmitigated, pest. The mistress and the master tried in every way to make up to Lad for the positive and negative afflictions he was enduring, but the sorrowing dog's unhappiness grew with the days.

Then one November morning Lady met Wolf's capering playfulness with a yell of rage so savage as to send the puppy scampering away in mortal terror, and to bring the master out from his study on a run. For no normal dog gives that hideous yell except in racking pain or in illness; and mere pain could not wring such a sound from a thoroughbred.

The master called Lady over to him. Sullenly she obeyed, slinking up to him in surly unwillingness. Her nose was hot and dry; her soft brown eyes were glazed, their whites a dull red. Her dense coat was tumbled.

After a quick examination, the master shut her into a kennel room and telephoned for a veterinarian.

"She is sickening for the worst form of distemper," reported the vet an hour later, "perhaps for something worse. Dogs seldom get distemper after they're a year old, but when they do it's dangerous. Better let me take her over to my hospital and isolate her there. Distemper runs through a kennel faster than cholera through a plague district. I may be able to cure her in a month or two—or I may not. Anyhow, there's no use in risking your other dogs' lives by leaving her here."

So it was that Lad saw his dear mate borne away from him in the back seat of a strange man's car.

Lady hated to go. She whimpered and hung back as the vet lifted her aboard. At sound of her whimper Lad started forward, head low, lips writhing back from his clenched teeth, his shaggy throat vibrant with growls. At a sharp word of command from the master, he checked his onset and stood uncertain. He looked at his departing mate, his dark eyes abrim with sorrow, then glanced at the master in an agony of appeal.

"It's all right, Laddie," the master tried to console him, stroking the dog's magnificent head as he spoke. "It's all right. It's the only chance of saving her."

Lad did not grasp the words, but their tone was reassuring. It told him, at least, that this kidnapping was legal and must not be prevented. Sorrowfully he watched the chugging car out of sight, up the drive. Then with a sigh he walked heavily back to his "cave" beneath the piano.

Lad, alone of the Place's dogs, was allowed to sleep in the house at night, and even had free access to that dog-forbidden spot, the dining room. Next morning, as soon as the doors were opened, he dashed out in search of Lady. With some faint hope that she might have been brought back in the night, he ransacked every corner of the Place for her.

He did not find Lady. But Wolf very promptly found Lad. Wolf was lonely, too—terribly lonely. He had just spent the first solitary night of his three-month life. He missed the furry warm body into whose shelter he had always cuddled for sleep. He missed his playmate—the pretty mother who had been his fond companion.

There are few things so mournful as the eyes of even the happiest collie pup; this morning, loneliness had intensified the melancholy expression in Wolf's eyes. But at sight of Lad, the puppy gamboled forward with a falsetto bark of joy. The world was not quite empty, after all. Though his mother had cruelly absented herself, here was a playfellow that was better than nothing. And up to Lad frisked the optimistic little chap.

Lad saw him coming. The older dog halted and instinctively turned aside to avoid the lively little nuisance. Then, halfway around, he stopped and turned back to face the puppy.

Lady was gone—gone, perhaps, forever. And all that was left to remind Lad of her was this bumptious and sharp-toothed little son of hers. Lady had loved the youngster—Lady, whom Lad so loved. Wolf alone was left; and Wolf was in some mysterious way a part of Lady.

So, instead of making his escape as the pest cantered toward him, Lad stood where he was. Wolf bounded upward and as usual nipped merrily at one of Lad's ears. Lad did not shake off his tormentor and stalk away. In spite of the pain to the sensitive flesh, he remained quiet, looking down at the joyful puppy with a sort of sorrowing friendliness. He seemed to realize that Wolf, too, was lonely and that the little dog was helpless.

Tired of biting an unprotesting ear, Wolf dived for Lad's white forelegs, gnawing happily at them with a playfully unconscious throwback to his wolf ancestors who sought thus to disable an enemy by breaking the foreleg bone. For all seemingly aimless puppy play had its origin in some ancestral custom.

Lad bore this new bother unflinchingly. Presently Wolf left off the sport. Lad crossed to the veranda and lay down. The puppy trotted over to him and stood for a moment with ears cocked and head on one side as if planning a new attack on his supine victim; then with a little satisfied whimper, he curled up close against his father's shaggy side and went to sleep.

Lad gazed down at the slumberer in some perplexity. He seemed even inclined to resent the familiarity of being used for a pillow. Then, noting that the fur on the top of the puppy's sleepy head was rumpled, Lad bent over and began softly to lick back the tousled hair into shape with his curving tongue—his raspberry-pink tongue with the single queer blue-black blot midway on its surface. The puppy mumbled drowsily in his sleep and nestled more snugly to his new protector.

And thus Lad assumed formal guardianship of his obstreperous little son. It was a guardianship more staunch by far than Lady's had been of late. For animal mothers early wear out their zealously self-sacrificing love for their young. By the time the latter are able to shift for themselves, the maternal care ceases. And, later on, the once-inseparable relationship drops completely out of mind.

Paternity, among dogs, is, from the very first, no tie at all. Lad, probably, had no idea of his relationship to his new ward. His adoption of Wolf was due solely to his own love for Lady and to the big heart and soul that stirred him into pity for anything helpless.

Lad took his new duties very seriously indeed. He not only accepted the annoyance of Wolf's undivided teasing, but he assumed charge of the puppy's education as well—this to the amusement of everyone on the Place. But everyone's amusement was kept from Lad. The sensitive dog would rather have been whipped than laughed at. So both the mistress and master watched the educational process with outwardly straight faces.

A puppy needs an unbelievable amount of educating. It is a task to wear threadbare the teacher's patience and to do all kinds of things to the temper. Small wonder that many humans lose patience and temper during the process and idiotically resort to the whip, to the boot toe and to bellowing—in which case the puppy is never decently educated, but emerges from the process with a cowed and broken spirit or with an incurable streak of meanness that renders him worthless.

Time, patience, firmness, wisdom, temper control, gentleness— these be the six absolute essentials for training a puppy. Happy the human who is blessed with any three of these qualities. Lad, being only a dog, was abundantly possessed of all six. And he had need of them.

To begin with, Wolf had a joyous yearning to tear up or bury every portable thing that could be buried or torn. He had a craze for destruction. A dropped lace handkerchief, a cushion left on the grass, a book or a hat lying on a veranda chair—these and a thousand other things he looked on as treasure-trove, to be destroyed as quickly and as delightedly as possible.

He also enjoyed taking a flying leap onto the face or body of any hammock-sleeper. He would howl long and lamentably, nearly every night, at the moon. If the night were moonless, he howled on general principles. He thrilled with bliss at a chance to harry and terrify the chickens or peacocks or pigeons or any others of the Place's Little People that were safe prey for him. He tried this form of bullying once—only once—on the mistress's temperamental gray cat, Peter Grimm. For the rest of the day Wolf nursed a scratched nose and a torn ear—which, for nearly a week, taught him to give all cats a wide berth; or, at most, to bark harrowingly at them from a safe distance.

Again, Wolf had an insatiable craving to find out for himself whether or not everything on earth was good to eat. Kipling writes of puppies' experiments in trying to eat soap and blacking. Wolf added to this limited fare a hundred articles, from clothespins to cigars. The climax came when he found on the veranda table a two-pound box of chocolates, from which the wrapping paper and gilt cord had not yet been removed. Wolf ate not only all the candy, but the entire box and the paper and the string—after which he was tumultuously and horribly ill.

The foregoing were but a small percentage of his gay sins. And on respectable, middle-aged Lad fell the burden of making him into a decent canine citizen. Lad himself had been one of those rare puppies to whom the Law is taught with bewildering ease. A single command or prohibition had ever been enough to fix a rule in his almost uncannily human brain. Perhaps if the two little brown pups had lived, one or both of them might have taken after their sire in character. But Wolf was the true son of temperamental, willful Lady, and Lad had his job cut out for him in educating the puppy.

It was a slow, tedious process. Lad went at it, as he went at everything—with a gallant dash, behind which was an endless supply of resource and endurance. Once, for instance, Wolf leaped barkingly upon a filmy square of handkerchief that had just fallen from the mistress's belt. Before the destructive little teeth could rip the fine cambric into rags, the puppy found himself, to his amazement, lifted gently from earth by the scruff of his neck and held thus, in midair, until he dropped the handkerchief.

Lad then deposited him on the grass—whereupon Wolf pounced once more upon the handkerchief, only to be lifted a second time, painlessly but terrifyingly, above earth. After this was repeated five times, a gleam of sense entered the puppy's fluff-brain, and he trotted sulkily away, leaving the handkerchief untouched.

Again, when he made a wild rush at the friendly covey of peacock chicks, he found he had hurled himself against an object as immobile as a stone wall. Lad had darted in between the pup and the chicks, opposing his own big body to the charge. Wolf was bowled clean over by the force of the impact, and lay for a minute on his back, the breath knocked clean out of his bruised body.

It was a longer but easier task to teach him at whom to bark and at whom not to bark. By a sharp growl or a menacing curl of the lips, Lad silenced the youngster's clamorous salvo when a guest or tradesman entered the Place, whether on foot or in a car. By his own thunderously menacing bark he incited Wolf to a like outburst when some peddler or tramp sought to slouch down the drive toward the house.

The full tale of Wolf's education would require many profitless pages in the telling. At times the mistress and the master, watching from the sidelines, would wonder at Lad's persistency and would despair of his success. Yet bit by bit—and in a surprisingly short time for so vast an undertaking—Wolf's character was rounded into form. True, he had the ever-goading spirits of a true puppy. And these spirits sometimes led him to smash even such sections of the law as he fully understood. But he was a thoroughbred, and the son of clever parents. So he learned, on the whole, with gratifying speed —far more quickly than he could have been taught by the wisest human.

Nor was his education a matter of constant drudgery. Lad varied it by taking the puppy for long runs in the December woods and relaxed to the extent of romping laboriously with him at times.

Wolf grew to love his sire as he had never loved Lady. For the discipline and the firm kindliness of Lad were having their effect on his heart as well as on his manners. They struck a far deeper note within him than ever had Lady's alternating affection and crossness.

In truth, Wolf seemed to have forgotten Lady. But Lad had not. Every morning, the moment he was released from the house, Lad would trot over to Lady's empty kennel to see if by any chance she had come back to him during the night. There was eager hope in his big dark eyes as he hurried over to the vacant kennel. There was dejection in every line of his body as he turned away from his hopeless quest.

Late gray autumn had emerged overnight into white early winter. The ground of the Place lay blanketed in snow. The lake at the foot of the lawn was frozen solid from shore to shore. The trees crouched away from the whirling north wind as if in shame at their own black nakedness. Nature, like the birds, had flown south, leaving the northern world as dead and as empty and as cheerless as a deserted bird's nest.

The puppy reveled in the snow. He would roll in it and bite it, barking all the while in an ecstasy of excitement. His gold-and-white coat was thicker and shaggier now, to ward off the stinging cold. And the snow and the roaring winds were his playfellows rather than his foes.

Most of all, the hard-frozen lake fascinated him. Earlier, when Lad had taught him to swim, Wolf had at first shrunk back from the chilly black water. Now, to his astonishment, he could run on that water as easily—if somewhat sprawlingly—as on land. It was a miracle he never tired of testing. He spent half his time on the ice, despite an occasional hard tumble or involuntary slide.

Once and once only—in all her six-week absence and in his own six-week loneliness—had Lad discovered anything to remind him of his lost mate; and that discovery caused him for the first time in his blameless life to break the most sacred of the Place's simple Laws—the inviolable Guest Law.

It was on a day in late November. A runabout came down the drive to the front door of the house. In it rode the vet who had taken Lady away. He had stopped for a moment on his way to Paterson, to report as to Lady's progress at his dog hospital.

Lad was in the living room at the time. As a maid answered the summons at the door, he walked hospitably forward to greet the unknown guest. The vet stepped into the room by one door as the master entered it by the other—which was lucky for the vet.

Lad took one look at the man who had stolen Lady. Then, without a sound or other sign of warning, he launched his mighty bulk straight at the vet's throat.

Accustomed though he was to the ways of dogs, the vet had barely time to brace himself and to throw one arm in front of his throat. And then Lad's eighty pounds smote him on the chest, and Lad's powerful jaws closed viselike on the forearm that guarded the man's throat. Deep into the thick ulster the white teeth clove their way—through ulster sleeve and undercoat sleeve and the sleeves of a linen shirt and of flannels—clear through to the flesh of the forearm.

"Lad!" shouted the master, springing forward.

In obedience to the sharp command, Lad loosed his grip and dropped to the floor—where he stood quivering with leashed fury.

Through the rage-mists that swirled over his brain, he knew he had broken the Law. He had never merited punishment. He did not fear it. But the master's tone of fierce disapproval cut the sensitive dog soul more painfully than any scourge could have cut his body.

"Lad!" cried the master again, in rebuking amazement.

The dog turned, walked slowly over to the master and lay down at his feet. The master, without another word, opened the front door and pointed outward. Lad rose and slunk out. He had been ordered from the house, and in a stranger's presence!

"He thinks I'm responsible for his losing Lady," said the vet, looking ruefully at his torn sleeve. "That's why he went for me. I don't blame the dog. Don't lick him."

"I'm not going to lick him," growled the master. "I'd as soon thrash a woman. Besides, I've just punished him worse than if I'd taken an ax handle to him. Send me a bill for your coat."

In late December came a thaw—a freak thaw that changed the white ground to brown mud and rotted the smooth surface of the lake ice to gray slush. All day and all night the trees and the eaves sent forth a dreary *drip-drip-drip*. It was the traditional January thaw—set forward a month.

On the third and last morning of the thaw Wolf galloped down to the lake as usual. Lad jogged along at his side. As they reached the margin, Lad sniffed and drew back. His weird sixth sense somehow told him—as it tells an elephant—that there was danger ahead.

Wolf, however, was at the stage of extreme youth when neither dogs nor humans are bothered by premonitions. Ahead of him stretched the huge sheet of ice whereon he loved to gambol. Straightaway he frisked out upon it.

A rough growl of warning from Lad made him look back, but the lure of the ice was stronger than the call of duty.

The current, at this point of the lake, twisted sharply landward in a half-circle. Thus, for a few yards out, the rotting ice was still thick, but where the current ran, it was thin, and as soggy as wet blotting paper—as Wolf speedily discovered.

He bounded on the thinner ice driving his hind claws into the slushy surface for his second leap. He was dismayed to find that the ice collapsed under the pounding feet. There was a dull, sloppy sound. A ten-foot ice cake broke off from the main sheet, breaking at once into a dozen smaller cakes; and Wolf disappeared, tail first, into the swift-running water beneath.

To the surface he came, at the outer edge of the hole. He was mad, clear through, at the prank his beloved lake had played on him. He struck out for shore. On the landward side of the opening his forefeet clawed helplessly at the unbroken ledge of ice. He had not the strength or the wit to crawl upon it and make his way to land. The bitter chill of the water was already paralyzing him. The strong current was tugging at his hindquarters. Anger gave way to panic. The puppy wasted much of his remaining strength by lifting up his voice in ear-splitting howls.

The mistress and the master, motoring into the drive from the highway nearly a quarter-mile distant, heard the racket. The lake was plainly visible to them through the bare trees, even at that distance, and they took in the impending tragedy at a glance. They jumped out of the car and set off at a run to the water edge. The way was long and the ground was heavy with mud. They could not hope to reach the lake before the puppy's strength should fail.

But Lad was already there. At Wolf's first cry, Lad sprang out on the ice that heaved and chucked and cracked under his greater weight. His rush carried him to the very edge of the hole, and there, leaning forward and bracing all four of his absurdly tiny white paws, he sought to catch the puppy by the neck and lift him to safety. But before his rescuing jaws could close on Wolf's fur, the decayed ice gave way beneath his weight, and the ten-foot hole was widened by another twenty feet of water.

Down went Lad with a crash, and up he came, in almost no time, a few feet away from where Wolf floundered helplessly among the chunks of drifting ice. The breaking off of the shoreward mass of ice, under Lad's pressure, had left the puppy with no foothold at all. It had ducked him and had robbed him even of the chance to howl.

His mouth and throat full of water, Wolf strangled and splashed in a delirium of terror. Lad struck out for him, butting aside the impending ice chunks with his great shoulders, and swimming with a rush that lifted a third of his tawny body out of water. His jaws gripped Wolf by the middle of the back, and he swam thus with him toward shore. At the edge of the shoreward ice he gave a heave which called on every numbing muscle of the huge frame, and which—in spite of the burden he held—again lifted his head and shoulders high above water.

He thus flung Wolf's body halfway up on the ledge of ice. The puppy's flying forepaws chanced to strike the ice surface. His sharp claws bit into its soft upper crust. With a frantic wriggle he was out of the water and on top of this thicker stratum of shore ice, and in a second he had regained shore and was careering wildly up the lawn toward the greater safety of his kennel.

Yet, halfway in his flight, courage returned to the sopping-wet baby. He halted, turned about and, with a volley of falsetto barks, challenged the offending water to come ashore and fight fair.

As Wolf's forepaws had gripped the ice, he had further aided his climb to safety by thrusting downward with his hind legs. Both his hind paws had struck Lad's head, their thrust had driven Lad clean under water. There the current caught him.

When Lad came up, it was not to the surface but under the ice, some yards below. The top of his head struck stunningly against the underpart of the ice sheet.

A lesser dog would then and there have given up the struggle, or else would have thrashed about futilely until he drowned. Lad, perhaps on instinct, perhaps on reason, struck out toward the light—the spot where the great hole had let in sunshine through the gray ice sheet.

The average dog is not trained to swim under water. To this day, it is a mystery how Lad had the sense to hold his breath. He fought his way on, inch by inch, against the current, beneath the scratching rough under-surface of the ice—always toward the light. And just as his lungs must have been ready to burst, he reached the open space.

Sputtering and panting, Lad made for shore. Presently he reached the ice ledge that lay between him and the bank. He reached it just as the master, squirming along, face downward and at full length, began to work his way out over the swaying shore ice toward him.

Twice the big dog raised himself almost to the top of the ledge. Once the ice broke under his weight, dousing him. The second time he got his forequarters well over the top of the ledge, and he was struggling upward with all his tired body when the master's hand gripped his soaked ruff.

With this new help, Lad made a final struggle—a struggle that laid him gasping but safe on the slushy surface of the thicker ice. Backward over the few yards that still separated them from land he and the master crawled to the bank.

Lad was staggering as he started forward to greet the mistress, and his eyes were still dim and bloodshot from his fearful ordeal. Midway in his progress toward the mistress another dog barred his path—a dog that fell upon him in an ecstasy of delighted welcome.

Lad cleared his waterlogged nostrils for a growl of protest. He had surely done quite enough for Wolf this day, without the puppy's trying to rob him now of the mistress's caress. He was tired, and he was dizzy; and he wanted such petting and comfort and praise as only the worshipped mistress could give.

Impatience at the puppy's interference cleared the haze a little from Lad's brain and eyes. He halted in his shaky walk and stared, dumbfounded. This dog which greeted him so rapturously was not Wolf. It was—why, it was—Lady! Oh, it was *Lady!*

"We've just brought her back to you, old friend," the master was telling him. "We went over for her in the car this morning. She's all well again, and—"

But Lad did not hear. All he realized—all he wanted to realize— was that his mate was ecstatically nipping one of his ears to make him romp with her.

It was a sharp nip; and it hurt like the very mischief.

Lad loved to have it hurt.

CHAPTER 5

FOR A BIT OF RIBBON

Lad had never been in a city or in a crowd. To him the universe was bounded by the soft green mountains that hemmed in the valley and the lake. The Place stood on the lake's edge, its meadows running back to the forest. There were few houses nearer than the mile-distant village. It was an ideal home for such a dog as Lad, even as Lad was an ideal dog for such a home.

A guest started all the trouble—a guest who spent a weekend at the Place and who loved dogs far better than he understood them. He made much of Lad, being loud-voiced in his admiration of the stately collie. Lad endured the caresses when he could not politely elude them.

"Say!" announced the guest just before he departed, "If I had a dog like Lad, I'd show him—at the big show at Madison Square, you know. It's booked for next month. Why not take a chance and exhibit him there? Think what it would mean to you people to have a Westminster blue ribbon the big dog had won! Why, you'd be as proud as Punch!"

It was a careless speech and well meant. No harm might have come from it, had not the master the next day chanced upon an advance notice of the dog show in his morning paper. He read the press agent's quarter column proclamation. Then he remembered what the guest had said. The mistress was called into consultation. And it was she, as ever, who cast the deciding vote.

"Lad is twice as beautiful as any collie we ever saw at the show," she declared, "and not one of them is half as wise or good or *human* as he is. And—a blue ribbon is the greatest honor a dog can have, I suppose. It would be something to remember."

After which, the master wrote a letter to a friend who kept a show kennel of Airedales. He received this answer:

I don't pretend to know anything, professionally, about collies—Airedales being my specialty. But Lad is a beauty, as I remember him, and his pedigree shows a bunch of old-time champions. I'd risk it, if I were you. If you are in doubt and don't want to plunge, why not just enter him for the Novice Class? That is a class for dogs that have never before been shown. It will cost you five dollars to enter him for a single class, like that. And in the Novice, he won't be up against any champions or other dogs that have already won prizes. That will make it easier. It isn't a grueling competition like the Open or even the Limit. If he wins as a Novice, you can enter him, another time, in something more important. I'm inclosing an application blank for you to fill out and send with your entrance fee, to the secretary. You'll find his address at the bottom of the blank. I'm showing four of my Airedales there— so we'll be neighbors.

Thus encouraged, the master filled in the blank and sent it with a check. And in due time word was returned to him that "Sunnybank Lad" was formally entered for the Novice Class, at the Westminster Kennel Club's annual show at Madison Square Garden.

By this time both the mistress and the master were infected with the most virulent type of the "show germ." They talked of little else than the forthcoming event. They read all the dog-show literature they could lay hands on.

As for Lad, he was mercifully ignorant of what was in store for him.

The mistress had an inkling of his fated ordeal when she read the Kennel Club rule that no dog could be taken from the Garden, except at stated times, from the moment the show should begin, at 10:00 A.M. Wednesday morning, until the hour of its close, at ten o'clock Saturday night. For twelve hours a day—for four consecutive days—every entrant must be there. By paying a forfeit fee, dog owners might take their pets to some nearby hotel or stable, for the remainder of the night and early morning—a permission which, for obvious reasons, would not affect most dogs.

"But Lad's never been away from home a night in his life!" exclaimed the mistress in dismay. "He'll be horribly lonely there, all that while—especially at night."

By this time, with the mysterious foreknowledge of the best type of thoroughbred collie, Lad began to be aware that something unusual had crept into the atmosphere of the Place. It made him restless, but he did not associate it with himself—until the mistress took to giving him daily baths and brushings.

Always she had brushed him once a day, to keep his shaggy coat fluffy and burnished; and the lake had supplied him with baths that made him as clean as any human. But never had he undergone such searching massage with comb and brush as was now his portion. Never had he known such soap-infested scrubbings as were now his daily fate, for the week preceding the show.

As a result of these ministrations his wavy fur was like spun silk in texture; and it stood out all over him like the hair of a Circassian beauty in a dime museum. The white chest and forepaws were like snow. And his sides and broad back and mighty shoulders shone like dark bronze.

He was magnificent—but he was miserable. He knew well enough, now, that he was in some way the center of all this unwonted stir and excitement which pervaded the Place. He loathed change of any sort—a thoroughbred collie being ever an ultraconservative. This particular change seemed to threaten his peace; also it kept his skin scraped with combs and his hair redolent of nasty-smelling soaps.

To humans there was no odor at all in the naphtha soap with which the mistress lathered the dog, and every visible atom of it was washed away at once with warm water. But a human's sense of smell, compared with the best type of collie's, is as a purblind puppy's power of sight in comparison to a hawk's.

All over the East, during these last days before the Show, hundreds of high-bred dogs were undergoing preparation for an exhibition which to the beholder is a delight—and which to many of the canine exhibits is a form of unremitting torture. To do justice to the master and the mistress, they had no idea—then—of this torture. Otherwise all the blue ribbons ever woven would not have tempted them to subject their beloved chum to it.

In some kennels Airedales were "plucked," by hand, to rid them of the last vestige of the soft gray outer coat which is an Airedale's chief natural beauty—and no hair of which must be seen in a show. "Plucking" a dog is like pulling live hairs from a human head, so far as the sensation goes. But show traditions demand the anguish.

In other kennels, bull terriers' white coats were still further whitened by the harsh rubbing of pipe clay into the tender skin. Sensitive tails and still more sensitive ears were sandpapered, for the victims' greater beauty—and agony. Ear interiors, also, were shaved close with safety razors.

Murderous little "knife combs" were tearing blithely away at collies' ear interiors and heads, to barber natural furriness into painful and unnatural trimness. Ears were "scrunched" until their wearers quivered with stark anguish—to impart the perfect tulip shape; ordained by fashion for collies.

And so on, through every breed to be exhibited—each to its own form of torment; torments compared to which Lad's gentle if bothersome brushing and bathing were a pure delight!

Few of these ruthlessly "prepared" dogs were personal pets. The bulk of them were "kennel dogs"—dogs bred and raised after the formula for raising and breeding prize hogs or chickens, and with little more of the individual element in it. The dogs were bred in a way to bring out certain arbitrary "points" which count in show judging, and which change from year to year.

Brain, fidelity, devotion, the *human* side of a dog—these were totally ignored in the effort to breed the perfect physical animal. The dogs were kept in kennel buildings and in wire runs like so many pedigreed cattle—looked after by paid attendants, and trained to do nothing but to be the best-looking of their kind, and to win ribbons. Some of them did not know their owners by sight—having been reared wholly by hirelings.

The body was everything; the heart, the mind, the namelessly delightful quality of the master-raised dog—these were nothing. Such traits do not win prizes at a bench show. Therefore fanciers, whose sole aim is to win ribbons and cups, do not bother to cultivate them. (All of this is extraneous; but may be worth your remembering, next time you go to a dog show.)

Early on the morning of the show's first day, the mistress and the master set forth for town with Lad. They went in their little car, that the dog might not risk the dirt and cinders of a train.

Lad refused to eat a mouthful of the tempting breakfast set before him that day. He could not eat, when foreboding was hot in his throat. He had often ridden in the car. Usually he enjoyed the ride; but now he crawled rather than sprang into the backseat. All the way up the drive, his great mournful eyes were turned back toward the house in dumb appeal. Every atom of spirit and gayety and dash were gone from him. He knew he was being taken away from the sweet Place he loved, and that the car was whizzing him along toward some dreaded fate. His heart was sick within him.

To the born and bred show dog this is an everyday occurrence—painful, but inevitable. To a chum dog like Lad, it is heartbreaking. The big collie buried his head in the mistress's lap and crouched hopelessly at her feet as the car chugged cityward.

A thoroughly unhappy dog is the most thoroughly unhappy thing on earth. All the adored mistress's coaxings and pettings could not rouse Lad from his dull apathy of despair. This was the hour when he was wont to make his stately morning rounds of the Place, at the heels of one of his two deities. And now, instead, these deities were carrying him away to something direfully unpleasant. A lesser dog would have howled or would have struggled crazily to break away. Lad stood his ground like a furry martyr, and awaited his fate.

In an hour or so the ride ended. The car drew up at Madison Square—beside the huge yellowish building, arcaded and Diana-capped, which goes by the name of Garden and which is as nearly historic as any landmark in feverish New York is permitted to be.

Ever since the car had entered Manhattan Island, unhappy Lad's nostrils had been aquiver with a million new and troublesome odors. Now, as the car halted, these myriad strange smells were lost in one—an all-pervasive scent of dog. To a human, out there in the street, the scent was not observable. To a dog it was overwhelming.

Lad, at the Master's word, stepped down from the backseat onto the sidewalk. He stood there, dazedly sniffing. The plangent roar of the city was painful to his ears, which had always been attuned to the deep silences of forest and lake. And through this din he caught the muffled noise of the chorused barks and howls of many of his own kind.

The racket that bursts so deafeningly on humans as they enter the Garden, during a dog show, was wholly audible to Lad out in the street itself. And, as instinct or scent makes a hog flinch at going into a slaughterhouse, so the gallant dog's spirit quailed for a moment as he followed the mistress and the master into the building.

A man who is at all familiar with the ways of dogs can tell at once whether a dog's bark denotes cheer or anger or terror or grief or curiosity. To such a man a bark is as expressive of meanings as are the inflections of a human voice. To another dog these meanings are far more intelligible. And in the timbre of the multiple barks and yells that now assailed his ears, Lad read nothing to allay his own fears.

He was the hero of a half-dozen hard-won fights. He had once risked his life to save life. He had attacked tramps and peddlers and other stick-wielding invaders who had strayed into the grounds of the Place. Yet the tiniest semblance of fear now crept into his heart.

He looked up at the mistress, a world of sorrowing appeal in his eyes. At her gentle touch on his head and at a whisper of her loved voice, he moved onward at her side with no further hesitation. If these, his gods, were leading him to death, he would not question their right to do it, but would follow on as befitted a good soldier.

Through a doorway they went. At a wicket a yawning veterinarian glanced uninterestedly at Lad. As the dog had no outward and glaring signs of disease, the vet did not so much as touch him, but with a nod suffered him to pass. The vet was paid to inspect all dogs as they entered the show. Perhaps some of them were turned back by him, perhaps not; but after this, as after many another show, scores of kennels were swept by distemper and by other canine maladies, scores of deaths followed. That is one of the risks a dog exhibitor must take—or rather that his luckless dogs must take —in spite of the fees paid to yawning veterinarians to bar out sick entrants.

As Lad passed in through the doorway, he halted involuntarily in dismay. Dogs—dogs—DOGS! More than two thousand of them, from Great Dane to toy terrier, benched in row after row throughout the vast floor space of the Garden! Lad had never known there were so many dogs on earth.

Fully five hundred of them were barking or howling. The hideous volume of sound swelled to the Garden's vaulted roof and echoed back again like innumerable hammer blows upon the eardrum.

The mistress stood holding Lad's chain and softly caressing the bewildered dog, while the master went to make inquiries. Lad pressed his shaggy body closer to her knee for refuge, as he gazed blinkingly around him.

In the Garden's center were several large enclosures of wire and reddish wood. Inside each enclosure were a table, a chair and a movable platform. The platform was some six inches high and four feet square. At corners of these "judging rings" were blackboards on which the classes next to be inspected were chalked up.

All around the central space were alleys, on each side of which were lines of raised benches, two feet from the ground. The benches were carpeted with straw and were divided off by high wire partitions into compartments about three feet in area. Each compartment was to be the abiding place of some unfortunate dog for the next four days and nights. By short chains the dogs were bound into these open-fronted cells.

The chains left their wearers just leeway enough to stand up or lie down or to move to the various limits of the tiny space. In front of some of the compartments a wire barrier was fastened. This meant that the occupant was savage—in other words, that under the four-day strain he was likely to resent the stares or pokes or ticklings or promiscuous alien pattings of fifty thousand curious visitors.

The master came back with a plumply tipped attendant. Lad was conducted through a babel of yapping and snapping thoroughbreds of all breeds, to a section at the Garden's northeast corner, above which, in large black letters on a white sign, was inscribed "COLLIES." Here his conductors stopped before a compartment numbered "658."

"Up, Laddie!" said the mistress, touching the straw-carpeted bench.

Usually, at this command, Lad was wont to spring to the indicated height—whether car floor or tabletop—with the lightness of a cat. Now, one foot after another, he very slowly climbed into the compartment he was already beginning to detest—the cell which was planned to be his only resting spot for four interminable days. There he, who had never been tied, was ignominiously chained as though he were a runaway puppy. The insult bit to the depths of his sore soul. He curled down in the straw.

The mistress made him as comfortable as she could. She set before him the breakfast she had brought and told the attendant to bring him some water.

The master, meantime, had met a collie man whom he knew, and in company with this acquaintance he was walking along the collie section examining the dogs tied there. A dozen times had the master visited dog shows; but now that Lad was on exhibition, he studied the other collies with new eyes.

"Look!" he said boastfully to his companion, pausing before a bench whereon were chained a half-dozen dogs from a single illustrious kennel. "These fellows aren't in it with old Lad. See—their noses are tapered like toothpicks, and the span of their heads, between the ears, isn't as wide as my palm; and their eyes are little and they slant unbecomingly; and their bodies are as curved as a grayhound's. Compared with Lad, some of them are freaks. That's all they are, just freaks—not all of them, of course, but a lot of them."

"That's the idea nowadays," laughed the collie man patronizingly. "The up-to-date collie—this year's style, at least—is bred with a borzoi (wolfhound) head and with graceful, small bones. What's the use of his having brain and scenting power? He's used for exhibition or kept as a pet nowadays—not to herd sheep. Long nose, narrow head—"

"But Lad once tracked my footsteps two miles through a snowstorm," bragged the master, "and again on a road where fifty people had walked since I had; and he understands the meaning of every simple word. He—"

"Yes?" said the collie man, quite unimpressed. "Very interesting —but not useful in a show. Some of the big exhibitors still care for sense in their dogs, and they make companions of them—Eileen Moretta, for instance, and Fred Leighton and one or two more; but I find most of the rest are just out for the prizes. Let's have a look at your dog. Where is he?"

On the way down the alley toward Cell 658 they met the worried mistress.

"Lad won't eat a thing," she reported, "and he wouldn't eat before we left home this morning, either. He drinks plenty of water, but he won't eat. I'm afraid he's sick."

"They hardly ever eat at a show," the collie man consoled her, "hardly a mouthful—most of the high-strung ones, but they drink quarts of water. This is your dog, hey?" he broke off, pausing at 658. "H'm!"

He stood, legs apart, hands behind his back, gazing down at Lad. The dog was lying, head between paws, as before. He did not so much as glance up at the stranger, but his great wistful eyes roved from the mistress to the master and back again. In all this horrible place they two alone were his salvation.

"H'm!" repeated the collie man thoughtfully. "Eyes too big and not enough slanted. Head too thick for length of nose. Ears too far apart. Eyes too far apart, too. Not enough 'terrier expression' in them. Too much bone, too much bulk. Wonderful coat, though—glorious coat! Best coat I've seen this five years. Great brush, too! What's he entered for? Novice, hey? May get a third with him at that. He's the true type—but old-fashioned. I'm afraid he's too old-fashioned for such fast company as he's in. Still, you never can tell. Only it's a pity he isn't a little more—"

"I wouldn't have him one bit different in any way!" flashed the mistress. "He's perfect as he is. You can't see that, though, because he isn't himself now. I've never seen him so crushed and woebegone. I wish we had never brought him here."

"You can't blame him," said the collie man philosophically. "Why, just suppose *you* were brought to a strange place like this and chained into a cage and were left there four days and nights while hundreds of other prisoners kept screaming and shouting and crying at the top of their lungs every minute of the time! And suppose about a hundred thousand people kept jostling past your cage night and day, rubbering at you and pointing at you and trying to feel your ears and mouth, and chirping at you to shake hands, would *you* feel very hungry or very chipper? A four-day show is the most fearful thing a high-strung dog can go through—next to vivisection. A little one-day show, for about eight hours, is no special ordeal, especially if the dog's master stays near him all the time; but a four-day show is—is Sheol! I wonder the SPCA doesn't do something to make it easier."

"If I'd known—if we'd known—" began the mistress.

"Most of these folks know!" returned the collie man. "They do it year after year. There's a mighty strong lure in a bit of ribbon. Why, look what an exhibitor will do for it! He'll risk his dog's health and make his dog's life a horror. He'll ship him a thousand miles in a tight crate from show to show. (Some dogs die under the strain of so many journeys.) And he'll pay five dollars for every class the dog's entered in. Some exhibitors enter a single dog in five or six classes. The Association charges one dollar admission to the show. Crowds of people pay the price to come in. The exhibitor gets none of the gate money. All he gets for his five dollars or his twenty-five dollars is an off chance at a measly scrap of colored silk worth maybe four cents. That, and the same off-chance at a tiny cash prize that doesn't come anywhere near to paying his expenses. Yet, for all, it's the straightest sport on earth. Not an atom of graft in it, and seldom any profit. . . . So long! I wish you folks luck with 658."

He strolled on. The mistress was winking very fast and was bending over Lad, petting him and whispering to him. The master looked in curiosity at a kennel man who was holding down a nearby collie while a second man was trimming the scared dog's feet and fetlocks with a pair of curved shears; and now the master noted that nearly every dog but Lad was thus clipped as to ankle.

At an adjoining cell a woman was sifting almost a pound of talcum powder into her dog's fur to make the coat fluffier. Elsewhere similar weird preparations were in progress. And Lad's only preparation had been baths and brushing! The master began to feel like a fool.

People all along the collie line presently began to brush dogs (smoothing the fur the wrong way to fluff it) and to put other finishing touches on the poor beasts' makeup. The collie man strolled back to 658.

"The Novice Class in collies is going to be called presently," he told the mistress. "Where's your exhibition leash and choke-collar? I'll help you put them on."

"Why, we've only this chain," said the mistress. "We bought it for

Lad yesterday, and this is his regular collar—though he never has
had to wear it. Do we have to have another kind?"

"You don't have to unless you want to," said the collie man, "but
it's best—especially, the choke-collar. You see, when exhibitors go
into the ring, they hold their dogs by the leash close to the neck.
And if their dogs have choke-collars, why, then they've *got* to hold
their heads high when the leash is pulled. They've got to, to keep
from strangling. It gives them a fine, proud carriage of the head,
that counts a lot with some judges. All dog photos are taken that
way. Then the leash is blotted out of the negative. Makes the dog
look showy, too—keeps him from slumping. Can't slump much
when you're trying not to choke, you know."

"It's horrible! *Horrible!*" shuddered the mistress. "I wouldn't put
such a thing on Lad for all the prizes on earth. When I read Davis's
wonderful 'Bar Sinister' story, I thought dog shows were a real treat
to dogs. I see, now, they're—"

"Your class is called!" interrupted the collie man. "Keep his head
high, keep him moving as showily as you can. Lead him close to you
with the chain as short as possible. Don't be scared if any of the
other dogs in the ring happen to fly at him. The attendants will look
out for all that. Good luck."

Down the aisle and to the wired gate of the northeastern ring the
unhappy mistress piloted the unhappier Lad. The big dog gravely
kept beside her, regardless of other collies moving in the same direction. The Garden had begun to fill with visitors, and the ring was
surrounded with interested "rail-birds." The collie classes, as usual,
were among those to be judged on the first day of the four.

Through the gate into the ring the mistress piloted Lad. Six other
Novice dogs were already there. Beautiful creatures they were, and
all but one were led by kennel men. At the table, behind a ledger
flanked by piles of multicolored ribbons, sat the clerk. Beside the
platform stood a wizened and elderly little man in tweeds. He was
McGilead, who had been chosen as judge for the collie division. He
was a Scot, and he was also a man with stubborn opinions of his
own as to dogs.

Around the ring, at the judge's order, the Novice collies were paraded. Most of them stepped high and fast and carried their heads proudly aloft—the thin choke-collars cutting deep into their furry necks. One entered was a harum-scarum puppy who writhed and bit and whirled about in ecstasy of terror.

Lad moved solemnly along at the mistress's side. He did not pant or curvet or look showy. He was miserable and every line of his splendid body showed his misery. The mistress, too, glancing at the more spectacular dogs, wanted to cry—not because she was about to lose, but because Lad was about to lose. Her heart ached for him. Again she blamed herself bitterly for bringing him here.

McGilead, hands in pockets, stood sucking at an empty brier pipe, and scanning the parade that circled around him. Presently he stepped up to the mistress, checked her as she filed past him, and said to her with a sort of sorrowful kindness, "Please take your dog over to the far end of the ring. Take him into the corner where he won't be in my way while I am judging."

Yes, he spoke courteously enough, but the mistress would rather have had him hit her across the face. Meekly she obeyed his command. Across the ring, to the very farthest corner, she went—poor beautiful Lad beside her, disgraced, weeded out of the competition at the very start. There, far out of the contest, she stood, a drooping little figure, feeling as though everyone were sneering at her dear dog's disgrace.

Lad seemed to sense her sorrow. For, as he stood beside her, head and tail low, he whined softly and licked her hand as if in encouragement. She ran her fingers along his silky head. Then, to keep from crying, she watched the other contestants.

No longer were these parading. One at a time and then in twos, the judge was standing them on the platform. He looked at their teeth. He pressed their heads between his hands. He "hefted" their hips. He ran his fingers through their coats. He pressed his palm upward against their underbodies. He subjected them to a score of such annoyances, but he did it all with a quick and sure touch that not even the crankiest of them could resent.

Then he stepped back and studied the quartet. After that he seemed to remember Lad's presence, and, as though by way of earning his fee, he slouched across the ring to where the forlorn mistress was petting her dear disgraced dog.

Lazily, perfunctorily, the judge ran his hand over Lad, with absolutely none of the thoroughness that had marked his inspection of the other dogs. Apparently there was no need to look for the finer points in a disqualified collie. The sketchy examination did not last three seconds. At its end the judge jotted down a number on a pad he held. Then he laid one hand heavily on Lad's head and curtly thrust out his other hand at the mistress.

"Can I take him away now?" she asked, still stroking Lad's fur.

"Yes," rasped the judge, "and take this along with him."

In his outstretched hand fluttered a little bunch of silk—dark blue, with gold lettering on it.

The blue ribbon! First prize in the Novice Class! And this grouchy little judge was awarding it—to *Lad!*

The mistress looked very hard at the bit of blue and gold in her fingers. She saw it through a queer mist. Then, as she stooped to fasten it to Lad's collar, she furtively kissed the tiny white spot on the top of his head.

"It's something like the 'Bar Sinister' victory after all!" she exclaimed joyously as she rejoined the delighted master at the ring gate. "But, oh, it was terrible for a minute or two, wasn't it?"

Now, Angus McGilead, Esq. (late of Linlithgow, Scotland), had a knowledge of collies such as is granted to few men, and this very fact made him a wretchedly bad dog show judge; as the Kennel Club, which—on the strength of his fame—had engaged his services for this single occasion, speedily learned. The greatest lawyer makes often the worst judge. Legal annals prove this; and the same thing applies to dog experts. They are sane rather than judicial.

McGilead had scant patience with the ultramodern, inbred and grayhoundlike collies which had so utterly departed from their ancestral standards. At one glimpse he had recognized Lad as a dog after his own heart—a dog that brought back to him the murk and magic of the Highland moors.

He had noted the deep chest, the mighty forequarters, the tiny white paws, the incredible wealth of outer- and under-coat, the brush, the grand head, and the soul in the eyes. This was such a dog as McGilead's shepherd ancestors had admitted as an honored equal, at hearth and board—such a dog, for brain and brawn and beauty, as a Highland master would no sooner sell than he would sell his own child.

McGilead, therefore, had waved Lad aside while he judged the lesser dogs of his class, lest he be tempted to look too much at Lad and too little at them; and he rejoiced, at the last, to give honor where all honor was due.

Through dreary hours that day Lad lay disconsolate in his cell, nose between paws, while the stream of visitors flowed sluggishly past him. His memory of the Guest Law prevented him from showing his teeth when some of these passing humans paused in front of the compartment to pat him or to consult his number in their catalogues. But he accorded not so much as one look—to say nothing of a handshake—to any of them.

A single drop of happiness was in his sorrow-cup. He had, seemingly, done something that made both the master and the mistress very, *very* proud of him. He did not know just why they should be for he had done nothing clever. In fact, he had been at his dullest. But they *were* proud of him—undeniably proud, and this made him glad, through all his black despondency.

Even the collie man seemed to regard him with more approval than before—not that Lad cared at all; and two or three exhibitors came over for a special look at him. From one of these exhibitors the mistress learned of a dog-show rule that was wholly new to her.

She was told that the winning dog of each and every class was obliged to return later to the ring to compete in what was known as the Winners' Class—a contest whose entrants included every class-victor from Novice to Open. Briefly, this special competition was to determine which class-winner was the best collie in the whole list of winners and, as such, entitled to a certain number of "points" toward a championship. There were eight of these winners.

One or two such world-famed champions as Grey Mist and

Southport Sample were in the show "for exhibition only." But the pick of the remaining leaders must compete in the Winners' Class —Sunnybank Lad among them. The master's heart sank at this news.

"I'm sorry!" he said. "You see, it's one thing to win as a Novice against a bunch of untried dogs, and quite another to compete against the best dogs in the show. I wish we could get out of it."

"Never mind!" answered the mistress. "Laddie has won his ribbon. They can't take that away from him. There's a silver cup for the Winners' Class, though. I wish there had been one for the Novices."

The day wore on. At last came the call for "Winners!" And for the second time poor Lad plodded reluctantly into the ring with the mistress. But now, instead of novice dogs, he was confronted by the cream of colliedom.

Lad's heartsick aspect showed the more intensely in such company. It grieved the mistress bitterly to see his disconsolate air. She thought of the three days and nights to come—the nights when she and the master could not be with him, when he must lie listening to the babel of yells and barks all around, with nobody to speak to him except some neglectful and sleepy attendant. And for the sake of a blue ribbon she had brought this upon him!

The mistress came to a sudden and highly unsportsmanlike resolution.

Again the dogs paraded the ring. Again the judge studied them from between half-shut eyes. But this time he did not wave Lad to one side. The mistress had noted, during the day, that McGilead had always made known his decisions by first laying his hand on the victor's head. And she watched breathless for such a gesture.

One by one the dogs were weeded out until only two remained. Of these two, one was Lad—the mistress's heart banged crazily— and the other was Champion Coldstream Guard. The Champion was a grand dog, gold-and-white of hue, perfect of coat and line, combining all that was best in the old and new styles of collies. He carried his head nobly aloft with no help from the choke-collar. His "tulip" ears hung at precisely the right curve.

Lad and Coldstream Guard were placed shoulder to shoulder on the platform. Even the mistress could not fail to contrast her pet's woebegone aspect with the Champion's alert beauty.

"Lad!" she said, very low, and speaking with slow intentness as McGilead compared the two. "Laddie, we're going home. Home! *Home,* Lad!"

Home! At the word, a thrill went through the great dog. His shoulders squared. Up went his head and his ears. His dark eyes fairly glowed with eagerness as he looked expectantly up at the mistress. *Home!*

Yet, despite the transformation, the other was the finer dog—from a mere show viewpoint. The mistress could see he was. Even the new uptilt of Lad's ears could not make those ears so perfect in shape and attitude as were the Champion's.

With almost a gesture of regret McGilead laid his hand athwart Coldstream Guard's head. The mistress read the verdict, and she accepted it.

"Come, Laddie, dear," she said tenderly. "You're second, anyway, Reserve-Winner. That's *something.*"

"Wait!" snapped McGilead.

The judge was seizing one of Champion Coldstream Guard's supershapely ears and turning it backward. His sensitive fingers, falling on the dog's head in token of victory, had encountered an odd stiffness in the curve of the ear. Now he began to examine that ear, and then the other, and thereby he disclosed a most clever bit of surgical bandaging.

Neatly crisscrossed, inside each of the Champion's ears, was a succession of adhesive strips cut thin and running from tip to orifice. The scientific applying of these strips had painfully imparted to the prick-ears (the dog's one flaw) the perfect tulip shape so desirable as a show quality. Champion Coldstream Guard's silken ears could not have had other than ideal shape and posture if he had wanted them to—while that crisscross of sticky strips held them in position!

Now, this was no new trick—the ruse that the Champion's handlers had employed. Again and again in bench shows, it had been employed upon bull terriers. A year or two ago a woman was ordered from the ring, at the Garden, when plaster was found inside her terrier's ears, but seldom before had it been detected in a collie—in which a prick-ear usually counts as a fatal blemish.

McGilead looked at the Champion. Long and searchingly he looked at the man who held the Champion's leash—and who fidgeted grinningly under the judge's glare. Then McGilead laid both hands on Lad's great honest head—almost as in benediction.

"Your dog wins, madam," he said, "and while it is no part of a judge's duty to say so, I am heartily glad. I won't insult you by asking if he is for sale, but if ever you have to part with him—"

He did not finish, but abruptly gave the mistress the Winners' Class rosette.

And now, as Lad left the ring, hundreds of hands were put out to pat him. All at once he was a celebrity.

Without returning the dog to the bench, the mistress went directly to the collie man.

"When do they present the cups?" she asked.

"Not until Saturday night, I believe," said the man. "I congratulate you both on—"

"In order to win his cup, Lad will have to stay in this—this inferno—for three days and nights longer?"

"Of course. All the dogs—"

"If he doesn't stay, he won't get the cup?"

"No. It would go to the Reserve, I suppose, or to—"

"Good!" declared the mistress in relief. "Then he won't be defrauding anyone, and they can't rob him of his two ribbons because I have those."

"What do you mean?" asked the puzzled collie man.

But the master understood—and approved.

"Good!" he said. "I wanted all day to suggest it to you, but I didn't have the nerve. Come around to the Exhibitors' Entrance. I'll go ahead and start the car."

"But what's the idea?" queried the collie man in bewilderment.

"The idea," replied the mistress, "is that the cup can go to any dog that wants it. Lad's coming *home*. He knows it, too. Just look at him. I promised him he should go home. We can get there by dinnertime, and he has a day's fast to make up for."

"But," expostulated the scandalized collie man, "if you withdraw your dog like that, the Association will never allow you to exhibit him at its shows again."

"The Association can have a pretty silver cup," retorted the mistress, "to console it for losing Lad. As for exhibiting him again— well, I wouldn't lose these two ribbons for a hundred dollars, but I wouldn't put my worst enemy's dog to the torture of winning them over again. Come along, Lad, we're going back home."

At the talisman word, Lad broke silence for the first time in all that vilely wretched day. He broke it with a series of thunderously trumpeting barks that quite put to shame the puny noisemaking efforts of every other dog in the show.

CHAPTER 6

LOST!

Four of us were discussing abstract themes, idly, as men will, after a good dinner and in front of a country-house fire. Someone asked, "What is the saddest sight in everyday life? I don't mean the most gloomily tragic, but the saddest."

A frivolous member of the fireside group cited a helpless man between two quarreling women. A sentimentalist said, "A lost child in a city street."

The dog master contradicted, "A lost *dog* in a city street."

Nobody agreed with him of course; but that was because none of the others chanced to know dogs—to know their psychology—their souls, if you prefer. The dog man was right. A lost dog in a city street is the very saddest and most hopeless sight in all a city street's abounding everyday sadness.

A man between two quarreling women is an object piteous enough, heaven knows. Yet his plight verges too much on the grotesque to be called sad.

A lost child? No. Let a child stand in the middle of a crowded sidewalk and begin to cry. In one minute fifty amateur and professional rescuers have flocked to the lost one's aid. An hour, at most, suffices to bring it in touch with its frenzied guardians.

A lost dog? Yes. No succoring cohort surges to the relief. A gang of boys, perhaps, may give chase, but assuredly not in kindness. A policeman seeking a record for "mad dog" shooting—a professional dogcatcher in quest of his dirty fee—these will show marked attention to the wanderer. But, again, not in kindness.

A dog, at some turn in the street, misses his master—doubles back to where the human demigod was last seen—darts ahead once more to find him, through the press of other human folk—halts, hesitates, begins the same maneuvers all over again; then stands, shaking in panic at his utter aloneness.

Get the look in his eyes, then—you who do not mind seeing such things—and answer, honestly: Is there anything sadder on earth? All this, before the pursuit of boys and the fever of thirst and the final knowledge of desolation have turned him from a handsome and prideful pet into a slinking outcast.

Yes, a lost dog is the saddest thing that can meet the gaze of a man or woman who understands dogs. As perhaps my story may help to show—or perhaps not.

Lad had been brushed and bathed, daily, for a week, until his mahogany-and-snow coat shone. All this, at the Place, far up in the North Jersey hinterland and all to make him presentable for the Westminster Kennel Show at New York's Madison Square Garden. After which, his two gods, the mistress and the master, took him for a thirty-mile ride in the Place's only car, one morning.

The drive began at the Place—the domain where Lad had ruled as king among the lesser folk for so many years. It ended at Madison Square Garden, where the annual four-day dog show was in progress.

You have read how Lad fared at that show—how, at the close of the first day, when he had two victories to his credit, the mistress had taken pity on his misery and had decreed that he should be taken home, without waiting out the remaining three days of torture ordeal.

The master went out first, to get the car and bring it around to the side exit of the Garden. The mistress gathered up Lad's belongings—his brush, his dog biscuits, etc., and followed, with Lad himself.

Out of the huge building, with its reverberating barks and yells from two thousand canine throats, she went. Lad paced, happy and majestic, at her side. He knew he was going home, and the unhappiness of the hideous day dropped from him.

At the exit, the mistress was forced to leave a deposit "to insure the return of the dog to his bench" (to which bench of agony she vowed, secretly, Lad should never return). Then she was told the law demands that all dogs in New York City streets shall be muzzled.

In vain she explained that Lad would be in the streets only for such brief time as the car would require to journey to the 130th Street ferry. The door attendant insisted that the law was inexorable. So, lest a policeman hold up the car for such disobedience to the city statutes, the mistress reluctantly bought a muzzle.

It was a big, awkward thing, made of steel, and bound on with leather straps. It looked like a rattrap. And it fenced in the nose and mouth of its owner with a wicked crisscross of shiny metal bars.

Never in all his years had Lad worn a muzzle. Never, until today, had he been chained. The splendid eighty-pound collie had been as free of the Place and of the forests as any human; and with no worse restrictions than his own soul and conscience put upon him.

To him this muzzle was a horror. Not even the loved touch of the mistress's dear fingers, as she adjusted the thing to his beautiful head, could lessen the degradation. And the discomfort of it—a discomfort that amounted to actual pain—was almost as bad as the humiliation.

With his absurdly tiny white forepaws, the huge dog sought to dislodge the torture implement. He strove to rub it off against the mistress's skirt. But beyond shifting it so that the forehead strap covered one of his eyes, he could not budge it.

Lad looked up at the mistress in wretched appeal. His look held no resentment, nothing but sad entreaty. She was his deity. All his life she had given him of her gentleness, her affection, her sweet understanding. Yet, today, she had brought him to this abode of noisy torment, and had kept him there from morning to dusk. And now—just as the vigil seemed ended—she was tormenting him, to nerverack, by this contraption she had fastened over his nose. Lad did not rebel. But he besought. And the mistress understood.

"Laddie, dear!" she whispered, as she led him across the sidewalk to the curb where the master waited for the car. "Laddie, old friend, I'm just as sorry about it as you are. But it's only for a few minutes. Just as soon as we get to the ferry, we'll take it off and throw it into the river. And we'll never bring you again where dogs have to wear such things. I promise. It's only for a few minutes."

The mistress, for once, was mistaken. Lad was to wear the accursed muzzle for much, *much* longer than "a few minutes."

"Give him the back seat to himself, and come in front here with me," suggested the master, as the mistress and Lad arrived alongside the car. "The poor old chap has been so cramped up and pestered all day that he'll like to have a whole seat to stretch out on."

Accordingly, the mistress opened the door and motioned Lad to the back seat. At a bound the collie was on the cushion, and proceeded to curl up thereon. The mistress got into the front seat with the master. The car set forth on its six-mile run to the ferry.

Now that his face was turned homeward, Lad might have found vast interest in his new surroundings, had not the horrible muzzle absorbed all his powers of emotion. The Milan Cathedral, the Taj Mahal, the Valley of the Arno at sunset—these be sights to dream of for years. But show them to a man who has an ulcerated tooth, or whose tight, new shoes pinch his soft corn, and he will probably regard them as Lad just then viewed the twilight New York streets.

He was a dog of forest and lake and hill, this giant collie with his mighty shoulders and tiny white feet and shaggy burnished coat and mournful eyes. Never before had he been in a city. The myriad blended noises confused and deafened him. The myriad blended smells assailed his keen nostrils. The swirl of countless multicolored lights stung and blurred his vision. Noises, smells, and lights were all jarringly new to him. So were the jostling masses of people on the sidewalk and the tangle and hustle of vehicular traffic through which the master was threading the car's way with such difficulty.

But, newest and most sickening of all the day's novelties was the muzzle.

Lad was quite certain the mistress did not realize how the muzzle was hurting him nor how he detested it. In all her dealings with him —or with anyone or anything else—the mistress had never been unkind; and most assuredly not cruel. It must be she did not understand. At all events, she had not scolded or forbidden, when he had tried to rub the muzzle off. So the wearing of this new torture was apparently no part of the Law. And Lad felt justified in striving again to remove it.

In vain he pawed the thing, first with one foot, then with both. He could joggle it from side to side, but that was all. And each shift of the steel bars hurt his tender nose and tenderer sensibilities worse than the one before. He tried to rub it off against the seat cushion—with the same distressing result.

Lad looked up at the backs of his gods, and whined very softly. The sound went unheard, in the babel of noise all around him. Nor did the mistress, or the master turn around, on general principles, to speak a word of cheer to the sufferer. They were in a mixup of crossways traffic that called for every atom of their attention, if they were to avoid collision. It was no time for conversation or for dog patting.

Lad got to his feet and stood, uncertainly, on the slippery leather cushion, seeking to maintain his balance, while he rubbed a corner of the muzzle against one of the supports of the car's lowered top. Working away with all his might, he sought to get leverage that would pry loose the muzzle.

Just then there was a brief gap in the traffic. The master put on speed, and, darting ahead of a delivery truck, sharply rounded the corner into a side street.

The car's sudden twist threw Lad clean off his precarious balance on the seat, and hurled him against one of the rear doors.

The door, insecurely shut, could not withstand the eighty-pound impact. It burst open. And Lad was flung out onto the greasy asphalt of the avenue.

He landed full on his side, in the muck of the roadway, with a force that shook the breath clean out of him. Directly above his head glared the twin lights of the delivery truck the master had just shot past. The truck was going at a good twelve miles an hour. And the dog had fallen within six feet of its fat front wheels.

Now, a collie is like no other animal on earth. He is, at worst, more wolf than dog. And, at best, he has more of the wolf's light-ning-swift instinct than has any other breed of canine. For which reason Lad was not, then and there, smashed, flat and dead, under the forewheels of a three-ton truck.

Even as the tires grazed his fur, Lad gathered himself compactly together, his feet well under him, and sprang far to one side. The lumbering truck missed him by less than six inches. But it missed him.

His leap brought him scramblingly down on all fours, out of the truck's way, but on the wrong side of the thoroughfare. It brought him under the very fender of a touring car that was going at a good pace in the opposite direction. And again, a leap that was inspired by quick instinct alone, lifted the dog free of this newest death menace.

He halted and stared piteously around in search of his deities. But in that glare and swelter of traffic, a trained human eye could not have recognized any particular car. Moreover, the mistress and master were a full half-block away, down the less crowded side street, and were making up for lost time by putting on all the speed they dared, before turning into the next westward traffic artery. They did not look back, for there was a car directly in front of them, whose driver seemed uncertain as to his wheel control, and the master was maneuvering to pass it in safety.

Not until they had reached the lower end of Riverside Drive, nearly a mile to the north, did either the master or mistress turn around for a word with the dog they loved.

Meantime, Lad was standing, irresolute and panting, in the middle of Columbus Circle. Cars of a million types seemed to be whizzing directly at him from every direction at once.

A bound, a dodge, or a deft shrinking back would carry him out of one such peril—barely out of it—when another, or fifty others, beset him.

And, all the time, even while he was trying to duck out of danger, his frightened eyes and his pulsing nostrils sought the mistress and the master.

His eyes, in that mixture of flare and dusk, told him nothing except that a host of motors were likely to kill him. But his nose told him what it had not been able to tell him since morning—namely, that, through the reek of gasoline and horseflesh and countless human scents, there was a nearness of fields and woods and water. And, toward that blessed mingling of familiar odors he dodged his threatened way.

By a miracle of luck and skill he crossed Columbus Circle, and came to a standstill on a sidewalk, beside a low gray stone wall. Behind the wall, his nose taught him, lay miles of meadow and wood and lake—Central Park. But the smell of the park brought him no scent of the mistress nor of the master. And it was they—infinitely more than his beloved countryside—that he craved. He ran up the street, on the sidewalk, for a little way, hesitant, alert, watching in every direction. Then, perhaps seeing a figure, in the other direction, that looked familiar, he dashed at top speed, eastward, for half a block. Then he made a peril-fraught sortie out into the middle of the traffic-humming street, deceived by the look of a passing car.

The car was traveling at twenty miles an hour. But, in less than a block, Lad caught up with it. And this, in spite of the many things he had to dodge, and the greasy slipperiness of the unfamiliar roadway. An upward glance, as he came alongside the car, told him his chase was in vain. And he made his precarious way to the sidewalk once more.

There he stood, bewildered, heartsick—lost!

Yes, he was lost. And he realized it—realized it as fully as would a city dweller snatched up by magic and set down amid the trackless Himalayas. He was lost. And horror bit deep into his soul.

The average dog might have continued to waste energy and risk life by galloping aimlessly back and forth, running hopefully up to every stranger he met; then slinking off in scared disappointment and searching afresh.

Lad was too wise for that. He was lost. His adored mistress had somehow left him, as had the master, in this bedlam place—all alone. He stood there, hopeless, head and tail adroop, his great heart dead within him.

Presently he became aware once more that he was still wearing his abominable muzzle. In the stress of the past few minutes Lad had actually forgotten the pain and vexation of the thing. Now, the memory of it came back, to add to his despair.

And, as a sick animal will ever creep to the woods and the waste places for solitude, so the soulsick Lad now turned from the clangor and evil odors of the street to seek the stretch of country land he had scented.

Over the gray wall he sprang, and came earthward with a crash among the leafless shrubs that edged the south boundary of Central Park.

Here in the park there were people and lights and motorcars, too, but they were few, and they were far off. Around the dog was a grateful darkness and aloneness. He lay down on the dead grass and panted.

The time was late February. The weather of the past day or two had been mild. The brown-gray earth and the black trees had a faint odor of slow-coming spring, though no nostrils less acute than a dog's could have noted it.

Through the misery at his heart and the carking pain from his muzzle, Lad began to realize that he was tired, also that he was hollow from lack of food. The long day's ordeal of the dog show had wearied him and had worn down his nerves more than could a fifty-mile run. The nasty thrills of the past half-hour had completed his fatigue. He had eaten nothing all day. Like most high-strung dogs at a show, he had drunk a great deal of water and had refused to touch a morsel of food.

He was not hungry even now for, in a dog, hunger goes only with peace of mind, but he was cruelly thirsty. He got up from his slushy couch on the dead turf and trotted wearily toward the nearest branch of the Central Park lake. At the brink he stooped to drink.

Soggy ice still covered the lake, but the mild weather had left a half-inch skim of water over it. Lad tried to lap up enough of this water to allay his craving thirst. He could not.

The muzzle protruded nearly an inch beyond his nose. Either through faulty adjustment or from his own futile efforts to scrape it off, the awkward steel hinge had become jammed and would not open. Lad could not get his teeth a half-inch apart.

After much effort he managed to protrude the end of his pink tongue and to touch the water with it, but it was a painful and drearily slow process absorbing water drop by drop in this way. More through fatigue than because his thirst was slaked, he stopped at last and turned away from the lake.

The next half-hour was spent in a diligent and torturing and wholly useless attempt to rid himself of his muzzle.

After which the dog lay panting and athirst once more; his tender nose sore and bruised and bleeding; the muzzle as firmly fixed in place as ever. Another journey to the lake and another Tantalus-effort to drink—and the pitifully harassed dog's uncanny brain began to work.

He no longer let himself heed the muzzle. Experience of the most painful sort had told him he could not dislodge it nor, in that clamorous and ill-smelling city beyond the park wall, could he hope to find the mistress and the master. These things being certain, his mind went on to the next step, and the next step was—home!

Home! The Place where his happy, beautiful life had been spent, where his two gods abode, where there were no clang and reek and peril as here in New York. Home—the House of Peace!

Lad stood up. He drew in great breaths of the muggy air, and he turned slowly about two or three times, head up, nostrils aquiver. For a full minute he stood thus. Then he lowered his head and trotted westward. No longer he moved uncertainly, but with as much sureness as if he were traversing the forest behind the Place —the forest that had been his roaming-ground since puppyhood.

(Now, this is not a fairy story, nor any other type of fanciful yarn, so I do not pretend to account for Lad's heading unswervingly toward the northwest in the exact direction of the Place, thirty miles distant, any more than I can account for the authenticated case of a collie who, in 1917, made his way four hundred miles from the home of a new owner in southern Georgia to the doorstep of his former and better loved master in the mountains of North Carolina; any more than I can account for the flight of a homing pigeon or for that of the northbound duck in spring. God gives to certain animals a whole set of mystic traits which He withholds utterly from humans. No dog student can doubt that, and no dog student or deep-delving psychologist can explain it.)

Northwestward jogged Lad, and in half a mile he came to the low western wall of Central Park. Without turning aside to seek a gateway, he cleared the wall and found himself on Eighth Avenue in the very middle of a block.

Keeping on the sidewalk and paying no heed to the few pedestrians, he moved along to the next westward street and turned down it toward the Hudson River. So calmly and certainly did he move that none would have taken him for a lost dog.

Under the roaring elevated road at Columbus Avenue, he trotted; his ears tormented by the racket of a train that reverberated above him; his sense so blurred by the sound that he all but forgot to dodge a southbound trolley car.

Down the cross street to Amsterdam Avenue he bore. A patrolman, on his way to the West Sixty-ninth Street police station to report for night duty, was so taken up by his own lofty thoughts that he quite forgot to glance at the big mud-spattered dog that padded past him.

For this lack of observation the patrolman was destined to lose a good opportunity for fattening his monthly pay. Because, on reaching the station, he learned that a distressed man and woman had just been there in a car to offer a fifty-dollar reward for the finding of a big mahogany-and-white collie, answering to the name of Lad.

As the dog reached Amsterdam Avenue a high little voice squealed delightedly at him. A three-year-old baby—a mere fluff of gold and white and pink—was crossing the avenue convoyed by a fat woman in black. Lad was jogging by the mother and child when the latter discovered the passing dog.

With a shriek of joyous friendliness the baby flung herself upon Lad and wrapped both arms about his shaggy neck.

"Why, *Doggie!*" she shrilled, ecstatically. "Why, dear, *dear* Doggie!"

Now Lad was in dire haste to get home, and Lad was in dire misery of mind and body, but his big heart went out in eagerly loving answer to the impulsive caress. He worshipped children, and would cheerfully endure from them any amount of mauling.

At the baby embrace and the baby voice, he stopped short in his progress. His plumy tail wagged in glad friendliness; his muzzled nose sought wistfully to kiss the pink little face on a level with his own. The baby tightened her hug, and laid her rose leaf cheek close to his own.

"I love you, Miss Doggie!" she whispered in Lad's ear.

Then the fat woman in black bore down upon them. Fiercely, she yanked the baby away from the dog. Then, seeing that the mud on Lad's shoulder had soiled the child's white coat, she whirled a string-fastened bundle aloft and brought it down with a resounding thwack over the dog's head.

Lad winced under the heavy blow, then hot resentment blazed through his first instant of grieved astonishment. This unpleasant fat creature in black was not a man, wherefore Lad contented himself by baring his white teeth, and with growling deep menace far down in his throat.

The woman shrank back scared, and she screamed loudly. On the instant the station-bound patrolman was beside her.

"What's wrong, ma'am?" asked the bluecoat.

The woman pointed a wobbly and fat forefinger at Lad, who had taken up his westward journey again and was halfway across the street.

"Mad dog!" she sputtered, hysterically. "He—he bit me! Bit *at* me, anyhow!"

Without waiting to hear the last qualifying sentence, the patrolman gave chase. Here was a chance for honorable blotter mention at the very least. As he ran he drew his pistol.

Lad had reached the westward pavement of Amsterdam Avenue and was in the side street beyond. He was not hurrying, but his short wolftrot ate up ground in deceptively quick time.

By the time the policeman had reached the west corner of street and avenue the dog was nearly a half-block ahead. The officer, still running, leveled his pistol and fired.

Now, anyone (but a very newly-appointed patrolman or a movie hero) knows that to fire a shot when running is worse than fatal to any chance of accuracy. No marksman—no one who has the remotest knowledge of marksmanship—will do such a thing. The very best pistol expert cannot hope to hit his target if he is joggling his own arm and his whole body by the motion of running.

The bullet flew high and to the right, smashing a second-story window and making the echoes resound deafeningly through the narrow street.

"What's up?" excitedly asked a boy, who stood beside a barrel bonfire with a group of chums.

"Mad dog!" puffed the policeman as he sped past.

At once the boys joined gleesomely in the chase, outdistancing the officer, just as the latter fired a second shot.

Lad felt a white-hot ridge of pain cut along his left flank like a whiplash. He wheeled to face his invisible foe, and he found himself looking at a half-dozen boys who charged whoopingly down on him. Behind the boys clumped a man in blue flourishing something bright.

Lad had no taste for this sort of attention. Always he had loathed strangers, and these new strangers seemed bent on catching him— on barring his homeward way.

He wheeled around again and continued his westward journey at a faster pace. The hue-and-cry broke into louder yells and three or four new recruits joined the pursuers. The yap of "Mad dog! *Mad dog!*" filled the air.

Not one of these people—not even the policeman himself—had any evidence that the collie was mad. There are not two really rabid dogs seen at large in New York or in any other city in the course of a year. Yet, at the back of the human throat ever lurks that fool cry of "Mad dog!"—ever ready to leap forth into shouted words at the faintest provocation.

One wonders, disgustedly, how many thousand luckless and totally harmless pet dogs in the course of a year are thus hunted down and shot or kicked or stoned to death in the sacred name of humanity, just because some idiot mistakes a hanging tongue or an uncertainty of direction for signs of that semiphantom malady known as "rabies."

A dog is lost. He wanders to and fro in bewilderment. Boys pelt or chase him. His tongue lolls and his eyes glaze with fear. Then, ever, rises the yell of "Mad dog!" And a friendly, lovable pet is joyfully done to death.

Lad crossed Broadway, threading his way through the trolley-and-taxi procession, and galloped down the hill toward Riverside Park. Close always at his heels followed the shouting crowd. Twice, by sprinting, the patrolman gained the front rank of the hunt, and twice he fired—both bullets going wide. Across West End Avenue and across Riverside Drive went Lad, hard-pressed and fleeing at top speed. The cross street ran directly down to a pier that jutted a hundred feet out into the Hudson River.

Along this pier flew Lad, not in panic terror, but none the less resolved that these howling New Yorkers should not catch him and prevent his going home.

Onto the pier the clattering hue-and-cry followed. A dock watchman, as Lad flashed by, hurled a heavy joist of wood at the dog. It whizzed past the flying hind legs, scoring the barest of misses.

And now Lad was at the pier end. Behind him the crowd raced; sure it had the dangerous brute cornered at last.

On the stringpiece the collie paused for the briefest of moments glancing to north and to south. Everywhere the wide river stretched away, unbridged. It must be crossed if he would continue his homeward course, and there was but one way for him to cross it.

The watchman, hard at his heels, swung upward the club he carried. Down came the club with murderous force—upon the stringpiece where Lad had been standing.

Lad was no longer there. One great bound had carried him over the edge and into the black water below.

Down he plunged into the river and far, far under it, fighting his way gaspingly to the surface. The water that gushed into his mouth and nostrils was salty and foul, not at all like the water of the lake at the edge of the Place. It sickened him. And the February chill of the river cut into him like a million ice needles.

To the surface he came, and struck out valorously for the opposite shore much more than a mile away. As his beautiful head appeared, a yell went up from the clustering riff-raff at the pier end. Bits of wood and coal began to shower the water all around him. A pistol shot plopped into the river a bare six inches away from him.

But the light was bad and the stream was a tossing mass of blackness and of light blurs, and presently the dog swam, unscathed, beyond the range of missiles.

Now a swim of a mile or of two miles was no special exploit for Lad—even in ice-cold water, but this water was not like any he had swum in. The tide was at the turn for one thing, and while, in a way, this helped him, yet the myriad eddies and crosscurrents engendered by it turned and jostled and buffeted him in a most perplexing way. And there were spars and barrels and other obstacles that were forever looming up just in front of him or else banging against his heaving sides.

Once a revenue cutter passed not thirty feet ahead of him. Its wake caught the dog and sucked him under and spun his body around and around before he could fight clear of it.

His lungs were bursting. He was worn out. He felt as sore as if he had been kicked for an hour. The bullet graze along his flank was hurting him as the salt water bit into it, and the muzzle half-blinded, half-smothered him.

But, because of his hero heart rather than through his splendid strength and wisdom, he kept on.

For an hour or more he swam until at last his body and brain were numb, and only the mechanical action of his wrenched muscles held him in motion. Twice tugs narrowly escaped running him down, and in the wake of each he waged a fearful fight for life.

After a century of effort his groping forepaws felt the impact of a submerged rock, then of another, and with his last vestige of strength Lad crawled feebly ashore on a narrow sandspit at the base of the elephant-gray Palisades. There, he collapsed and lay shivering, panting, struggling for breath.

Long he lay there, letting nature bring back some of his wind and his motive-power, his shaggy body one huge pulsing ache.

When he was able to move, he took up his journey. Sometimes swimming, sometimes on ground, he skirted the Palisades-foot to northward, until he found one of the several precipice-paths that Sunday picnickers love to climb. Up this he made his tottering way, slowly; conserving his strength as best he could.

On the summit he lay down again to rest. Behind him, across the stretch of black and lamp-flecked water, rose the inky skyline of the city with a lurid furnace glow between its crevices that smote the sky. Ahead was a plateau with a downward slope beyond it.

Once more, getting to his feet, Lad stood and sniffed, turning his head from side to side, muzzled nose aloft. Then, his bearings taken, he set off again, but this time his jog-trot was slower and his light step was growing heavier. The terrible strain of his swim was passing from his mighty sinews, but it was passing slowly because he was so tired and empty and in such pain of body and mind. He saved his energies until he should have more of them to save.

Across the plateau, down the slope, and then across the interminable salt meadows to westward he traveled; sometimes on road or path, sometimes across field or hill, but always in an unswerving straight line.

It was a little before midnight that he breasted the first rise of Jersey hills above Hackensack. Through a lightless one-street village he went, head low, stride lumbering, the muzzle weighing a ton and composed of molten iron and hornet stings.

It was the muzzle—now his first fatigue had slackened—that galled him worst. Its torture was beginning to do queer things to his nerves and brain. Even a stolid, nerveless dog hates a muzzle. More than one sensitive dog has been driven crazy by it.

Thirst—intolerable thirst—was torturing Lad. He could not drink at the pools and brooks he crossed. So tight-jammed was the steel jaw hinge now that he could not even open his mouth to pant, which is the cruelest deprivation a dog can suffer.

Out of the shadows of a ramshackle hovel's front yard dived a monstrous shape that hurled itself ferociously on the passing collie.

A mongrel watchdog—part mastiff, part hound, part anything you choose—had been dozing on his squatter-owner's doorstep when the pad-pad-pad of Lad's wearily jogging feet had sounded on the road.

Other dogs, more than one of them, during the journey had run out to yap or growl at the wanderer, but as Lad had been big and had followed an unhesitant course they had not gone to the length of actual attack.

This mongrel, however, was less prudent. Or, perhaps, dog-fashion, he realized that the muzzle rendered Lad powerless and therefore saw every prospect of a safe and easy victory. At all events, he gave no warning bark or growl as he shot forward to the attack.

Lad—his eyes dim with fatigue and road dust, his ears dulled by water and by noise—did not hear nor see the foe. His first notice of the attack was a flying weight of seventy-odd pounds that crashed against his flank. A double set of fangs in the same instant, sank into his shoulder.

Under the onslaught Lad fell sprawlingly into the road on his left side, his enemy upon him.

As Lad went down the mongrel deftly shifted his unprofitable shoulder grip to a far more promisingly murderous hold on his fallen victim's throat.

A cat has five sets of deadly weapons—its four feet and its jaws. So has every animal on earth—human and otherwise—except a dog. A dog is terrible by reason of its teeth. Encase the mouth in a muzzle and a dog is as helpless for offensive warfare as is a new-born baby.

And Lad was thus pitiably impotent to return his foe's attack. Exhausted, flung prone to earth, his mighty jaws muzzled, he seemed as good as dead.

But a collie down is not a collie beaten. The wolf strain provides against that. Even as he fell Lad instinctively gathered his legs under him as he had done when he tumbled from the car.

And, almost at once, he was on his feet again, snarling horribly and lunging to break the mongrel's throat grip. His weariness was forgotten and his wondrous reserve strength leaped into play. Which was all the good it did him; for he knew as well as the mongrel that he was powerless to use his teeth.

The throat of a collie—except in one small vulnerable spot—is armored by a veritable mattress of hair. Into this hair the mongrel had driven his teeth. The hair filled his mouth, but his grinding jaws encountered little else to close on.

A lurching jerk of Lad's strong frame tore loose the savagely inefficient hold. The mongrel sprang at him for a fresh grip. Lad reared to meet him, opposing his mighty chest to the charge and snapping powerlessly with his close-locked mouth.

The force of Lad's rearing leap sent the mongrel spinning back by sheer weight, but at once he drove in again to the assault. This time he did not give his muzzled antagonist a chance to rear, but sprang at Lad's flank. Lad wheeled to meet the rush and, opposing his shoulder to it, broke its force.

Seeing himself so helpless, this was of course the time for Lad to take to his heels and try to outrun the enemy he could not out-fight. To stand his ground was to be torn, eventually, to death. Being anything but a fool Lad knew that; yet he ignored the chance of safety and continued to fight the worse-than-hopeless battle.

Twice and thrice his wit and his uncanny swiftness enabled him to block the big mongrel's rushes. The fourth time, as he sought to rear, his hind foot slipped on a skim of puddle ice.

Down went Lad in a heap, and the mongrel struck.

Before the collie could regain his feet the mongrel's teeth had found a hold on the side of Lad's throat. Pinning down the muzzled dog, the mongrel proceeded to improve his hold by grinding his way toward the jugular. Now his teeth encountered something more solid than mere hair. They met upon a thin leather strap.

Fiercely the mongrel gnawed at this solid obstacle, his rage-hot brain possibly mistaking it for flesh. Lad writhed to free himself and to regain his feet, but seventy-five pounds of fighting weight were holding his neck to the ground.

Of a sudden, the mongrel growled in savage triumph. The strap was bitten through!

Clinging to the broken end of the leather the victor gave one final tug. The pull drove the steel bars excruciatingly into Lad's bruised nose for a moment. Then, by magic, the torture implement was no longer on his head but was dangling by one strap between the mongrel's jaws.

With a motion so swift that the eye could not follow it, Lad was on his feet and plunging deliriously into the fray. Through a miracle, his jaws were free; his torment was over. The joy of deliverance sent a glow of berserk vigor sweeping through him.

The mongrel dropped the muzzle and came eagerly to the battle. To his dismay he found himself fighting not a helpless dog, but a maniac wolf. Lad sought no permanent hold. With dizzying quickness his head and body moved—and kept moving, and every motion meant a deep slash or a ragged tear in his enemy's short-coated hide.

With ridiculous ease the collie eluded the mongrel's awkward counter-attacks, and ever kept boring in. To the quivering bone his short front teeth sank. Deep and bloodily his curved tusks slashed —as the wolf and the collie alone can slash.

The mongrel, swept off his feet, rolled howling into the road; and Lad tore grimly at the exposed underbody.

Up went a window in the hovel. A man's voice shouted. A woman in a house across the way screamed. Lad glanced up to note this new diversion. The stricken mongrel yelping in terror and agony seized the second respite to scamper back to the doorstep, howling at every jump.

Lad did not pursue him, but jogged along on his journey without one backward look.

At a rivulet, a mile beyond, he stopped to drink. And he drank for ten minutes. Then he went on. Unmuzzled and with his thirst slaked, he forgot his pain, his fatigue, his muddy and blood-caked and abraded coat, and the memory of his nightmare day.

He was going home!

At gray dawn the mistress and the master turned in at the gateway of the Place. All night they had sought Lad; from one end of Manhattan Island to the other—from police Headquarters to dog pound—they had driven. And now the master was bringing his tired and heartsore wife home to rest, while he himself would return to town and to the search.

The car chugged dispiritedly down the driveway to the house, but before it had traversed half the distance the dawn hush was shattered by a thunderous bark of challenge to the invaders.

Lad, from his post of guard on the veranda, ran stiffly forward to bar the way. Then as he ran his eyes and nose suddenly told him these mysterious newcomers were his gods.

The mistress, with a gasp of rapturous unbelief, was jumping down from the car before it came to a halt. On her knees, she caught Lad's muddy and bloody head tight in her arms.

"Oh, Lad," she sobbed incoherently. "Laddie! *Laddie!*"

Whereat, by another miracle, Lad's stiffness and hurts and weariness were gone. He strove to lick the dear face bending so tearfully above him. Then, with an abandon of puppylike joy, he rolled on the ground waving all four soiled little feet in the air pretending to snap at the loving hands that caressed him.

Which was ridiculous conduct for a stately and full-grown collie. But Lad didn't care, because it made the mistress stop crying and laugh. And that was what Lad most wanted her to do.

CHAPTER 7

THE THROWBACK

The Place was nine miles north of the county seat city of Paterson. And yearly, near Paterson, was held the great North Jersey Live-stock Fair—a fair whose awards established for the next twelve-month the local rank of purebred cattle and sheep and pigs for thirty miles in either direction.

From the Ramapo hill pastures, south of Suffern, two days before the fair, descended a flock of twenty prize sheep—the play-things of a man to whom the title of Wall Street Farmer had a lure of its own—a lure that cost him something like thirty thousand dollars a year; and which made him a scourge to all his few friends.

Among these luckless friends chanced to be the mistress and the master of the Place. And the gentleman farmer had decided to break his sheep's fairward journey by a twenty-four-hour stop at the Place.

The master, duly apprised of the sorry honor planned for his home, set aside a disused horse paddock for the woolly visitors' use. Into this their shepherd drove his dusty and bleating charges on their arrival.

The shepherd was a somber Scot. Nature had begun the work of

109

somberness in his Highland heart. The duty of working for the Wall
Street Farmer had added tenfold to the natural tendency. His name
was McGillicuddy.

Now, in northern New Jersey a live sheep is well nigh as rare as a
pterodactyl. This flock of twenty had cost their owner their weight
in merino wool. A dog—especially a collie—that does not know
sheep is prone to consider them his lawful prey, in other words, the
sight of a sheep has turned many an otherwise law-abiding dog into
a killer.

To avoid so black a smirch on the Place's hospitality, the master
had loaded all his collies, except Lad, into the car, and had shipped
them off, that morning, for a three-day sojourn at the boarding
kennels, ten miles away.

"Does the old dog go, too, sir?" asked the Place's foreman, with
a questioning nod at Lad, after he had lifted the others into the
backseat.

Lad was viewing the procedings from the top of the veranda
steps. The master looked at him, then at the car, and answered,
"No. Lad has more right here than any measly imported sheep. He
won't bother them if I tell him not to. Let him stay."

The sheep, convoyed by the misanthropic McGillicuddy, filed
down the drive, from the highroad, an hour later, and were mar-
shaled into the corral.

As the jostling procession, followed by its dour shepherd, turned
in at the gate of the Place, Lad rose from his rug on the veranda.
His nostrils itching with the unfamiliar odor, his soft eyes outraged
by the bizarre sight, he set forth to drive the intruders out into the
main road.

Head lowered, he ran, uttering no sound. This seemed to him an
emergency which called for drastic measures rather than for moni-
tory barking. For all he knew, these twenty fat, woolly, white things
might be fighters who would attack him in a body, and who might
even menace the safety of his gods; and McGillicuddy did not im-
press him at all favorably. Hence the silent charge at the foe—a
charge launched with the speed and terrible menace of a thunder-
bolt.

McGillicuddy sprang swiftly to the front of his flock, staff upwhirled; but before the staff could descend on the furry defender of the Place, a sweet voice called imperiously to the dog.

The mistress had come out upon the veranda and had seen Lad dash to the attack.

"Lad!" she cried. *"Lad!"*

The great dog halted midway in his rush.

"Down!" called the mistress. "Leave them alone! Do you hear, Lad? *Leave them alone!* Come back here!"

Lad heard, and Lad obeyed. Lad always obeyed. If these twenty malodorous strangers and their staff-brandishing guide were friends of the mistress he must not drive them away. The order "Leave them alone!" was one that could not be disregarded.

Trembling with anger, yet with no thought of rebelling, Lad turned and trotted back to the veranda. He thrust his cold nose into the mistress's warm little hand and looked up eagerly into her face, seeking a repeal of the command to keep away from the sheep and their driver.

But the mistress only patted his silken head and whispered, "We don't like it any more than you do, Laddie; but we mustn't let anyone know we don't. Leave them alone!"

Past the veranda filed the twenty priceless sheep, and on to the paddock.

"I suppose they'll carry off all the prizes at the fair, won't they?" asked the mistress civilly, as McGillicuddy plodded past her at the tail of the procession.

"Aiblins, aye," grunted McGillicuddy, with the exquisite courtesy of one who feels he is being patronized. "Aiblins, aye. Aiblins, na'. Aiblins—ugh-uh."

Having thus safeguarded his statement against assault from any side at all, the Scot moved on. Lad strolled down toward the paddock to superintend the task of locking up the sheep. The mistress did not detain him. She felt calmly certain her order of "Leave them alone!" had renderd the twenty visitors inviolate from him.

Lad walked slowly around the paddock, his gaze on the sheep. These were the first sheep he had ever seen. Yet his ancestors, for a thousand years or more, had herded and guarded flocks on the moors.

Atavism is mysteriously powerful in dogs, and it takes strange forms. A collie, too, has a queer strain of wolf in him—not only in body but in brain, and the wolf was the sheep's official murderer, as far back as the days when a humpbacked Greek slave, named Aesop, used to beguile his sleepless nights with writing fables.

Round and round the paddock prowled Lad; his eyes alight with a myriad half-memories; his sensitive nostrils quivering at the scents that enveloped them.

McGillicuddy, from time to time, eyed the dog obliquely, and with a scowl. These sheep were not the pride of his heart. His conscientious heart possessed no pride—pride being one of the seven deadly sins, and the sheep not being his own; but the flock represented his livelihood—his comfortably overpaid job with the Wall Street Farmer. He was responsible for their welfare.

And McGillicuddy did not at all like the way this beautiful collie eyed the prize merinos, nor was the Scot satisfied with the strength of the corral. Its wire fencing was rusty and sagging from long disuse, its gate hung crookedly and had a crazy hasp.

A sheep is one of the least intelligent creatures on earth. Should the flock's leader decide at any time during the night to press his heavy bulk against the gate or against some of the rustier wire strands, there would presently be a gap through which the entire twenty could amble forth. Once outside—

Again McGillicuddy glowered dourly at Lad. The collie returned the look with interest; a well-bred dog being as skilled in reading human faces as is any professional dead beat. Lad saw the dislike in McGillicuddy's heavy-thatched eyes; cordially he yearned to prove his own distaste for the shepherd, but the mistress's command had immuned this stranger.

So Lad merely turned his back on the man, sat down, flattened his furry ears close against his head, thrust his pointed nose skyward, and sniffed. McGillicuddy was too much an animal man not to read the insult in the dog's posture and action, and the shepherd's fist tightened longingly round his staff.

Half an hour later the Wall Street Farmer himself arrived at the Place. He came in a runabout. On the seat beside him sat his pasty-faced, four-year-old son. At his feet was something which, at first glance, might have been either a quadruped or a rag bag.

The mistress and the master, with dutiful hypocrisy, came smilingly out on the veranda to welcome the guests. Lad, who had returned from the impromptu sheepfold, stood beside them. At sight and scent of this new batch of visitors the collie doubtless felt what old-fashioned novelists used to describe as "mingled emotions."

There was a child in the car. And though there had been few children in Lad's life, yet he loved them, loved them as a big-hearted and big-bodied dog always loves the helpless. Wherefore, at sight of the child, Lad rejoiced.

But the animal crouching at the Wall Street Farmer's feet was quite a different form of guest. Lad recognized the thing as a dog—yet no such dog as ever he had seen. An unwholesome-looking dog. Even as the little boy was an unwholesome looking child.

"Well!" sonorously proclaimed the Wall Street Farmer as he scrambled out of the runabout and bore down upon his hosts. "Here I am! The sheep got here all safe? Good! I knew they would. McGillicuddy's a genius; nothing he can't do with sheep. You remember Mortimer?"—lifting the lanky youngster from the seat. "He teased so to come along, his mother said I'd better bring him. I knew you'd be glad. Shake hands with them, Morty, darling."

"I wun't!" snarled Morty darling, hanging back.

Then he caught sight of Lad. The collie came straight up to the child, grinning from ear to ear, and wrinkling his nose so delightedly that every white front tooth showed. Morty flung himself forward to greet the huge dog, but the Wall Street Farmer, with a shout of warning, caught the boy in his arms and bravely interposed his own fat body between Mortimer and Lad.

"What does the beast mean by snarling at my son?" fiercely demanded the Wall Street Farmer. "You people have no right to leave such a savage dog at large."

"He's not snarling," the mistress indignantly declared, "he's smiling. That's Lad's way. Why, he'd let himself be cut up into squares sooner than hurt a child."

Still doubtful, the Wall Street Farmer cautiously set down his son on the veranda. Morty flung himself bodily upon Lad; hauling and mauling the stately collie this way and that.

Had any grown person, save only the mistress or the master, attempted such treatment, the curving white eyeteeth would have buried themselves very promptly in the offender.

Indeed, the master now gazed, with some nervousness, at the performance; but the mistress was not worried as to her adored pet's behavior; and the mistress, as ever, was right.

For Lad endured the mauling—not patiently, but blissfully. He fairly writhed with delight at the painful tugging of hair and ears; and moistly he strove to kiss the wizened little face that was on a level with his own. Morty repaid this attention by slapping Lad across the mouth. Lad only wagged his plumy tail the more ecstatically and snuggled closer to the preposterous baby.

Meantime, the Wall Street Farmer, in clarion tones, was calling attention to the second of the two treasures he had brought along.

"Melisande!" he cried.

At the summons, the fuzzy monstrosity in the car ceased peering snappishly over the doortop at Lad, and condescended to turn toward its owner. It looked like something between an Old English sheepdog and a dachshund; straw-colored fur enveloped the scrawny body; a miserable apology for a bushy tail hung limply between crooked hind legs; evil little eyes peered forth from beneath a scarecrow stubble of head fringe; it was not a pretty dog, this canine the Wall Street Farmer had just addressed by the poetic title of Melisande.

"What in blazes is he?" asked the master.

"She is a Prussian sheepdog," proudly replied the Wall Street Farmer. "She is the first of her breed ever imported to America. Cost me a clean $1,100 to buy her from a Chicago man who brought her over. I'm going to exhibit her at the Garden Show next winter. What do you think of her, old man?"

"I'd hate to tell you," said the master, "but I'll gladly tell you what I think of that Chicago man. He's the original genius who sold all the land between New York and Jersey City for a thousand dollars an acre and issued the series of ten-dollar season admission tickets to Central Park."

Being the Wall Street Farmer's host the master said this in the recesses of his own heart. Aloud, he blithered some complimentary lie and watched the visitor lift the scraggy nondescript out of the car.

The moment she was on the ground, Melisande made a wild dash at Lad. Snarling, she snapped ferociously at his throat. Lad merely turned his shaggy shoulder to meet the onslaught. And Melisande found herself gripping nothing but a mouthful of his soft hair. He made no move to resent the attack. And the Wall Street Farmer, shouting unobeyed mandates to his pet, dragged away the pugnacious Melisande by the scruff of the neck.

The $1,100 Prussian sheepdog next caught a glimpse of one of the half-grown peacock chicks—the joy of the mistress's summer—strutting across the lawn. Melisande, with a yap of glee, rushed off in pursuit.

The chick had no fear. The dogs of the Place had always been trained to give the fowls a wide berth; so the pretty little peacock fell a pitifully easy prey to the first snap of Melisande's jaws.

Lad growled, deep down in his throat, at this gross lawlessness. The mistress bit her lip to keep her self-control at the slaughter of her pet. The master hastily said something that was lost in the louder volume of the Wall Street Farmer's bellow as he sought to call back his $1,100 treasure from further slaying.

"Well, well, well!" the guest exclaimed as at last he returned to the veranda, dragging Melisande along in his wake. "I'm sorry this happened, but you must overlook it. You see, Melisande is so high spirited she is hard to control. That's the way with thoroughbred dogs. Don't you find it so?"

The master, thus appealed to, glanced at his wife. She was momentarily out of earshot, having gone to pick up the killed peacock and stroke its rumpled plumage. So the master allowed himself the luxury of plainer speech than if she had been there to be grieved over the breach of hospitality.

"A thoroughbred dog," he said oracularly, "is either the best dog on earth, or else he is the worst. If he is the best he learns to mind, and to behave himself in every way like a thoroughbred. He learns it without being beaten or sworn at. If he is the worst—then it's wisest for his owner to hunt up some easy mark and sell the cur to him for $1,100. You'll notice I said his owner—not his master. There's all the difference in the world between those two terms. Anybody, with price to buy a dog, can be an owner, but all the cash coined won't make a man a dog's master—unless he's that sort of man. Think it over."

The Wall Street Farmer glared apoplectically at his host, who was already sorry that the sneer at Lad and the killing of his wife's pet had made him speak so to a guest—even to a self-invited and unde-sired guest. Then the Wall Street Man, with a grunt, put a leash on Melisande and gruffly asked that she be fastened to one of the vacant kennels.

The mistress came back to the group as the $1,100 beast was led away, kennelward, by the gardener. Recovering her self-possession, the mistress said to her guest, "I never heard of a Prussian sheep-dog before. Is she trained to herd your sheep?"

"No," replied the Wall Street Farmer, his rancor forgotten in the prospect of exploiting his wondrous dog, "not yet. In fact, she hates the sheep. She's young, so we haven't tried to train her for shepherding. Two or three times we have taken her into the pasture —always on leash—but she flies at the sheep and goes almost crazy with anger. McGillicuddy says it's bad for the sheep to be scared by her. So we keep her away from them. But by next season—"

He got no further. A sound of lamentation—prolonged and leather-lunged lamentation—smote upon the air.

"Morty!" ejaculated the visitor in panic. "It's Morty! Quick!"

Following the easily traceable direction of the squalling, he ran up the veranda steps and into the house—closely followed by the mistress and the master.

The engaging Mortimer was of the stuff whereof explorers are made. No pent-up Utica—nor veranda—contracted his powers. Bored by the stupid talk of grown folk, wearying of Lad's friendly advances, he had slipped through the open house door into the living room.

There, for the day was cool, a jolly wood fire blazed on the hearth. In front of the fireplace was an enormous and cavernous couch. In the precise center of the couch was curled something that looked like a ball of the grayish fluff a maid sweeps under the bed.

As Mortimer came into the room, the infatuated Lad at his heels, the fluffy ball lazily uncurled and stretched—thereby revealing itself as no ball, but a superfurry gray kitten—the mistress's temperamental new Persian kitten rejoicing in the dreamily romantic name of Tipperary.

With a squeal of glad discovery, Mortimer grabbed Tipperary with both hands, essaying to pull her fox-brush tail. Now, no sane person needs to be told the basic difference between the heart of a cat and the heart of a dog. Nor will any student of Persian kittens be surprised to hear that Tipperary's reception of the ruffianly baby's advances was totally different from Lad's.

A lightning stroke of one of her shapeless forepaws, and Tipperary was free. Morty stood blinking in amazement at four geometrically regular red marks on the back of his own pudgy hand. Tipperary had not done her persecutor the honor to run away. She merely moved to the far end of the couch and lay down there to renew her nap.

A mad fury fired the brain of Mortimer; a fury goaded by the pain of his scratches. Screaming in rage he seized the cat by the nape of the neck—to be safe from teeth and whizzing claws—and stamped across toward the high-burning fire with her. His arm was drawn back to fling the squirming and offending kitten into the scarlet heart of the flames. And then Lad intervened.

Now Lad was not in the very least interested in Tipperary; treating the temperamental Persian always with marked coldness. It is even doubtful if he realized Morty's intent.

But one thing he did realize—that a silly baby was toddling

straight toward the fire. As many another wise dog has done, before and since, Lad quietly stepped between Morty and the hearth. He stood, broadside to the fire and to the child—a shaggy wall between the peril and the baby.

But so quickly had anger carried Mortimer toward the hearth that the dog had not been able to block his progress until only a bare eighteen inches separated the youngster from the blaze.

Thus Lad found the heat from the burning logs all but intolerable. It bit through his thick coat and into the tender flesh beneath. Like a rock he stood there.

Mortimer, his gentle plan of kitten killing foiled, redoubled his screeches. Lad's back was higher than the child's eyes. Yet Morty sought to hurl the kitten over this stolid barrier into the fire.

Tipperary fell short; landing on the dog's shoulders, digging her needle claws viciously therein, and thence leaping to the floor, from which she sprang to the top of the bookshelves, spitting back blasphemously at her tormentor.

Morty's interest in the fire had been purely as a piece of immolation for the cat, but finding his path to it barred, he straightway resolved to go thither himself.

He started to move round to it, in front of Lad. The dog took a forward step that again barred the way. Morty went insane with wrath at this new interference with his sweet plans. His howls swelled to a sustained roar that reached the ears of the grown-ups on the lawn.

He flew at Lad, beating the dog with all the puny force of his fists, sinking his milk teeth into the collie's back, wrenching and tearing at the thick fur, stamping with his booted heels upon the absurdly tiny white forepaws, kicking the short ribs and the tender stomach.

Never for an instant did the child slacken his howls as he punished the dog that was saving him from death. Rather, he increased their volume from moment to moment. Lad did not stir. The kicking and beating and gouging and hair-pulling were not pleasant, but they were wholly bearable. The heat was not. The smell of singed hair began to fill the room, but Lad stood firm.

And then in rushed the relief expedition, the Wall Street Farmer at its head.

At once concluding that Lad had bitten his son's bleeding hand, the irate father swung aloft a chair and strode to the rescue.

Lad saw him coming.

With the lightning swiftness of his kind he whirled to one side as the mass of wood descended. The chair missed him by a fraction of an inch and splintered into pieces. It was a Chippendale, and had belonged to the mistress's great grandparents.

For the first time in all his blameless life Lad broke the sacred Guest Law by growling at a vouched-for visitor. But surely this fat bellower was no guest! Lad looked at his gods for information.

"Down, Lad!" said the master very gently, his voice not quite steady.

Lad, perplexed but obedient, dropped to the floor.

"The brute tried to kill my boy!" stormed the Wall Street Farmer right dramatically as he caught the howling Morty up in his arms to study the extent of the wound.

"He's my guest! *He's my guest!* HE'S MY GUEST!" the master was saying over and over to himself. "Lord, help me to keep on remembering he's my GUEST!"

The mistress came forward.

"Lad would sooner die than hurt a child," she declared, trying not to think of the wrecked heirloom chair. "He loves children. Here, let me see Morty's hand. Why, those are claw-marks! Cat scratches!"

"Ve nassy cat scwatched me!" bawled Morty. "Kill her, daddy! I twied to. I twied to frow her in ve fire. But ve mizz'ble dog wouldn't let me! Kill her, daddy! Kill ve dog too!"

The master's mouth flew wide open.

"Won't you go down to the paddock, dear," hastily interposed the mistress, "and see if the sheep are all right? Take Lad along with you."

Lad, alone of all the Place's dogs, had the run of the house, night and day, of the scared dining room. During the rest of that day he did not avail himself of his high privilege. He kept out of the way—

perplexed, woebegone, his burns still paining him despite the master's ministrations.

After talking long and loudly all evening of his sheep's peerless quality and of their certain victory over all comers in the fair the Wall Street Farmer consented at last to go to bed. And silence settled over the Place.

In the black hour before dawn, that same silence was split in a score of places—split into a most horrible cacophony of sound that sent sleep scampering to the winds.

It was the mingling of yells and bleats and barks and the scurry of many feet. It burst out all at once in full force, lasting for some seconds with increasing clangor; then died to stillness.

By that time every human on the Place was out of bed. In more or less rudimentary attire the house's inhabitants trooped down into the lower hall. There the Wall Street Farmer was raving noisily and was yanking at a door bolt whose secret he could not fathom.

"It's my sheep!" he shouted. "That accursed dog of yours has gotten at them. He's slaughtering them. I heard the poor things bleating and I heard him snarling among them. They cost me—"

"If you're speaking of Lad," blazed the master, "he's—"

"Here are the flashlights," interposed the mistress. "Let me open that door for you. I understand the bolt."

Out into the dark they went, all but colliding with McGillicuddy. The Scot, awakened like the rest, had gone to the paddock. He had now come back to report the paddock empty and all the sheep gone.

"It's the collie tike!" spouttered McGillicuddy. "I'll tak' oath to it. I ken it's him. I suspeecioned him a' long, from how he garred at oor sheep the day. He—"

"I said so!" roared the Wall Street Farmer. "The murderous brute! First, he tries to kill Morty. And now he slaughters my sheep. You—"

The Master started to speak. But a white little hand, in the darkness, was laid gently across his mouth.

"You told me he always slept under the piano in your music

room!" accused the guest as the four made their way paddockward, lighting a path with the electric flashlights. "Well, I looked there just now. He isn't under the piano. He—He—"

"Lad!" called the master; then at the top of his lungs. *"Lad!"*

A distant growl, a snarl, a yelp, a scramble—and presently Lad appeared in the farthest radius of the flashlight flare.

For only a moment he stood there. Then he wheeled about and vanished in the dark. Nor had the master the voice to call him back. The momentary glimpse of the great collie, in the merciless gleam of the lights, had stricken the whole party into an instant's speechlessness.

Vividly distinct against the darkness they had seen Lad. His wellgroomed coat was rumpled. His eyes were fireballs. And—his jaws were red with blood. Then he had vanished.

A groan from the master—a groan of heartbreak —was the first sound from the four. The dog he loved was a killer.

"It isn't true! It isn't true!" stoutly declared the mistress.

The Wall Street Farmer and McGillicuddy had already broken into a run. The shepherd had found the tracks of many little hoofs on the dewy ground. And he was following the trail. The guest, swearing and panting, was behind him. The mistress and the master brought up the rear.

At every step they peered fearfully around them for what they dreaded to see—the mangled body of some slain sheep. But they saw none. And they followed the trail.

In a quarter mile they came to its end.

All four flashlights played simultaneously upon a tiny hillock that rose from the meadow at the forest edge. The hillock was usually green. Now it was white.

Around its short slopes was huddled a flock of sheep, as closeringed as though by a fence. At the hillock's summit sat Lad. He was sitting there in a queer attitude, one of his snowy forepaws pinning something to the ground—something that could not be clearly distinguished through the huddle, but which, evidently, was no sheep.

The Wall Street Farmer broke the tense silence with a gobbled exclamation.

"Whisht!" half reverently interrupted the shepherd, who had been circling the hillock on census duty. "There's na a sheep gone, nor—so far's I can see—a sheep hurted. The fu' twenty is there."

The master's flashlight found a gap through which its rays could reach the hillock crest. The light revealed, under Lad's gently pinioning forepaw, the crouching and badly scared Melisande—the $1,100 Prussian sheepdog.

McGillicuddy, with a grunt, was off on another and longer tour of inspection. Presently he came back. He was breathing hard.

Even before McGillicuddy made his report the master had guessed at the main points of the mystery's solution.

Melisande, weary of captivity, had gnawed through her leash. Seeking sport, she had gone to the paddock. There she had easily worried loose the crazy gate latch. Just as she was wriggling through, Lad appeared from the veranda.

He had tried to drive back the would-be killer from her prey. Lad was a veteran of several battles. But, apart from her sex, Melisande was no opponent for him. And he had treated her accordingly. Melisande had snapped at him, cutting him deeply in the underjaw. During the scrimmage the panic-urged sheep had bolted out of the paddock and had scattered.

Remember, please, that Lad, ten hours earlier, had never in his life seen a sheep. But remember, too, that a million of his ancestors had won their right to a livelihood by their almost supernatural skill at herding flocks. Let this explain what actually happened—the throwback of a great collie's instinct.

Driving the scared and subdued Melisande before him—and ever hampered by her unwelcome presence—Lad proceeded to round up the scattered sheep. He was in the midst of the process when the master called him. Merely galloping back for an instant, and finding the summons was not repeated, he returned to his atavistic task.

In less than five minutes the twenty scampering runaways were "ringed" on the hillock. And, still keeping the Prussian sheepdog out of mischief, Lad established himself in the ring's center.

Further than that, and the keeping of the ring intact, his primal instincts did not serve him. Having rounded up his flock Lad had not the remotest idea what to do with them. So he merely held them there until the noisily gabbling humans should decide to take the matter out of his care.

McGillicuddy examined every sheep separately and found not a scratch or a stain on any of them. Then he told in effect what has here been set down as to Lad's exploit.

As he finished his recital McGillicuddy looked shamefacedly around him as though gathering courage for an irksome task. A sickly yellow dawn was crawling over the eastern mountains, throwing a ghostly glow on the shepherd's dour and craggy visage. Drawing a long breath of resolve he advanced upon Lad. Dropping on one knee, his eyes on a level with the unconcernedly observant collie's, McGillicuddy intoned, "Laddie, ye're a braw, braw dog. Ou, a canny dog! A sonsie dog, Laddie! I hae na met yer match this side o' Kirkcaldy Brae. Gin ye'll tak' an auld ·fule's apology for wrangin' ye, an' an auld fule's hand in gude fellowship, 'twill pleasure me, Laddie. Winna ye let bygones be bygones, an' shake?"

Yes, the speech was ridiculous, but no one felt like laughing, not even the Wall Street Farmer. The shepherd was gravely sincere and he knew that Lad would understand his burring words.

And Lad did understand. Solemnly he sat up. Solemnly he laid one white forepaw in the gnarled palm the kneeling shepherd outstretched to him. His eyes glinted in wise friendliness as they met the admiring gaze of the old man. Two born shepherds were face to face. Deep was calling unto deep.

Presently McGillicuddy broke the spell by rising abruptly to his feet. Gruffly he turned to the master.

"There's na wit, sir," he growled, "in speirin' will ye sell him. But —but I compliment ye on him, nanetheless."

"That's right; McGillicuddy's right!" boomed the Wall Street Farmer, catching but part of his shepherd's mumbled words. "Good idea! He is a fine dog. I see that now. I was prejudiced. I freely admit it. A remarkable dog. What'll you take for him? Or—better yet, how would you like to swap, even, for Melisande?"

The master's mouth again flew ajar, and many sizzling words jostled each other in his throat. Before any of these could shame his hospitality by escaping, the mistress hurriedly interposed, "Dear, we left all the house doors wide open. Would you mind hurrying back ahead of us and seeing that everything is safe? And—will you take Lad with you?"

CHAPTER 8

THE GOLD HAT

The Place was in the North Jersey hinterland, backed by miles of hill and forest, facing the lake that divided it from the village and the railroad and the other new-made smears which had been daubed upon Mother Nature's smiling face in the holy name of civilization. The lonely situation of the Place made Lad's self-appointed guardianship of its acres no sinecure at all. The dread of his name spread far—carried by hobo and by less harmless intruder.

Ten miles to northward of the Place, among the mountains of this same North Jersey hinterland, a man named Glure had bought a rambling old wilderness farm. By dint of much money, more zeal and most dearth of taste, he had caused the wilderness to blossom like the Fifth Proposition of Euclid. He had turned bosky wildwood into chaste picnicgrove pleasure grounds, lush meadows into sunken gardens, a roomy colonial farmstead into something between a feudal castle and a roadhouse. And, looking on his work, he had seen that it was good.

This beautifier of the wilderness was a financial giantlet, who had lately chosen to amuse himself, after work hours, by what he called

125

"farming." Hence the purchase and renovation of the five-hundred-acre tract, the building of model farms, the acquisition of priceless livestock, and the hiring of a battalion of skilled employees. Hence, too, his dearly loved and self-given title of Wall Street Farmer. His name, I repeat, was Glure.

Having established himself in the region, the Wall Street Farmer undertook most earnestly to reproduce the storybook glories of the life supposedly led by mid-Victorian country gentlemen. Not only in respect to keeping open-house and in alternately patronizing and bullying the peasantry, but in filling his gunroom shelves with cups and other trophies won by his livestock.

To his "open house" few of the neighboring families came. The local peasantry—Jersey mountaineers of Revolutionary stock, who had not the faintest idea they were "peasantry" and who, indeed, had never heard of the word—alternately grinned and swore at the Wall Street Farmer's treatment of them, and mulcted him of huge sums for small services. But Glure's keenest disappointment—a disappointment that crept gradually up toward the monomania point —was the annoyingly continual emptiness of his trophy shelves.

When, for instance, he sent to the Paterson Livestock Show a score of his pricelessly imported merino sheep, under his more pricelessly imported Scotch shepherd, Mr. McGillicuddy—the sheep came ambling back to Glure Towers Farm bearing no worthier reward than a single third-prize yellow silk rosette and a Commended ribbon. First and second prizes, as well as the challenge cup had gone to flocks owned by vastly inferior folk—small farmers who had no money wherewith to import the pick of the Scottish moors—farmers who had bred and developed their own sheep, with no better aid than personal care and personal judgment.

At the Hohokus Fair, too, the country gentleman's imported Holstein bull, Tenebris, had had to content himself with a measly red rosette in token of second prize, while the silver cup went to a bull owned by an elderly North Jersey man of low manners, who had bred his own entry and had bred the latter's ancestors for forty years back.

It was discouraging, it was mystifying. There actually seemed to be a vulgar conspiracy among the down-at-heel rural judges—a conspiracy to boost second-rate stock and to turn a blind eye to the virtues of overpriced transatlantic importations.

It was the same in the poultry shows and in hog exhibits. It was the same at the County Fair horsetrots. At one of these trots,the Wall Street Farmer, in person, drove his $9,000 English colt. And a rangy Hackensack gelding won all three heats. In none of the three did Glure's colt get within hailing distance of the wire before at least two other trotters had clattered under it.

(Glure's English head groom was called on the carpet to explain why a colt that could do a neat 2.13 in training was beaten out in a 2.17 trot. The groom lost his temper and his place. For he grunted, in reply, "The colt was all there. It was the driving did it.")

The gun room's glassed shelves in time were gay with ribbon. But only two of the three primary colors were represented there—blue being conspicuously absent. As for cups—the burglar who should break into Glure Towers in search of such booty would find himself the worse off by a wageless night's work.

Then it was that the Wall Street Farmer had his inspiration. Which brings us by easy degrees to the Hampton Dog Show.

Even as the Fiery Cross among the Highland crags once flashed signal of war, so, when World War I swirl sucked nation after nation into its eddy, the Red Cross flamed from one end of America to the other, as the common rallying point for those who, for a time, must do their fighting on the hither side of the gray seas. The country bristled with a thousand money-getting functions of a thousand different kinds, with one objective—the Red Cross.

So it happened at last that North Jersey was posted, on state road and byway, with flaring placards announcing a Mammoth Outdoor Specialty Dog Show, to be held under the auspices of the Hampton Branch of the American National Red Cross, on Labor Day.

Mr. Hamilcar Q. Glure, the announcement continued, had kindly donated the use of his beautiful grounds for the event, and had subscribed three hundred dollars toward its running expenses and prizes.

Not only were the usual dog classes to be judged, but an added interest was to be supplied by the awarding of no less than fifteen Specialty trophies.

Mr. Glure, having offered his grounds and the initial three hundred dollars, graciously turned over the details of the show to a committee, whose duty it was to suggest popular specialties and to solicit money for the cups.

Thus, one morning, an official letter was received at the Place, asking the master to enter all his available dogs for the show—at one dollar apiece for each class—and to contribute, if he should so desire, the sum of fifteen dollars, besides, for the purchase of a Specialty Cup.

The mistress was far more excited over the coming event than was the master. And it was she who suggested the nature of the specialty for which the fifteen-dollar cup should be offered.

The next outgoing mail bore the master's check for a cup. "To be awarded to the oldest and best-cared-for dog, of any breed, in the show."

It was like the mistress to think of that, and to reward the dog owner whose pet's old age had been made happiest. Hers was destined to be the most popular specialty of the entire show.

The master, at first, was disposed to refuse the invitation to take any of his collies to Hampton. The dogs were, for the most part, out of coat. The weather was warm. At these amateur shows—as at too many professional exhibits—there was always danger of some sick dog spreading epidemic. Moreover, the living room trophy shelf at the Place was already comfortably filled with cups, won at similar contests. Then, too, the master had somehow acquired a most causeless and cordial dislike for the Wall Street Farmer.

"I believe I'll send an extra ten dollars," he told the mistress, "and save the dogs a day of torment. What do you think?"

By way of answer, the mistress sat down on the floor where Lad was sprawled, asleep. She ran her fingers through his forest of ruff.

The great dog's brush pounded drowsily against the floor at the loved touch; and he raised his head for further caress.

"Laddie's winter coat is coming in beautifully," she said at last. "I don't suppose there'll be another dog there with such a coat. Besides, it's to be outdoors, you see. So he won't catch any sickness. If it were a four-day show—if it were anything longer than a one-day show—he shouldn't go a step. But, you see, I'd be right there with him all the time. And I'd take him into the ring myself, as I did at Madison Square Garden. And he won't be unhappy or lonely or —or anything. And I always love to have people see how splendid he is. And those Specialty Trophies are pretty, sometimes. So—so we'll do just whatever you say about it."

Which, naturally, settled the matter, once and for all.

When a printed copy of the Specialty Lists arrived, a week later, the mistress and the master scanned eagerly its pages.

There were cups offered for the best tricolor collie, for the best mother-and-litter, for the collie with the finest under-and-outer coat, for the best collie exhibited by a woman, for the collie whose get had won most prizes in other shows. At the very bottom of the section, and in type six points larger than any other announcement on the whole schedule, were the words:

Presented by the Hon. Hugh Lester Maury of New York City— 18-KARAT GOLD SPECIALTY CUP, FOR COLLIES (conditions announced later).

"A gold cup!" sighed the mistress, yielding to delusions of grandeur, "A *gold* cup! I never heard of such a thing, at a dog show. And—and won't it look perfectly gorgeous in the very center of our trophy shelf, there—with the other cups radiating from it on each side? And—"

"Hold on!" laughed the master, trying to mask his own thrill, by wetblanketing his wife's enthusiasm. "Hold on! We haven't got it, yet. I'll enter Lad for it, of course. But so will every other collie owner who reads that. Besides, even if Lad should win it, we'd have

to buy a microscope to see the thing. It will probably be about half
the size of a thimble. Gold cups cost gold money, you know. And I
don't suppose this 'Hon. Hugh Lester Maury of New York City' is
squandering more than ten or fifteen dollars at most on a country
dog show. Even for the Red Cross. I suppose he's some Wall Street
chum that Glure has wheedled into giving a Specialty. He's a novelty to me. I never heard of him before. Did you?"

"No," admitted the mistress. "But I feel I'm beginning to love
him. Oh, Laddie," she confided to the dog, "I'm going to give you a
bath in naphtha soap every day till then; and brush you, two hours
every morning; and feed you on liver and—"

" 'Conditions announced later,' " quoted the master, studying the
big-type offer once more. "I wonder what that means. Of course, in
a Specialty Show, anything goes. But—"

"I don't care what the conditions are," interrupted the mistress,
refusing to be disheartened. "Lad can come up to them. Why, there
isn't a greater dog in America than Lad. And you know it."

"I know it," assented the pessimistic master. "But will the judge?
You might tell him so."

"Lad will tell him," promised the Mistress. "Don't worry."

On Labor Day morning a thousand cars, from a radius of fifty
miles, were converging upon the much-advertised village of Hampton; whence, by climbing a tortuous first-speed hill, they present
chugged into the still-more-advertised estate of Hamilcar Q. Glure,
Wall Street Farmer.

There, the sylvan stillness was shattered by barks in every key,
from Pekingese falsetto to St. Bernard bass thunder. An open
stretch of shaded sward—backed by a stable that looked more like
a dissolute cathedral—had been given over to ten double rows of
benches, for the anchorage of the show's three hundred exhibits.
Above the central show ring a banner was strung between two tree
tops. It bore a blazing red cross at either end. In its center was the
legend:

WELCOME TO GLURE TOWERS!

The Wall Street Farmer, as I have hinted, was a man of much taste—of a sort.

Lad had enjoyed the ten-mile spin through the cool morning air, in the backseat of the Place's only car—albeit the course of baths and combings of the past week had long since made him morbidly aware that a detested dog show was somewhere at hand. Now, even before the car entered the fearsome feudal gateway of Glure Towers, the collie's ears and nose told him the hour of ordeal was at hand.

His zest in the ride vanished. He looked reproachfully at the mistress and tried to bury his head under her circling arm. Lad loathed dog shows; as does every dog of high-strung nerves and higher intelligence. The mistress, after one experience, had refrained from breaking his heart by taking him to those horrors known as "two-or-more-day shows." But, as she herself took such childish delight in the local one-day contests, she had schooled herself to believe Lad must enjoy them, too.

Lad, as a matter of fact, preferred these milder ordeals, merely as a man might prefer one day of jail or toothache to two or more days of the same misery. But—even as he knew many lesser things —he knew the adored mistress and master reveled in such atrocities as dog shows; and that he, for some reason, was part of his two gods' pleasure in them. Therefore, he made the best of the nuisance. Which led his owners to a certainty that he had grown to like it.

Parking the car, the mistress and master led the unhappy dog to the clerk's desk, received his number tag and card, and were shown where to bench him. They made Lad as nearly comfortable as possible, on a straw-littered raised stall; between a supercilious Merle and a fluffily disconsolate sable-and-white six-month puppy that howled ceaselessly in an agony of fright.

The master paused for a moment in his quest of water for Lad, and stared open-mouthed at the Merle.

"Good Lord!" he mumbled, touching the mistress's arm and pointing to the gray dog. "That's the most magnificent collie I ever set eyes on. It's farewell to poor old Laddie's hopes, if he is in any of the same classes with that marvel. Say goodbye, right now, to your hopes of the Gold Cup; and to Winners in the regular collie division."

"I won't say goodbye to it," refused the mistress. "I won't do anything of the sort. Lad's every bit as beautiful as that dog. Every single bit."

"But not from the show judge's view," said the master. "This Merle's a gem. Where in blazes did he drop from, I wonder? These 'no-point' out-of-town Specialty Shows don't attract the stars of the Kennel Club circuits. Yet, this is as perfect a dog as ever Grey Mist was. It's a pleasure to see such an animal. Or," he corrected himself, "it would be, if he wasn't pitted against dear old Lad. I'd rather be kicked than take Lad to a show to be beaten. Not for my sake or even yours. But for his. Lad will be sure to know. He knows everything. Laddie, old friend, I'm sorry. Dead *sorry.*"

He stooped down and patted Lad's satin head. Both master and mistress had always carried their fondness for Lad to an extent that perhaps was absurd. Certainly absurd to the man or woman who has never owned such a super-dog as Lad. As not one man or woman in a thousand has.

Together, the mistress and the master made their way along the collie section, trying to be interested in the line of barking or yelling entries.

"Twenty-one collies in all," summed up the master, as they reached the end. "Some quality dogs among them, too. But not one of the lot, except the Merle, that I'd be afraid to have Lad judged against. The Merle's our Waterloo. Lad is due for his first defeat. Well, it'll be a fair one. That's one comfort."

"It doesn't comfort *me,* in the very least," returned the mistress, adding, "Look! There is the trophy table. Let's go over. Perhaps the Gold Cup is there. If it isn't too precious to leave out in the open."

The Gold Cup was there. It was plainly—or, rather, flamingly— visible. Indeed, it smote the eye from afar. It made the surrounding array of pretty silver cups and engraved medals look tawdrily insignificant. Its presence had, already, drawn a goodly number of admirers—folk at whom the guardian village constable, behind the table, stared with sour distrust.

The Gold Cup was a huge bowl of unchased metal, its softly glowing surface marred only by the script words: *"Maury Specialty Gold Cup. Awarded to ————"*

There could be no shadow of doubt as to the genuineness of the claim that the trophy was of eighteen-karat gold. Its value spoke for itself. The vessel was like a half melon in contour and was supported by four severely plain claws. Its rim flared outward in a wide curve.

"It's—it's all the world like an inverted derby hat!" exclaimed the mistress, after one long dumb look at it. "And it's every bit as big as a derby hat. Did you ever see anything so ugly—and so Croesusful? Why, it must have cost—it must have cost—"

"Just sixteen hundred dollars, ma'am," supplemented the constable, beginning to take pride in his office of guardian to such a treasure. "Sixteen hundred dollars, flat. I heard Mr. Glure sayin' so myself. Don't go handlin' it, please."

"Handling it?" repeated the mistress. "I'd as soon think of handling the national debt!"

The superintendent of the show strolled up and greeted the mistress and the master. The latter scarce heard the neighborly greeting. He was scowling at the precious trophy as at a personal foe.

"I see you've entered Lad for the Gold Cup," said the superintendent. "Sixteen collies, in all, are entered for it. The conditions for the Gold Cup contest weren't printed till too late to mail them. So I'm handing out the slips this morning. Mr. Glure took charge of their printing. They didn't get here from the job shop till half an hour ago. And I don't mind telling you they're causing a lot of kicks. Here's one of the copies. Look it over, and see what Lad's up against."

"Who's the Hon. Hugh Lester Maury, of New York?" suddenly demanded the master, rousing himself from his glum inspection of the cup. "I mean the man who donated that—that Gold Hat?"

"Gold Hat!" echoed the superintendent, with a chuckle of joy. "Gold Hat! Now you say so, I can't make it look like anything else. A derby, upside down, with four—"

"Who's Maury?" insisted the master.

"He's the original Man of Mystery," returned the superintendent, dropping his voice to exclude the constable. "I wanted to get in touch with him about the delayed set of conditions. I looked him up. That is, I tried to. He is advertised in the premium list, as a New Yorker. You'll remember that, but his name isn't in the New York City directory or in the New York City telephone book or in the suburban telephone book. He can afford to give a sixteen-hundred-dollar cup for charity, but it seems he isn't important enough to get his name in any directory. Funny, isn't it? I asked Glure about him. That's all the good it did me."

"You don't mean—?" began the mistress, excitedly.

"I don't mean anything," the superintendent hurried to forestall her. "I'm paid to take charge of this show. It's no affair of mine if—"

"If Mr. Glure chooses to invent Hugh Lester Maury and make him give a Gold Hat for a collie prize?" suggested the mistress. "But—"

"I didn't say so," denied the superintendent. "And it's none of my business, anyhow. Here's—"

"But why should Mr. Glure do such a thing?" asked the mistress, in wonder. "I never heard of his shrinking coyly behind another name when he wanted to spend money. I don't understand why he—"

"Here is the conditions list for the Maury Specialty Cup," interposed the superintendent with extreme irrelevance, as he handed her a pink slip of paper. "Glance over it."

The mistress took the slip and read aloud for the benefit of the master who was still glowering at the Gold Hat: *Conditions of Contest for Hugh Lester Maury Gold Cup:* 'First—No collie shall be eligible that has not already taken at least one blue ribbon at a licensed American or British Kennel Club Show.' "

"That single clause has barred out eleven of the sixteen entrants," commented the superintendent. "You see, most of the dogs at these local shows are pets, and hardly any of them have been to Madison Square Garden or to any of the other AKC shows. The few that have been to them seldom got a Blue."

"Lad did!" exclaimed the mistress joyfully. "He took two Blues at the Garden last year; and then, you remember, it was so horrible for him there we broke the rules and brought him home without waiting for—"

"I know," said the superintendent, "but read the rest."

"'Second,'" read the mistress. "'Each contestant must have a certified five-generation pedigree, containing the names of at least ten champions.' Lad had twelve in his pedigree," she added, "and it's certified."

"Two more entrants were killed out by *that* clause," remarked the superintendent, "leaving only three out of the original sixteen. Now go ahead with the clause that puts poor old Lad and one other out of the running. I'm sorry."

"'Third,'" the mistress read, her brows crinkling and her voice trailing as she proceeded. "'Each contestant must go successfully through the preliminary maneuvers prescribed by the Kirkaldie Association, Inc., of Great Britain, for its Working Sheepdog Trials.' But," she protested, "Lad isn't a 'working' sheepdog! Why, this is some kind of a joke! I never heard of such a thing—even in a Specialty Show."

"No," agreed the superintendent, "nor anybody else. Naturally, Lad isn't a 'working' sheepdog. There probably haven't been three 'working' sheepdogs born within a hundred miles of here, and it's a mighty safe bet that no 'working' sheepdog has ever taken a Blue at an AKC Show. A 'working' dog is almost never a show dog. I know of only one either here or in England; and he's a freak—a miracle. So much so, that he's famous all over the dog world."

"Do you mean Champion Lochinvar III?" asked the mistress. "The dog the Duke of Hereford used to own?"

"That's the dog. The only—"

"We read about him in the *Collie Folio,*" said the mistress. "His picture was there, too. He was sent to Scotland when he was a puppy, the *Folio* said, and trained to herd sheep before ever he was shown. His owner was trying to induce other collie fanciers to make their dogs useful and not just show exhibits. Lochinvar is an international champion, too, isn't he?"

The superintendent nodded.

"If the Duke of Hereford lived in New Jersey," pursued the mistress, trying to talk down her keen chagrin over Lad's mishap, "Lochinvar might have a chance to win a nice Gold Hat."

"He has," replied the superintendent. "He has every chance, and the only chance."

"*Who* has?" queried the puzzled mistress.

"Champion Lochinvar III," was the answer. "Glure bought him by cable. Paid $7,000 for him. That eclipses Untermeyer's record price of $6,500 for old Squire of Tytton. The dog arrived last week. He's here. A big Blue Merle. You ought to look him over. He's a wonder. He—"

"*Oh!*" exploded the mistress. "You can't mean it. You *can't!* Why, it's the most—the most hideously unsportsmanlike thing I ever heard of in my life! Do you mean to tell me Mr. Glure put up this sixteen-hundred-dollar cup and then sent for the only dog that could fulfill the Trophy's conditions? It's unbelievable!"

"It's Glure," tersely replied the superintendent. "Which perhaps comes to the same thing."

"Yes!" spoke up the master harshly, entering the talk for the first time, and tearing his disgusted attention from the Gold Hat. "Yes, it's Glure, and it's unbelievable! And it's worse than either of those, if anything can be. Don't you see the full rottenness of it all? Half the world is starving or sick or wounded. The other half is working its fingers off to help the Red Cross make Europe a little less like hell; and, when every cent counts in the work, this—this Wall Street Farmer spends sixteen hundred precious dollars to buy himself a Gold Hat; and he does it under the auspices of the Red Cross, in the holy name of charity. The unsportsmanlikeness of it is nothing to that. It's—it's an unpardonable sin, and I don't want to endorse it by staying here. Let's get Lad and go home."

"I wish to heaven we could!" flamed the mistress, as angry as he. "I'd do it in a minute if we were able to. I feel we're insulting loyal old Lad by making him a party to it all. But we can't go. Don't you see? Mr. Glure is unsportsmanlike, but that's no reason we should be. You've told me, again and again, that no true sportsman will back out of a contest just because he finds he has no chance of winning it."

"She's right," chimed in the superintendent. "You've entered the dog for the contest, and by all the rules he'll have to stay in it. Lad doesn't know the first thing about 'working.' Neither does the only other local entrant that the first two rules have left in the competition. And Lochinvar is perfect at every detail of sheep-work. Lad and the other can't do anything but swell his victory. It's rank bad luck, but—"

"All right! All right!" growled the master. "We'll go through with it. Does anyone know the terms of a Kirkaldie Association's Preliminaries, for Working Sheepdog Trials? My own early education was neglected."

"Glure's education wasn't," said the superintendent. "He has the full set of rules in his brand new Sportsman Library. That's, no doubt, where he got the idea. I went to him for them this morning, and he let me copy the laws governing the preliminaries. They're absurdly simple for a 'working' dog and absurdly impossible for a nonworker. Here, I'll read them over to you."

He fished out a folded sheet of paper and read aloud a few lines of pencil scribblings:

"Four posts shall be set up, at ninety yards apart, at the corners of a square enclosure. A fifth post shall be set in the center. At this fifth post the owner or handler of the contestant shall stand with his dog. Nor shall such owner or handler move more than three feet from the post until his dog shall have completed the trial.

"Guided only by voice and by signs, the dog shall go alone from the center post to the post numbered '1'. He shall go thence, in the order named, to Posts 2, 3, and 4, without returning to within fifteen feet of the central post until he shall have reached Post 4.

"Speed and form shall count as seventy points in these evolutions. Thirty points shall be added to the score of the dog or dogs which shall make the prescribed tour of the posts directed wholly by signs and without the guidance of voice.

"There," finished the superintendent, "you see it is as simple as a kindergarten game. But a child who had never been taught could not play puss-in-the-corner. I was talking to the English trainer that Glure bought along with the dog. The trainer tells me Lochinvar can go through those maneuvers and a hundred harder ones without a word being spoken. He works entirely by gestures. He watches the trainer's hand. Where the hand points he goes. A snap of the fingers halts him. Then he looks back for the next gesture. The trainer says it's a delight to watch him."

"The delight is all his," grumbled the master. "Poor, poor Lad! He'll get bewildered and unhappy. He'll want to do whatever we tell him to, but he can't understand. It was different the time he rounded up Glure's flock of sheep—when he'd never seen a sheep before. That was ancestral instinct. A throwback. But ancestral instinct won't teach him to go to Post 1 and 2 and 3 and 4. He—"

"Hello, people!" boomed a jarringly cordial voice. "Welcome to the Towers!"

Bearing down upon the trio was a large person, round and yellow of face and clad elaborately in a morning costume that suggested a stud-groom with ministerial tendencies. He was dressed for the occasion. Mr. Glure was always dressed for the occasion.

"Hello, people!" repeated the Wall Street Farmer, alternately pump-handling the totally unresponsive mistress and master. "I see you've been admiring the Maury Trophy. Magnificent, eh? Oh, Maury's a prince, I tell you! A prince! A bit eccentric, perhaps—as you'll have guessed by the conditions he's put up for the cup. But a prince. A prince! We think everything of him on the Street. Have you seen my new dog? Oh, you must go and take a look at Lochinvar! I'm entering him for the Maury Trophy, you know."

"Yes," assented the master dully, as Mr. Glure paused to breathe. "I know."

He left his exultant host with some abruptness, and piloted the mistress back to the Collie Section. There they came upon a scene of dire wrath. Disgruntled owners were loudly denouncing the Maury conditions list, and they redoubled their plaint at sight of the two new victims of the trick.

Folks who had bathed and brushed and burnished their pets for days, in eager anticipation of a neighborhood contest, gargled in positive hatred at the glorious Merle. They read the pink slips over and over with more rage at each perusal.

One pretty girl had sat down on the edge of a bench, gathering her beloved gold-and-white collie's head in her lap, and was crying unashamed. The master glanced at her. Then he swore softly, and set to work helping the mistress in the task of fluffing Lad's glossy coat to a final soft shagginess.

Neither of them spoke. There was nothing to say; but Lad realized more keenly than could a human that both his gods were wretchedly unhappy, and his great heart yearned pathetically to comfort them.

"There's one consolation," said a woman at work on a dog in the opposite bench. "Lochinvar's not entered for anything except the Maury Cup. The clerk told me so."

"Little good that will do any of us!" retorted her bench-neighbor. "In an All-Specialty Show, the winner of the Maury Trophy will go up for the Winners' Class, and that means Lochinvar will get the cup for the Best Collie, as well as the Maury Cup and probably the cup for Best Dog of Any Breed, too. And—"

"The Maury Cup is the first collie event on the program," lamented the other. "It's slated to be called before even the Puppy and the Novice classes. Mr. Glure has—"

"Contestants for the Maury Trophy—all out!" bawled an attendant at the end of the section.

The master unclasped the chain from Lad's collar, snapped the light show-ring leash in its place and handed the leash to the mistress.

"Unless you'd rather have me take him in?" he whispered. "I hate to think of your handling a loser."

"I'd rather take Lad to defeat than any other dog to—a Gold Hat," she answered, sturdily. "Come along, Laddie!"

The Maury contest, naturally, could not be decided in the regular show-ring. Mr. Glure had thoughtfully set aside a quadrangle of greensward for the event—a quadrangle bounded by four white and numbered posts, and bearing a larger white post in its center.

A throng of people was already banked deep on all four sides of the enclosure when the mistress arrived. The collie judge standing by the central post declaimed loudly the conditions of the contest. Then he asked for the first entrant.

This courtier of failure chanced to be the only other local dog besides Lad that had survived the first two clauses of the conditions. He chanced also to be the dog over which the pretty girl had been crying.

The girl's eyes were still red through a haze of powder as she led her slender little gold-and-snow collie into the ring. She had put on a filmy white muslin dress with gold ribbons that morning with the idea of matching her dog's coloring. She looked very sweet and dainty—and heartsore.

At the central post she glanced up hopelessly at the judge who stood beside her. The judge indicated Post No. 1 with a nod. The girl blinked at the distant post, then at her collie, after which she pointed to the post.

"Run on over there, Mac!" she pleaded. "That's a good boy!"

The little collie wagged his tail, peered expectantly at her, and barked. But he did not stir. He had not the faintest idea what she wanted him to do, although he would have been glad to do it. Wherefore, the bark.

Presently (after several more fruitless entreaties which reduced the dog to a paroxysm of barking) she led her collie out of the enclosure, strangling her sobs as she went. And again the master swore softly, but with much venomous ardor.

And now, at the judge's command, the mistress led Lad into the quadrangle and up to the central post. She was very pale, but her thoroughbred nerves were rocklike in their steadiness. She, like Lad, was of the breed that goes down fighting. Lad walked majestically beside her, his eyes dark with sorrow over his goddess's unhappiness, which he could not at all understand and which he so longed to lighten. Hitherto, at dog shows, Lad had been the only representative of the Place to grieve.

He thrust his nose lovingly into the mistress's hand, as he moved along with her to the post; and he whined, under his breath.

Ranging up beside the judge, the mistress took off Lad's leash and collar. Stroking the dog's upraised head, she pointed to the No. 1 post.

"Over there," she bade him.

Lad looked in momentary doubt at her, and then at the post. He did not see the connection, nor know what he was expected to do. So, again he looked at the sorrowing face bent over him.

"Lad!" said the mistress gently, pointing once more to the post. "Go!"

Now, there was not one dog at the Place that had not known from puppyhood the meaning of the word "Go!" coupled with the pointing of a finger. Fingers had pointed, hundreds of times, to kennels or to the open doorways or to canoe bottoms or to car backseats or to whatsoever spot the dog in question was desired to betake himself. And the word "Go!" had always accompanied the motion.

Lad still did not see why he was to go where the steady finger indicated. There was nothing of interest over there; no one to attack at command. But he went.

He walked for perhaps fifty feet; then he turned and looked back.

"Go on!" called the voice that was his loved Law.

And he went on. Unquestionably, as uncomprehendingly, he

went, because the mistress told him to! Since she had brought him out before this annoying concourse of humans to show off his obedience all he could do was to obey. The knowledge of her mysterious sadness made him the more anxious to please her.

So on he went. Presently, as his progress brought him alongside a white post, he heard the mistress call again. He wheeled and started toward her at a run. Then he halted again, almost in midair.

For her hand was up in front of her, palm forward, in a gesture that meant "Stop!" from the time he had been wont to run into the house with muddy feet, as a puppy.

Lad stood, uncertain. And now the mistress was pointing another way and calling, "Go on! Lad! Go on!"

Confused, the dog started in the new direction. He went slowly. Once or twice he stopped and looked back in perplexity at her; but, as often, came the steady-voiced order, "Go on! Lad! Go *on!*"

On plodded Lad. Vaguely, he was beginning to hate this new game played without known rules and in the presence of a crowd. Lad abominated a crowd.

But it was the mistress's bidding, and in her dear voice his quick hearing could read what no human could read—a hard-fought longing to cry. It thrilled the big dog, this subtle note of grief. And all he could do to ease her sorrow, apparently, was to obey this queer new whim of hers as best he might.

He had continued his unwilling march as far as another post when the welcome word of recall came—the recall that would bring him close again to his sorrowing deity. With a bound he started back to her.

But, for the second time, came that palm-forward gesture and the cry of "Stop! Go *back!*"

Lad paused reluctantly and stood panting. This thing was getting on his fine-strung nerves. And nervousness ever made him pant.

The mistress pointed in still another direction, and she was calling almost beseechingly, "Go on, Lad! Go *on!*"

Her pointing hand waved him ahead and, as before, he followed its guidance. Walking heavily, his brain more and more befogged, Lad obeyed. This time he did not stop to look to her for instructions. From the new vehemence of the mistress's gesture she had apparently been ordering him off the field in disgrace, as he had seen puppies ordered from the house. Head and tail down, he went.

But, as he passed by the third of those silly posts, she recalled him. Gleeful to know he was no longer in disgrace he galloped toward the mistress; only to be halted again by that sharp gesture and sharper command before he had covered a fifth of the distance from the post to herself.

The mistress was actually pointing again—more urgently than ever—and in still another direction. Now her voice had in it a quiver that even the humans could detect; a quiver that made its sweetness all but sharp.

"Go on, Lad! Go *on!*"

Utterly bewildered at his usually moodless mistress's crazy mood and spurred by the sharp reprimand in her voice Lad moved away at a crestfallen walk. Four times he stopped and looked back at her, in piteous appeal, asking forgiveness of the unknown fault for which she was ordering him away; but always he was met by the same fierce "Go *on!*"

And he went.

Of a sudden, from along the tight-crowded edges of the quadrangle, went up a prodigious handclapping punctuated by such foolish and ear-grating yells as "Good *boy!*" "*Good* old Laddie!" "He *did* it!"

And through the looser volume of sound came the mistress's call of, "Laddie! Here, *Lad!*"

In doubt, Lad turned to face her. Hesitatingly he went toward her expecting at every step that hateful command of "Go *back!*"

But she did not send him back. Instead, she was running forward to meet him. And out of her face the sorrow—but not the desire to cry—had been swept away by a tremulous smile.

Down on her knees beside Lad the mistress flung herself, and gathered his head in her arms and told him what a splendid, dear dog he was and how proud she was of him.

All Lad had done was to obey orders, as any dog of his brain and heart and home training might have obeyed them. Yet, for some unexplained reason, he had made the mistress wildly happy. And that was enough for Lad.

Forgetful of the crowd, he licked at her caressing hands in puppylike ecstasy; then he rolled in front of her; growling ferociously and catching one of her little feet in his mighty jaws, as though to crush it. This foot-seizing game was Lad's favorite romp with the mistress. With no one else would he condescend to play it, and the terrible white teeth never exerted the pressure of a tenth of an ounce on the slipper they gripped.

"Laddie!" the mistress was whispering to him, *"Laddie!* You did it, old friend. You did it terribly badly I suppose, and of course we'll lose. But we'll 'lose right.' We've made the contest. You *did* it!"

And now a lot of noisy and bothersome humans had invaded the quadrangle and wanted to paw him and pat him and praise him. Wherefore Lad at once got to his feet and stood aloofly disdainful of everything and everybody. He detested pawing; and, indeed, any outsider's handling.

Through the congratulating knot of folk the Wall Street Farmer elbowed his way to the mistress.

"Well, well!" he boomed. "I must compliment you on Lad! A really intelligent dog. I was surprised. I didn't think any dog could make the round unless he'd been trained to it. Quite a dog! But, of course, you had to call to him a good many times. And you were signaling pretty steadily every second. Those things count heavily against you, you know. In fact, they goose-egg your chances if another entrant can go the round without so much coaching. Now my dog Lochinvar never needs the voice at all and he needs only one slight gesture for each maneuver. Still, Lad did very nicely. He— why does the sulky brute pull away when I try to pat him?"

"Perhaps," ventured the mistress, "perhaps he didn't catch your name."

Then she and the master led Lad back to his bench where the local contingent made much of him, and where—after the manner of a high-bred dog at a show—he drank much water and would eat nothing.

When the mistress went again to the quadrangle, the crowd was banked thicker than ever, for Lochinvar III was about to compete for the Maury Trophy.

The Wall Street Farmer and the English trainer had delayed the event for several minutes while they went through a strenuous dispute. As the mistress came up she heard Glure end the argument by booming, "I tell you that's all rot. Why shouldn't he 'work' for me just as well as he'd 'work' for you? I'm his master, ain't I?"

"No, sir," replied the trainer, glumly. "Only his *owner.*"

"I've had him a whole week," declared the Wall Street Farmer, "and I've put him through those rounds a dozen times. He knows me and he goes through it all like clockwork for me. Here! Give me his leash!"

He snatched the leather cord from the protesting trainer and, with a yank at it, started with Lochinvar toward the central post. The aristocratic Merle resented the uncalled-for tug by a flash of teeth. Then he thought better of the matter, swallowed his resentment and paced along beside his visibly proud owner.

A murmur of admiration went through the crowd at sight of Lochinvar as he moved forward. The dog was a joy to look on. Such a dog as one sees perhaps thrice in a lifetime. Such a dog for perfect beauty, as were Southport Sample, Grey Mist, Howgill Rival, Sunnybank Goldsmith, or Squire of Tytton. A dog, for looks, that was the despair of all competing dogdom.

Proudly perfect in carriage, in mist-gray coat, in a hundred points —from the noble pale-eyed head to the long massy brush— Lochinvar III made people catch their breath and stare. Even the mistress's heart went out—though with a tinge of shame for disloyalty to Lad—at his beauty.

Arrived at the central post, the Wall Street Farmer unsnapped the leash. Then, one hand on the Merle's head and the other holding a half-smoked cigar between two pudgy fingers, he smiled upon the tense onlookers.

This was his moment. This was the supreme moment which had cost him nearly ten thousand dollars in all. He was due, at last, to win a trophy that would be the talk of all the sporting universe.

These country-folk who had won lesser prizes from under his very
nose—how they would stare, after this, at his gun-room treasures!

"Ready, Mr. Glure?" asked the judge.

"All ready!" graciously returned the Wall Street Farmer.

Taking a pull at his thick cigar, and replacing it between the first
two fingers of his right hand, he pointed majestically with the same
hand to the first post.

No word of command was given; yet Lochinvar moved off at a
sweeping run directly in the line laid out by his owner's gesture.

As the Merle came alongside the post the Wall Street Farmer
snapped his fingers. Instantly Lochinvar dropped to a halt and
stood moveless, looking back for the next gesture.

This "next gesture" was wholly impromptu. In snapping his fingers the Wall Street Farmer had not taken sufficient account of the
cigar stub he held. The snapping motion had brought the fire end
of the stub directly between his first and second fingers, close to the
palm. The red coal bit deep into those two tenderest spots of all the
hand.

With a reverberating snort the Wall Street Farmer dropped the
cigar butt and shook his anguished hand rapidly up and down, in
the first sting of pain. The loose fingers slapped together like the
strands of an obese cat-of-nine-tails.

And this was the gesture which Lochinvar beheld, as he turned to
catch the signal for his next move.

Now, the frantic St. Vitus shaking of the hand and arm, accompanied by a clumsy step-dance and a mouthful of rich oaths, forms
no signal known to the very cleverest of "working" collies. Neither
does the inserting of two burned fingers into the signaler's mouth—
which was the second motion the Merle noted.

Ignorant as to the meaning of either of these unique signals the
dog stood, puzzled. The Wall Street Farmer recovered at once from
his fit of babyish emotion, and motioned his dog to go on to the
next post.

The Merle did not move. Here, at last, was a signal he understood perfectly well. Yet, after the manner of the best-taught

"working" dogs, he had been most rigidly trained from earliest days to finish the carrying out of one order before giving heed to another.

He had received the signal to go in one direction. He had obeyed. He had then received the familiar signal to halt and to await instructions. Again he had obeyed. Next, he had received a wildly emphatic series of signals whose meaning he could not read. A long course of training told him he must wait to have these gestures explained to him before undertaking to obey the simple signal that had followed.

This, in his training kennel, had been the rule. When a pupil did not understand an order he must stay where he was until he could be made to understand. He must not dash away to carry out a later order that might perhaps be intended for some other pupil.

Wherefore, the Merle stood stock still. The Wall Street Farmer repeated the gesture of pointing toward the next post. Inquiringly, Lochinvar watched him. The Wall Street Farmer made the gesture a third time—to no purpose other than to deepen the dog's look of inquiry. Lochinvar was abiding, steadfastly, by his hard-learned lessons of the Scottish moorland days.

Someone in the crowd tittered. Someone else sang out delightedly, "Lad wins!"

The Wall Street Farmer heard. And he proceeded to mislay his easily losable self control. Again, these inferior country folk seemed about to wrest from him a prize he had deemed all his own, and to rejoice in the prospect.

"You mongrel cur!" he bellowed. "Get along there!"

This diction meant nothing to Lochinvar, except that his owner's temper was gone—and with it his scanty authority.

Glure saw red—or he came as near to seeing it as can anyone outside a novel. He made a plunge across the quadrangle, seized the beautiful Merle by the scruff of the neck and kicked him.

Now, here was something the dog could understand with entire ease. This loud-mouthed vulgarian giant, whom he had disliked from the first, was daring to lay violent hands on him—on

Champion Lochinvar III, the dog-aristocrat that had always been handled with deference and whose ugly temper had never been trained out of him.

As a growl of hot resentment went up from the onlookers, a far more murderously resentful growl went up from the depths of Lochinvar's furry throat.

In a flash, the Merle had wrenched free from his owner's neck grip. And, in practically the same moment, his curved eye-teeth were burying themselves deep in the calf of the Wall Street Farmer's leg.

Then the trainer and the judge seized on the snarlingly floundering pair. What the outraged trainer said, as he ran up, would have brought a blush to the cheek of a waterside bartender. What the judge said (in a tone of no regret, whatever) was, "Mr. Glure, you have forfeited the match by moving more than three feet from the central post. But your dog had already lost it by refusing to 'work' at your command. Lad wins the Maury Trophy."

So it was that the Gold Hat, as well as the modest little silver Best Collie cup, went to the Place that night. Setting the golden monstrosity on the trophy shelf, the master surveyed it for a moment; then said, "That Gold Hat is even bigger than it looks. It is big enough to hold a thousand yards of surgical dressings, and gallons of medicine and broth, besides. And that's what it is going to hold. Tomorrow I'll send it to Vanderslice, at the Red Cross Headquarters."

"Good!" applauded the mistress. "Oh, *good!* Send it in Lad's name."

"I shall. I'll tell Vanderslice how it was won; and I'll ask him to have it melted down to buy hospital supplies. If that doesn't take off its curse of unsportsmanliness, nothing will. I'll get you something to take its place, as a trophy."

But there was no need to redeem that promise. A week later, from headquarters, came a tiny scarlet enamel cross, whose silver back bore the inscription:

To SUNNYBANK LAD; in memory of a generous gift to Humanity.

"It's face value is probably fifty cents, Lad, dear," commented the mistress, as she strung the bit of scarlet on the dog's shaggy throat. "But its heart value is at least a billion dollars. Besides—you can wear it. And nobody, outside a nightmare, could possibly have worn kind, good Mr. Hugh Lester Maury's Gold Hat. I must write to Mr. Glure and tell him all about it. How tickled he'll be! Won't he, Laddie?"

CHAPTER 9

SPEAKING OF UTILITY

The man huddled frowzily in the tree crotch, like a rumpled and sick raccoon. At times he would crane his thin neck and peer about him, but more as if he feared rescue than as though he hoped for it.

Then, before slumping back to his sick-raccoon pose, he would look murderously earthward and swear with lurid fervor.

At the tree foot the big dog wasted neither time nor energy in frantic barking or in capering excitedly about. Instead, he lay at majestic ease, gazing up toward the treed man with grave attentiveness.

Thus, for a full half-hour, the two had remained—the treer and the treed. Thus, from present signs, they would continue to remain until Christmas.

There is, by tradition, something intensely comic in the picture of a man treed by a dog. The man, in the present case, supplied the only element of comedy in the scene. The dog was anything but comic, either in looks or in posture.

He was a collie, huge of bulk, massive of shoulder, deep and shaggy of chest. His forepaws were snowy and absurdly small. His eyes were seal-dark and sorrowful—eyes that proclaimed not only

an uncannily wise brain, but a soul as well. In brief, he was Lad;
official guard of the Place's safety.

It was in this role of guard that he was now serving as jailer to
the man he had seen slouching through the undergrowth of the
forest which grew close up to the Place's outbuildings.

From his two worshipped deities—the mistress and the master—
Lad had learned in puppyhood the simple provisions of the Guest
Law. He knew, for example, that no one openly approaching the
house along the driveway from the furlong-distant highroad was to
be molested. Such a visitor's advent—especially at night—might
lawfully be greeted by a salvo of barks. But the barks were a mere
announcement, not a threat.

On the other hand, the Law demanded the instant halting of all
prowlers, or of anyone seeking to get to the house from road or
lake by circuitous and stealthy means. Such roundabout methods
spell trespass. Every good watchdog knows that. But wholly good
watchdogs are far fewer than most people—even their owners—
realize. Lad was one of the few.

Today's trespasser had struck into the Place's grounds from an
adjoining bit of woodland. He had moved softly and obliquely and
had made little furtive dashes from one bit of cover to another, as
he advanced toward the outbuildings a hundred yards north of the
house.

He had moved cleverly and quietly. No human had seen or heard
him. Even Lad, sprawling half-asleep on the veranda, had not seen
him. For, in spite of theory, a dog's eye by daylight is not so keen
nor so far-seeing as is a human's. But the wind had brought news of
a foreign presence on the Place—a presence which Lad's hasty
glance at driveway and lake edge did not verify.

So the dog had risen to his feet, stretched himself, collie fashion,
fore and aft, and trotted quickly away to investigate. Scent, and
then sound, taught him which way to go.

Two minutes later he changed his wolf trot to a slow and unwont-
edly stiff-legged walk, advancing with head lowered, and growling
softly far down in his throat. He was making straight for a patch of

sumac, ten feet in front of him and a hundred feet behind the stables.

Now, when a dog bounds toward a man, barking and with head up, there is nothing at all to be feared from his approach. But when the pace slackens to a stiff walk and his head sinks low, that is a very good time, indeed, for the object of his attentions to think seriously of escape or of defense.

Instinct or experience must have imparted this useful truth to the lurker in the sumac patch, for as the great dog drew near the man incontinently wheeled and broke cover. At the same instant Lad charged.

The man had a ten-foot start. This vantage he utilized by flinging himself bodily at a low-forked hickory tree directly in his path.

Up the rough trunk to the crotch he shinned with the speed of a chased cat. Lad arrived at the tree bole barely in time to collect a mouthful of cloth from the climber's left trouser ankle.

After which, since he was not of the sort to clamor noisily for what lurked beyond his reach, the dog yawned and lay down to keep guard on his arboreal prisoner. For half an hour he lay thus, varying his vigil once or twice by sniffing thoughtfully at a ragged scrap of trouser cloth between his little white forepaws. He sniffed the thing as though trying to commit its scent to memory.

The man did not seek help by shouting. Instead, he seemed oddly willing that no other human should intrude on his sorry plight. A single loud yell would have brought aid from the stables or from the house or even from the lodge up by the gate. Yet, though the man must have guessed this, he did not yell. Instead, he cursed whisperingly at intervals and snarled at his captor.

At last, his nerve going, the prisoner drew out a jackknife, opened a blade at each end of it and hurled the ugly missile with all his force at the dog. As the man had shifted his position to get at the knife, Lad had risen expectantly to his feet with some hope that his captive might be going to descend.

It was lucky for Lad that he was standing when the knife was thrown for the aim was not bad, and a dog lying down cannot easily dodge. A dog standing on all fours is different, especially if he is a collie.

Lad sprang to one side instinctively as the thrower's arm went back. The knife whizzed, harmless, into the sumac patch. Lad's teeth bared themselves in something that looked like a smile and was not. Then he lay down again on guard.

A minute later he was up with a jump. From the direction of the house came a shrill whistle followed by a shout of "Lad! *La-ad!*"

It was the master calling him. The summons could not be ignored. Usually it was obeyed with eager gladness, but now—Lad looked worriedly up into the tree. Then, coming to a decision, he galloped away at top speed.

In ten seconds he was at the veranda where the master stood talking with a newly arrived guest. Before the master could speak to the dog, Lad rushed up to him, whimpering in stark appeal, then ran a few steps toward the stables, paused, looked back and whimpered again.

"What's the matter with him?" loudly demanded the guest—an obese and elderly man, right sportily attired. "What ails the silly dog?"

"He's found something," said the master. "Something he wants me to come and see—and he wants me to come in a hurry."

"How do you know?" asked the guest.

"Because I know his language as well as he knows mine," retorted the master.

He set off in the wake of the excited dog. The guest followed in more leisurely fashion complaining: "Of all the idiocy! To let a measly dog drag you out of the shade on a red-hot day like this just to look at some dead chipmunk he's found!"

"Perhaps," stiffly agreed the master, not slackening his pace. "But if Lad behaves like that, unless it's pretty well worthwhile, he's changed a lot in the past hour. A man can do worse sometimes than follow a tip his dog gives him."

"Have it your own way," grinned the guest. "Perhaps he may lead us to a treasure cave or to a damsel in distress. I'm with you."

"Guy me if it amuses you," said the master.

"It does," his guest informed him. "It amuses me to see any grown man think so much of a dog as you people think of Lad. It's maudlin."

"My house is the only one within a mile on this side of the lake that has never been robbed," was the master's reply. "My stable is the only one in the same radius that hasn't been rifled by harness-and-tire thieves. Thieves who seem to do their work in broad day-light, too, when the stables won't be locked. I have Lad to thank for all that. He—"

The dog had darted far ahead. Now he was standing beneath a low-forked hickory tree staring up into it.

"He's treed a cat!" guffawed the guest, his laugh as irritating as a kick. "Extra! Come out and get a nice sunstroke, folks! Come and see the cat Lad has treed!"

The master did not answer. There was no cat in the tree. There was nothing visible in the tree. Lad's aspect shrank from hope to depression. He looked apologetically at the master. Then he began to sniff once more at a scrap of cloth on the ground.

The master picked up the cloth and presently walked over to the tree. From a jut of bark dangled a shred of the same cloth. The master's hand went to Lad's head in approving caress.

"It was not a cat," he said. "It was a man. See the rags of—"

"Oh, piffle!" snorted the guest. "Next you'll be reconstructing the man's middle name and favorite perfume from the color of the bark on the tree. You people are always telling about wonderful stunts of Lad's. And that's all the evidence there generally is to it."

"No, Mr. Glure," denied the master, taking a strangle hold on his temper. "No. That's not quite all the evidence that we have for our brag about Lad. For instance, we had the evidence of your own eyes when he herded that flock of stampeded prize sheep for you last spring, and of your own eyes again when he won the Gold Hat cup at the Labor Day Dog Show. No, there's plenty of evidence that Lad is worth his salt. Let it go at that. Shall we get back to the house? It's fairly cool on the veranda. By the way, what was it you wanted me to call Lad for? You aked to see him. And—"

"Why, here's the idea," explained Glure, as they made their way through the heat back to the shade of the porch. "It's what I drove over here to talk with you about. I'm making the rounds of all this region. And, say, I didn't ask to see Lad. I asked if you still had him. I asked because—"

"Oh," apologized the master. "I thought you wanted to see him. Most people ask to if he doesn't happen to be round when they call. We—"

"I asked you if you still had him," expounded Mr. Glure, "because I hoped you hadn't. I hoped you were more of a patriot."

"Patriot?" echoed the master, puzzled.

"Yes. That's why I'm making this tour of the country: to rouse dog owners to a sense of their duty. I've just formed a local branch of the Food Conservation League and—"

"It's a splendid organization," warmly approved the master, "but what have dog owners to—"

"To do with it?" supplemented Glure. "They have nothing to do with it, more's the pity. But they ought to. That's why I volunteered to make this canvass. It was my own idea. Some of the others were foolish enough to object, but as I had founded and financed this Hampton branch of the league—"

"What 'canvass' are you talking about?" asked the master, who was far too familiar with Glure's ways to let the man become fairly launched on a pan of self-adulation. "You say it's 'to rouse dog owners to a sense of their duty.' Along what line? We dog men have raised a good many thousand dollars this past year by our Red Cross shows and by our subscriptions to all sorts of war funds. The Blue Cross, too, and the Collie Ambulance Fund have—"

"This is something better than the mere giving of surplus coin," broke in Glure. "It is something that involves sacrifice. A needful sacrifice for our country. A sacrifice that may win the war."

"Count me in on it, then!" cordially approved the master. "Count in all real dog men. What is the 'sacrifice'?"

"It's my own idea," modestly boasted Glure, adding, "that is, of course, it's been agitated by other people in letters to newspapers and all that, but I'm the first to go out and put it into actual effect."

"Shoot!" suggested the weary master.

"That's the very word!" exclaimed Glure. "That's the very thing I want dog owners to combine in doing. To shoot!"

"To—what?"

"To shoot—or poison—or asphyxiate," expounded Glure, warming to his theme. "In short, to get rid of every dog."

The master's jaw swung ajar and his eyes bulged. His face began to assume an unbecoming bricky hue. Glure went on, "You see, neighbor, our nation is up against it. When war was declared last month it found us unprepared. We've got to pitch in and economize. Every mouthful of food wasted here is a new lease of life to the kaiser. We're cutting down on sugar and meat and fat, but for every cent we save that way we're throwing away a dollar in feeding our dogs. Our dogs that are a useless, senseless, costly luxury! They serve no utilitarian end. They eat food that belongs to soldiers. I'm trying to brighten the corner where I am by persuading my neighbors to get rid of their dogs. When I've proved what a blessing it is I'm going to inaugurate a nationwide campaign from California to New York, from—"

"Hold on!" snapped the master, finding some of his voice and, in the same effort, mislaying much of his temper. "What wall-eyed idiocy do you think you're trying to talk? How many dog men do you expect to convert to such a crazy doctrine? Have you tried any others? Or am I the first mark?"

"I'm sorry you take it this way," reproved Glure. "I had hoped you were more broad minded, but you are pig-headed as the rest."

"The 'rest,' hey?" the master caught him up. "The 'rest?' Then I'm not the first? I'm glad they had sense enough to send you packing."

"They were blind animal worshipers, both of them," said Glure aggrievedly, "just as you are. One of them yelled something after me that I sincerely hope I didn't hear aright. If I did, I have a strong action for slander against him. The other chucklehead so far forgot himself as to threaten to take a shotgun to me if I didn't get off his land."

"I'm sorry!" sighed the master. "For both of them seem to have covered the ground so completely that there isn't anything unique for me to say—or do. Now listen to me for two minutes. I've read a few of those antidog letters in the newspapers, but you're the first person I've met in real life who backs such rot. And I'm going—"

"It is not a matter for argument," loftily began Glure.

"Yes it is," asserted the master. "Everything is, except religion and love and toothache. You say dogs ought to be destroyed as a patriotic duty because they aren't utilitarian. There's where you're wrong at the very beginning. Dead wrong. I'm not talking about the big kennels where one man keeps a hundred dogs as he'd herd so many prize hogs. Though look what the owners of such kennels did for the country at the last New York show at Madison Square Garden! Every penny of the thousands and thousands of dollars in profits from the show went to the Red Cross. I'm speaking of the man who keeps one dog or two or even three dogs, and keeps them as pets. I'm speaking of myself, if you like. Do you know what it costs me per week to feed my dogs?"

"I'm not looking for statistics in—"

"No, I suppose not. Few fanatics are. Well, I figured it out a few weeks ago, after I read one of those antidog letters. The total upkeep of all my dogs averages just under a dollar a week. A bare fifty dollars a year. That's true. And—"

"And that fifty dollars," interposed Glure eagerly, "would pay for a soldier's—"

"It would not!" contradicted the master, trying to keep some slight grip on his sliding temper. "But I can tell you what it *would* do. Part of it would go for burglar insurance, which I don't need now, because no stranger dares to sneak up to my house at night. Part of it would go to make up for things stolen around the Place. For instance, in the harness room of my stable there are five sets of good harness and two or three extra automobile tires. Unless I'm very much mistaken, the best of those would be gone now if Lad hadn't just treed the man who was after them."

"Pshaw!" exploded Glure in fine scorn. "We saw no man there. There was no proof of—"

"There was proof enough for me," continued the master. "And if Lad hadn't scented the fellow one of the other dogs would. As I told you, mine is the only house—and mine is the only stable—on this side of the lake that has never been looted. Mine is the only orchard—and mine is the only garden—that is never robbed. And this is the only place, on our side of the lake, where dogs are kept at large for twelve months of the year. My dogs' entry fees at Red Cross shows have more than paid for their keep, and those fees went straight to charity."

"But—"

"The women of my family are as safe here, day and night, as if I had a machine-gun company on guard. That assurance counts for more than a little, in peace of mind, back here in the North Jersey hinterland. I'm not taking into account the several other ways the dogs bring in cash income to us. Not even the cash Lad turned over to the Red Cross when we sent that $1,600 Gold Hat cup he won, to be melted down. And I'm not speaking of our dogs' comradeship, and what that means to us. Our dogs are an asset in every way—not a liability. They aren't deadheads either. For I pay the state tax on them every year. They're true, loyal, companionable chums, and they're an ornament to the Place as well as its best safeguard. All in return for table scraps and skim milk and less than a weekly dollar's worth of stale bread and castoff butcher-shop bones. Where do you figure out the 'saving' for the war chest if I got rid of them?"

"As I said," repeated Glure with cold austerity, "it's not a matter for argument. I came here hoping to—"

"I'm not given to mawkish sentiment," went on the master shamefacedly, "but on the day your fool law for dog exterminating goes into effect there'll be a piteous crying of little children all over the whole world—of little children mourning for the gentle protecting playmates they loved. And there'll be a million men and women whose lives have all at once become lonely and empty and miserable. Isn't this war causing enough crying and loneliness and misery without your adding to it by killing our dogs? For the matter of that, haven't the army dogs over in Europe been doing enough for mankind to warrant a square deal for their stay-at-home brothers? Haven't they?"

"That's a mass of sentimental bosh," declared Glure. "All of it."

"It is," willingly confessed the master. "So are most of the worth-while things in life, if you reduce them to their lowest terms."

"You know what a fine group of dogs I had," said Glure, starting off on a new tack. "I had a group that cost me, dog for dog, more than any other kennel in the state. Grand dogs too. You remember my wonderful Merle, for instance, and—"

"And your rare 'Prussian sheepdog'—or was it a prune-hound—that a Chicago man sold to you for $1,100," supplemented the master, swallowing a grin. "I remember. I remember them all. What then?"

"Well," resumed Glure, "no one can accuse me of not practicing what I preach. I began this splendid campaign by getting rid of every dog I owned. So I—"

"Yes," agreed the master. "I read all about that last month in your local paper. Distemper had run through your kennel, and you tried doctoring the dogs on a theory of your own instead of sending for a vet. So they all died. Tough luck! Or perhaps you got rid of them that way on purpose? For the good of the cause? I'm sorry about the Merle. He was—"

"I see there's no use talking to you," sighed Glure in disgust, ponderously rising and waddling toward his car. "I'm disappointed; because I hoped you were less bone-brained and more patriotic than these yokels round here."

"I'm not," cheerily conceded the master. "I'm not, I'm glad to say. Not a bit."

"Then," pursued Glure, climbing into the car, "since you feel that way about it, I suppose there's no use asking you to come to the little cattle show I'm organizing for week after next, because that's for the Food Conservation League too. And since you're so out of sympathy with—"

"I'm not out of sympathy with the league," asserted the master. "Its card is in our kitchen window. We've signed its pledge and we're boosting it in every way we know how, except by killing our dogs; and that's no part of the league's program, as you know very well. Tell me more about the cattle show."

"It's a neighborhood affair," said Glure sulkily, yet eager to secure any possible entrants. "Just a bunch of home-raised cattle. Cup and rosette for best of each recognized breed, and the usual ribbons for second and third. Three dollars an entry. Only one class for each breed. Every entrant must have been raised by the exhibitor. Gate admission fifty cents. Red Cross to get the gross proceeds. I've offered the use of my south meadow at Glure Towers—just as I did for the Specialty Dog Show. I've put up a hundred dollars toward the running expenses too. Micklesen's to judge."

"I don't go in for stock raising," said the master. "My little Alderney heifer is the only head of quality stock I ever bred. I doubt if she is worth taking up there, but I'll be glad to take her if only to swell the competition list. Send me a blank, please."

Lad trotted dejectedly back to the house as Glure's car chugged away up the drive. Lad was glumly unhappy. He had had no trouble at all in catching the scent of the man he had treed. He had followed the crashingly made trail through undergrowth and woodland until it had emerged into the highroad.

And there, perforce, Lad had paused. For, taught from puppyhood, he knew the boundaries of the Place as well as did the mistress or the master, and he knew equally well that his own jurisdiction ended at those boundaries. Beyond them he might not chase even the most loathed intruder. The highroad was sanctuary.

Wherefore at the road edge he stopped and turned slowly back. His pursuit was ended, but not his anger, nor his memory of the marauder's scent. The man had trespassed slyly on the Place. He had gotten away unpunished. These things rankled in the big dog's mind. . . .

It was a pretty little cattle show and staged in a pretty setting withal—at Glure Towers, two weeks later. The big sunken meadow on the verge of the Ramapo River was lined on two sides with impromptu sheds. The third side was blocked by something be-

tween a grand stand and a marquee. The tree-hung river bordered
the fourth side. In the field's center was the roped-off judging enclosure into which the cattle, class by class, were to be led.

Above the pastoral scene brooded the architectural crime, known
as the Towers—homestead and stronghold of Hamilcar Q. Glure,
Esquire.

Glure had made much money in Wall Street—a crooked little
street that begins with a graveyard and ends in a river. Having
waxed indecently rich, he had erected for himself a hideously expensive estate among the Ramapo Mountains and had settled down
to the task of patronizing his rural neighbors. There he elected to
be known as the Wall Street Farmer, a title that delighted not only
himself but everyone else in the region.

There was, in this hinterland stretch, a friendly and constant ri-
valry among the natives and other old residents in the matter of
stock raising. Horses, cattle, pigs, chickens, even a very few sheep
were bred for generations along lines which their divers owners had
laid out—lines which those owners fervently believed must some
day produce perfection.

Each owner or group of owners had his own special ideas as to
the best way to produce this super-stock result. The local stock
shows formed the only means of proving or disproving the excel-
lence of the varied theories. Hence these shows were looked upon
as barnyard supreme courts.

Mr. Glure had begun his career in the neighborhood with a laud-
able aim of excelling everybody else in everything. He had gone,
heart and soul, into stock producing and as he had no breeding
theories of his own he proceeded to acquire a set. As it would
necessarily take years to work out these beliefs, he bridged the gap
neatly by purchasing and importing prize livestock and by entering
it against the home-raised products of his neighbors.

Strangely enough, this did not add to the popularity which he did
not possess. Still more strangely, it did not add materially to his
prestige as an exhibitor, for the judges had an exasperating way of
handing him a second or third prize ribbon and then of awarding

the coveted blue rosette to the owner and breeder of some local exhibit.

After a long time it began to dawn upon Glure that narrow neighborhood prejudice deemed it unsportsmanlike to buy prize stock and exhibit it as one's own. At approximately the same time three calves were born to newly imported prize cows in the two-acre model barns of Glure Towers, and with them was born Glure's newest idea.

No one could deny he had bred these calves himself. They were born on his own place and of his own high-pedigreed cattle. Three breeds were represented among the trio of specimens. By points and by lineage they were well-nigh peerless. Wherefore the plan for a show of neighborhood "home-raised" cattle. At length Glure felt he was coming into his own.

The hinterland folk had fought shy of Glure since the dog show wherein he had sought to win the capital prize by formulating a set of conditions that could be filled by no entrant except a newly imported champion Merle of his own.

But the phrase "home-raised" now proved a bait that few of the region's stock lovers could resist; and on the morning of the show no fewer than fifty-two cattle of standard breeds were shuffling or lowing in the big impromptu sheds.

A farmhand, the day before, had led to the show ground the Place's sole entrant—the pretty little Alderney heifer of which the master had spoken to Glure and which, by the way, was destined to win nothing higher than a third-prize ribbon.

For that matter, to end the suspense, the best of the three Glure calves won only a second prize, all the first for their three breeds going to two nonplutocratic North Jerseymen who had bred the ancestors of their entrants for six generations.

The mistress and the master motored over to Glure Towers on the morning of the show in their one car. Lad went with them. He always went with them.

Not that any dog could hope to find interest in a cattle show, but a dog would rather go anywhere with his master than to stay at home without him. Witness the glad alacrity wherewith the weariest dog deserts a snug fireside in the vilest weather for the joy of a master-accompanying walk.

A tire puncture delayed the trip. The show was about to begin when the car was at last parked behind the sunken meadow. The mistress and the master, with Lad at their heels, started across the meadow afoot toward the well-filled grandstand.

Several acquaintances in the stand waved to them as they advanced. Also, before they had traversed more than half the meadow's area their host bore down upon them.

Mr. Glure (dressed, as usual, for the occasion) looked like a blend of Landseer's *Edinburgh Drover* and a theater-program picture of *What the Man Will Wear*.

He had been walking beside a garishly liveried groom who was leading an enormous Holstein bull toward the judging enclosure. The bull was steered by a five-foot bar, the end snapped to a ring in his nose.

"Hello, good people!" Mr. Glure boomed, pump-handling the unenthusiastic mistress's right hand and bestowing a jarringly annoying slap upon the master's shoulder. "Glad to see you! You're late. Almost too late for the best part of the show. Before judging begins, I'm having some of my choicest European stock paraded in the ring. Just for exhibition, you know. Not for a contest. I like to give a treat to some of these farmers who think they know how to breed cattle."

"Yes?" queried the master, who could think of nothing cleverer to say.

"Take that bull, Tenebris, of mine, for instance," proclaimed Glure, with a wave toward the approaching Holstein and his guide. "Best ton of livestock that ever stood on four legs. Look how he—"

Glure paused in his lecture for he saw that both the mistress and the master were staring, not at the bull, but at the beast's leader. The spectacle of a groom in gaudy livery, on duty at a cattle show, was all but too much for their gravity.

"You're looking at that boy of mine, hey? Fine, well-set-up chap, isn't he? A faithful boy. Devoted to me. Slavishly devoted. Not like most of these grumpy, independent Jersey rustics. Not much. He's a treasure, Winston is. Used to be chief handler for some of the biggest cattle breeders in the East he tells me. I got hold of him by chance, and just by the sheerest good luck, a week or so ago. Met him on the road and he asked for a lift. He—"

It was then that Lad disgraced himself and his deities, and proved himself all unworthy to appear in so refined an assembly. The man in livery had convoyed the bull to within a few feet of the proudly exhorting Glure. Now, without growl or other sign of warning, the hitherto peaccable dog changed into a murder machine.

In a single mighty bound he cleared the narrowing distance between himself and the advancing groom.

The leap sent him hurtling through the air, an eighty-pound furry catapult, straight for the man's throat.

Over and beyond the myriad cattle odors, Lad had suddenly recognized a scent that spelt deathless hatred. The scent had been verified by a single glance at the brilliantly clad man in livery. Wherefore the mad charge.

The slashing jaws missed their mark in the man's throat by a bare half inch. That they missed it at all was because the man also recognized Lad, and shrank back in mortal terror.

Even before the eighty-pound weight, smashing against his chest, sent the groom sprawling backward to the ground, Lad's slashing jaws had found a hold in place of the one they had missed.

This grip was on the liveried shoulder, into which the fangs sank to their depth. Down went the man, screaming, the dog atop of him.

"Lad!" cried the mistress, aghast. *"Lad!"*

Through the avenging rage that misted his brain the great dog heard. With a choking sound that was almost a sob he relinquished his hold and turned slowly from his prey.

The master and Glure instinctively took a step toward the approaching dog and the writhingly prostrate man. Then, still more instinctively, and without even coming to a standstill before going into reverse, they both sprang back. They would have sprung further had not the roped walls of the show ring checked them.

For Tenebris had taken a sudden and active part in the scene.

The gigantic Holstein during his career in Europe had trebly won his title to champion. And during the three years before his exportation to America he had gored to death no fewer than three over-confident stable attendants. The bull's homicidal temper, no less than the dazzling price offered by Glure, had caused his owner to sell him to the transatlantic bidder.

A bull's nose is the tenderest spot of his anatomy. Next to his eyes, he guards its safety most zealously. Thus, with a stout leading-bar between him and his conductor, Tenebris was harmless enough.

But the conductor just now had let go of that bar, as Lad's weight had smitten him. Freed, Tenebris had stood for an instant in perplexity.

Fiercely he flung his gnarled head to one side to see the cause of the commotion. The gesture swung the heavy leading-bar, digging the nose ring cruelly into his sensitive nostrils. The pain maddened Tenebris. A final plunging twist of the head—and the bar's weight tore the nose ring free from the nostrils.

Tenebris bellowed thunderously at the climax of pain. Then he realized he had shaken off the only thing that gave humans a control over him. A second bellow—a furious pawing of the earth—and the bull lowered his head. His evil eyes glared about him in search of something to kill.

It was the sight of this motion which sent the master and Glure recoiling against the show-ring ropes.

In almost the same move the master caught up his wife and swung her over the top rope, into the ring. He followed her into that refuge's fragile safety with a speed that held no dignity whatever. Glure, seeing the action, wasted no time in wriggling through the ropes after him.

Tenebris did not follow them.

One thing and only one his red eyes saw: On the ground, not six feet away, rolled and moaned a man. The man was down. He was helpless. Tenebris charged.

A bull plunging at a nearby object shuts both eyes. A cow does not. Which may—or may not—explain the Spanish theory that bullfights are safer than cowfights. To this eye-closing trait many a hard-pressed matador has owed his life.

Tenebris, both eyes screwed shut, hurled his two-thousand-pound bulk at the prostrate groom. Head down, nose in, short horns on a level with the earth and barely clearing it, he made his rush.

But at the very first step he became aware that something was amiss with his pleasantly anticipated charge. It did not follow specifications or precedent.

All because a heavy something had flung its weight against the side of his lowered head, and a new and unbearable pain was torturing his blood-filled nostrils.

Tenebris swerved. He veered to one side, throwing up his head to clear it of this unseen torment.

As a result, the half-lifted horns grazed the fallen man. The pointed hoofs missed him altogether. At the same moment the weight was gone from against the bull's head, and the throbbing stab from his nostrils.

Pausing uncertainly, Tenebris opened his eyes and glared about him. A yard or two away a shaggy dog was rising from the tumble caused by the jerky uptossing of the bull's head.

Now, were this a fiction yarn, it would be interesting to devise reasons why Lad should have flown to the rescue of a human whom he loathed, and arrayed himself against a fellow beast toward which he felt no hatred at all.

To dogs all men are gods. And perhaps Lad felt the urge of saving even a detested god from the onslaught of a beast. Or perhaps not. One can go only by the facts. And the facts were that the collie had checked himself in the reluctant journey toward the mistress and had gone to his foe's defense.

With a flash of speed astonishing in so large and sedate a dog, he had flown at the bull in time—in the barest time—to grip the torn nostrils and turn the whirlwind charge.

And now Tenebris shifted his baleful glare from the advancing dog to the howling man. The dog could wait. The bull's immediate pleasure and purpose were to kill the man.

He lowered his head again. But before he could launch his

enormous bulk into full motion—before he could shut his eyes—
the dog was between him and his quarry.

In one spring Lad was at the bull's nose. And again his white eye
teeth slashed the ragged nostrils. Tenebris halted his own incipient
rush and strove to pin the collie to the ground. It would have been
as easy to pin a whizzing hornet.

Tenebris thrust at the clinging dog, once more seeking to smash
Lad against the sod with his battering-ram forehead and his short
horns. But Lad was not there. Instead, he was to the left, his body
clean out of danger, his teeth in the bull's left ear.

A lunge of the tortured head sent Lad rolling over and over. But
by the time he stopped rolling he was on his feet again. Not only on
his feet, but back to the assault. Back, before his unwieldly foe
could gauge the distance for another rush at the man. And a keen
nip in the bleeding nostrils balked still one more charge.

The bull, snorting with rage, suddenly changed his plan of campaign. Apparently his first ideas had been wrong. It was the man
who could wait, and the dog that must be gotten out of the way.

Tenebris wheeled and made an express-train rush at Lad. The
collie turned and fled. He did not flee with tail down, as befits a
beaten dog. Brush wavingly aloft, he gamboled along at top speed,
just a stride or two ahead of the pursuing bull. He even looked
back encouragingly over his shoulder as he went.

Lad was having a beautiful time. Seldom had he been so riot-
ously happy. All the pent-up mischief in his soul was having a glorious airing.

The bull's blind charge was short, as a bull's charge always is.
When Tenebris opened his eyes he saw the dog, not ten feet in
front of him, scampering for dear life toward the river. And again
Tenebris charged.

Three such charges, one after another, brought pursuer and pursued to within a hundred feet of the water.

Tenebris was not used to running. He was getting winded. He
came to a wavering standstill, snorting loudly and pawing up great
lumps of sod.

But he had not stood thus longer than a second before Lad was at him. Burnished shaggy coat abristle, tail delightedly wagging, the dog bounded forward. He set up an earsplitting fanfare of barking.

Round and round the bull he whirled, never letting up on that deafening volley of barks; nipping now at ears, now at nose, now at heels; dodging in and out under the giant's clumsy body; easily avoiding the bewilderingly awkward kicks and lunges of his enemy. Then, forefeet crouching and muzzle close to the ground, like a playful puppy, he waved his plumed tail violently and, in a new succession of barks, wooed his adversary to the attack.

It was a pretty sight. And it set Tenebris into active motion at once.

The bull doubtless thought he himself was doing the driving, by means of his panting rushes, and by his lurches to one side or another to keep away from the dog's sharp bites. But he was not. It was Lad who chose the direction in which they went. And he chose it deliberately.

Presently the two were but fifteen feet away from the river, at a point where the bank shelved, clifflike, for two or three yards, down to a wide pool.

Feinting for the nose, Lad induced Tenebris to lower his tired head. Then he sprang lightly over the threatening horns, and landed, ascramble, with all four feet, on the bull's broad shoulders.

Scurrying along the heaving back, the dog nipped Tenebris on the hip, and dropped to earth again.

The insult, the fresh pain, the astonishment combined to make Tenebris forget his weariness. Beside himself with maniac wrath, he shut both eyes and launched himself forward. Lad slipped, eellike, to one side. Carried by his own blind momentum, Tenebris shot over the bank edge.

Too late the bull looked. Half sliding, half scrambling, he crashed down the steep sides of the bank and into the river.

Lad, tongue out, jogged over to the top of the bank, where, with head to one side and ears cocked, he gazed interestedly down into the wildly churned pool.

Tenebris had gotten to his feet after the ducking; and he was floundering pastern-deep in stickily soft mud. So tightly bogged down that it later took the efforts of six farmhands to extricate him, the bull continued to flounder and to bellow.

A stream of people were running down the meadow toward the river. Lad hated crowds. He made a loping detour of the nearest runners and sought to regain the spot where last he had seen the mistress and master. Also, if his luck held good, he might have still another bout with the man he had once treed. Which would be an ideal climax to a perfect day.

He found all the objects of his quest together. The groom, hysterical, was swaying on his feet, supported by Glure.

At sight of the advancing collie the bitten man cried aloud in fear and clutched his employer for protection.

"Take him away, sir!" he babbled in mortal terror. "He'll kill me! He hates me, the ugly hair devil! He *hates* me. He tried to kill me once before! He—"

"H'm!" mused the master. "So he tried to kill you once before, eh? Aren't you mistaken?"

"No, I ain't!" wept the man. "I'd know him in a million! That's why he went for me again today. He remembered me. I seen he did. That's no dog. It's a *devil!*"

"Mr. Glure," asked the master, a light dawning, "when this chap applied to you for work, did he wear grayish tweed trousers? And were they in bad shape?"

"His trousers were in rags," said Glure. "I remember that. He said a savage dog had jumped into the road from a farmhouse somewhere and gone for him. Why?"

"Those trousers," answered the master, "weren't entire strangers to you. You'd seen the missing parts of them—on a tree and on the ground near it, at the Place. Your 'treasure' is the harness thief Lad treed the day you came to see me. So—"

"Nonsense!" fumed Glure. "Why, how absurd! He—"

"I hadn't stolen anything!" blubbered the man. "I was coming cross-lots to a stable to ask for work. And the brute went for me. I had to run up a tree and—"

"And it didn't occur to you to shout for help?" sweetly urged the master. "I was within call. So was Mr. Glure. So was at least one of my men. An honest seeker for work needn't have been afraid to halloo. A thief would have been afraid to. In fact, a thief *was!*"

"Get out of here, you!" roared Glure, convinced at last. "You measly sneak thief! Get out or I'll have you jailed! You're an imposter! A panhandler! A—"

The thief waited to hear no more. With an apprehensive glance to see that Lad was firmly held, he bolted for the road.

"Thanks for telling me," said Glure. "He might have stolen everything at Glure Towers if I hadn't found out. He—"

"Yes. He might even have stolen more than the cost of our nonutilitarian Lad's keep," unkindly suggested the master. "For that matter, if it hadn't been for a nonutilitarian dog, that mad bull's horns, instead of his nostrils, would be red by this time. At least one man would have been killed. Perhaps more. So, after all—"

He stopped. The mistress was tugging surreptitiously at his sleeve. The master, in obedience to his wife's signal, stepped aside, to light a cigar.

"I wouldn't say any more, dear, if I were you," the mistress was whispering. "You see, if it hadn't been for Lad, the bull would never have broken loose in the first place. By another half-hour that fact may dawn on Mr. Glure, if you keep rubbing it in. Let's go over to the grandstand. Come, Lad!"

CHAPTER 10

THE KILLER

One of the jolliest minutes in Lad's daily cross-country tramp with the mistress and the master was his dash up Mount Pisgah. This mount was little more than a foothill. It was treeless, and covered with short grass and mullein; a slope where no crop but buckwheat could be expected to thrive. It rose out of the adjoining mountain forests in a long and sweeping ascent.

Here, with no trees or undergrowth to impede him, Lad, from puppyhood, had ordained a racecourse of his own. As he neared the hill he would always dash forward at top speed; flying up the rise like a tawny whirlwind, at unabated pace, until he stopped, panting and gloriously excited, on the summit; to await his slower-moving human escorts.

One morning in early summer, Lad, as usual, bounded ahead of the mistress and the master, as ever, he rushed gleefully forward for his daily breather, up the long slope. But, before he had gone fifty yards, he came to a scurrying halt, and stood at gaze. His back was bristling and his lips curled back from his white teeth in sudden annoyance.

His keen nostrils, even before his eyes, told him something was amiss with his cherished racetrack. The eddying shift of the breeze, from west to north, had brought to his nose the odor which had checked his onrush; an odor that wakened all sorts of vaguely formless memories far back in Lad's brain; and which he did not at all care for.

Scent is ten times stronger, to a dog, than is sight. The best dog is nearsighted. And the worst dog has a magic sense of smell. Wherefore, a dog almost always uses his nose first and his eyes last. Which Lad now proceeded to do.

Above him was the pale green hillside, up which he loved to gallop. But its surface was no longer smoothly unencumbered. Instead, it was dotted and starred—singly or in groups—with fluffy grayish-white creatures.

Lad was almost abreast of the lowest group of sheep when he paused. Several of the feeding animals lifted their heads, snortingly, from the short herbage, at sight of him and fled up the hill. The rest of the flock joined them in the silly stampede.

The dog made no move to follow. Instead, his forehead creased and his eyes troubled, he stared after the gray-white surge that swept upward toward the summit of his favored coursing ground. The mistress and the master, too, at sight of the woolly avalanche, stopped and stared.

From over the brow of Mount Pisgah appeared the nonpicturesque figure of a man in blue denim overalls—one Titus Romaine, owner of the sparse-grassed hill. Drawn by the noisy multiple patter of his flock's hoofs, he emerged from under a hilltop boulder's shade to learn the cause of their flight.

Now, in all his life, Lad had seen sheep just once before. That one exception had been when Hamilcar Q. Glure, the Wall Street Farmer, had corralled a little herd of his prize merinos, overnight, at the Place, on the way to the Paterson Livestock Show. On that occasion, the sheep had broken from the corral, and Lad, acting on ancestral instinct, had rounded them up, without injuring or scaring one of them.

The memory was not pleasing to Lad, and he wanted nothing more to do with such stupid creatures. Indeed, as he looked now upon the sheep that were obstructing his run, he felt a distinct aversion to them. Whining a little, he trotted back to where stood the mistress and the master. And, as they waited, Titus Romaine bore wrathfully down upon them.

"I've been expectin' something like that!" announced the land-owner. "Ever since I turned these critters out here, this mornin'. I ain't surprised a bit. I—"

"What is it you've been expecting, Romaine?" asked the master. "And how long have you been a sheep raiser? A sheep, here in the North Jersey hinterland, is as rare as—"

"I been expectin' some savage dog would be runnin' 'em," retorted the farmer. "Just like I've read they do. An' now I've caught him at it!"

"Caught whom—at what?" queried the perplexed mistress; failing to note the man's baleful glower at the contemptuous Lad.

"That big ugly brute of your'n, of course," declared Romaine. "I caught him, red-handed, runnin' my sheep. He—"

"Lad did nothing of the kind," denied the mistress. "The instant he caught sight of them he stopped running. Lad wouldn't hurt anything that is weak and helpless. Your sheep saw him and they ran away. He didn't follow them an inch."

"I seen what I seen," cryptically answered the man. "An' I give you fair warnin', if any of my sheep is killed, I'll know right where to come to look for the killer."

"If you mean Lad—" began the master, hotly.

But the mistress intervened.

"I am glad you have decided to raise sheep, Mr. Romaine," she said. "Everyone ought to, who can. I read, only the other day, that America is using up more sheep than it can breed; and that the price of fodder and the scarcity of pasture were doing terrible things to the mutton-and-wool supply. I hope you'll have all sorts of good luck. And you are wise to watch your sheep so closely. But don't be afraid of Lad harming any of them. He wouldn't, for worlds, I know. Because I know Lad. Come along, Laddie!" she finished, as she turned to go away.

But Titus Romaine stopped her.

"I've put a sight of money into this flock of sheep," he declared. "More'n I could reely afford. An' I've been readin' up on sheep, too. I've been readin' that the worst en'my to sheep is 'pred'tory dogs.' An' if that big dog of your'n ain't 'pred'tory,' then I never seen one that was. So I'm warnin' you, fair—"

"If your sheep come to any harm, Mr. Romaine," returned the mistress, again forestalling an untactful outbreak from her husband, "I'll guarantee Lad will have nothing to do with it."

"An' I'll guarantee to have him shot an' have you folks up in court, if he does," chivalrously retorted Mr. Titus Romaine.

With which exchange of good fellowship, the two groups parted, Romaine returning to his scattered sheep, while the mistress, Lad at her heels, lured the master away from the field of encounter. The master was fuming.

"Here's where good old Mr. Trouble drops in on us for a nice long visit!" he grumbled, as they moved homeward. "I can see how it is going to turn out. Because a few stray curs have chased or killed sheep, now and then, every decent dog is under suspicion as a sheep killer. If one of Romaine's male sheep gets a scratch on its leg, from a bramble, Lad will be blamed. If one of the mongrels from over in the village should chase his sheep, Lad will be accused. And we'll be in the first 'neighborhood squabble' of our lives."

The master spoke with a pessimism his wife did not share, and which he, himself, did not really believe. The folk at the Place had always lived in good fellowship and peace with their few rural neighbors, as well as with the several hundred inhabitants of the mile-distant village, across the lake. And, though livestock is the foundation of ninety rustic feuds out of ninety-one, the dogs of the Place had never involved their owners in any such row.

Yet, barely three days later, Titus Romaine bore down upon the Place, before breakfast, breathing threats and complaining of slaughter.

He was waiting on the veranda in blasphemous converse with the

Place's foreman, when the master came out. At Titus's heels stood his hired man—a huge and sullen person named Schwartz, who possessed a scarce-conquered accent that fit the name.

"Well!" orated Romaine, in glum greeting, as he sighted the master. "Well, I guessed right! He done it, after all! He done it. We all but caught him, red-handed. Got away with four of my best sheep! Four of 'em. The cur!"

"What are you talking about?" demanded the master, as the mistress, drawn by the visitor's plangent tones, joined the veranda group. " 'Bout that ugly big dog of your'n!" answered Romaine. "I knew what he'd do, if he got the chance. I knew it, when I saw him runnin' my poor sheep, last week. I warned you then. The two of you. An' now he's done it!"

"Done what?" insisted the master, impatient of the man's noise and fury.

"What dog?" asked the mistress, at the same time.

"Are you talking about Lad? If you are—"

"I'm talkin' about your big brown collie cur!" snorted Titus. "He's gone an' killed four of my best sheep. Did it in the night an' early this mornin'. My man here caught him at the last of 'em, an' drove him off, just as he was finishin' the poor critter. He got away with the rest of 'em."

"Nonsense!" denied the master. "You're talking rot. Lad wouldn't touch a sheep. And—"

"That's what all folks say when they dogs or their children is charged with doin' wrong!" scoffed Romaine. "But this time it won't do no good to—"

"You say this happened last night?" interposed the mistress.

"Yes, it did. Last night an 'early in the mornin', too. Schwartz, here—"

"But Lad sleeps in the house, every night," objected the mistress. "He sleeps under the piano, in the music room. He has slept there every night since he was a puppy. The maid who dusts the downstairs rooms before breakfast lets him out, when she begins work. So he—"

"Bolster it up any way you like!" broke in Romaine. "He was out last night, all right. An' early this morning, too."

"How early?" questioned the master.

"Five o'clock," volunteered Schwartz, speaking up, from behind his employer. "I know, because that's the time I get up. I went out, first thing, to open the barnyard gate and drive the sheep to the pasture. First thing I saw was that big dog growling over a sheep he'd just killed. He saw me, and he wiggled out through the barnyard bars—same way he had got in. Then I counted the sheep. One was dead—the one he had just killed—and three were gone. We've been looking for their bodies ever since, and we can't find them."

"I suppose Lad swallowed them," ironically put in the Place's foreman. "That makes about as much sense as the rest of the yarn. The old dog would no sooner—"

"Do you really mean to say you saw Lad—saw and *recognized* him—in Mr. Titus's barnyard, growling over a sheep he had just killed?" demanded the mistress.

"I sure do," affirmed Schwartz. "And I—"

"An' he's ready to go on th' stand an' take oath to it!" supplemented Titus. "Unless you'll pay me the damages out of court. Them sheep cost me exac'ly $12.10 a head, in the Pat'son market, one week ago. An' sheep on the hoof has gone up a full forty cents more since then. You owe me for them four sheep exac'ly—"

"I owe you not one red cent!" denied the master. "I hate law worse than I hate measles. But I'll fight that idiotic claim all the way up to the Appellate Division before I'll—"

The mistress lifted a little silver whistle that hung at her belt and blew it. An instant later Lad came galloping gaily up the lawn from the lake, adrip with water from his morning swim. Straight, at the mistress's summons, he came, and stood, expectant, in front of her, oblivious of others.

The great dog's mahogany-and-snow coat shone wetly in the sunshine. Every line of his splendid body was tense. His eyes looked up into the face of the loved mistress in eager anticipation. For a whistle-call usually involved some matter of more than common interest.

"That's the dog!" cried Schwartz, his thick voice betraying a shade more of its half-lost German accent, in the excitement of the minute. "That's the one. He has washed off the blood. But that is the one. I could know him anywhere at all. And I knew him, already. And Mr. Romaine told me to be looking out for him, about the sheep, too. So I—"

The master had bent over Lad, examining the dog's mouth. "Not a trace of blood or of wool!" he announced. "And look how he faces us! If he had anything to be ashamed of—"

"I got a witness to prove he killed my sheep," cut in Romaine. "Since you won't be honest enough to square the case out of court, then the law'll take a tuck in your wallet for you. The law will look after a poor man's int'rest. I don't wonder there's folks who want all dogs done 'way with. Pesky curs! Here, the papers say we are short on sheep, an' they beg us to raise 'em, because mutton is worth double what it used to be, in open market. Then, when I buy sheep, on that sayso, your dog gets four of 'em the very first week. Think what them four sheep would 'a meant to—"

"I'm sorry you lost them," the master interrupted. "Mighty sorry. And I'm still sorrier if there is a sheep-killing dog at large anywhere in this region. But Lad never—"

"I tell ye, he *did!*" stormed Titus. "I got proof of it. Proof good enough for any court. An' the court is goin' to see me righted. It's goin' to do more. It's goin' to make you shoot that killer, there, too. I know the law. I looked it up. An' the law says if a sheep-killin' dog—"

"Lad is not a sheep-killing dog!" flashed the mistress.

"That's what he is!" snarled Romaine. "An', by law, he'll be shot as sech. He—"

"Take your case to law, then!" retorted the master, whose last shred of patience went by the board, at the threat. "And take it and yourself off my Place! Lad doesn't 'run' sheep. But, at the word from me, he'll ask nothing better than to 'run' you and the German every step of the way to your own woodshed. Clear out!"

He and the mistress watched the two irately mumbling intruders plod out of sight up the drive. Lad, at the master's side, viewed the accusers' departure with sharp interest. Schooled in reading the human voice, he had listened alertly to the master's speech of dismissal. And, as the dog listened, his teeth had come slowly into view from beneath a menacingly upcurled lip. His eyes, half shut, had been fixed on Titus with an expression that was not pretty.

"Oh, dear!" sighed the mistress miserably, as she and her husband turned indoors and made their way toward the breakfast room. "You were right about 'good old Mr. Trouble dropping in on us.' Isn't it horrible? But it makes my blood boil to think of Laddie being accused of such a thing. It is crazily absurd, of course. But—"

"Absurd?" the master caught her up. "It's the most absurd thing I ever heard of. If it was about any other dog than Lad, it would be good for a laugh. I mean, Romaine's charge of the dog's doing away with no less than four sheep and not leaving a trace of more than one of them. That, alone, would get his case laughed out of court. I remember, once in Scotland, I was stopping with some people whose shepherd complained that three of the sheep had fallen victim to a 'killer.' We all went up to the moor-pasture to look at them. They weren't a pretty sight, but they were all *there*. A dog doesn't devour a sheep he kills. He doesn't even lug it away. Instead, he just—"

"Perhaps you'd rather describe it *after* breakfast," suggested the mistress, hurriedly. "This wretched business has taken away all of my appetite that I can comfortably spare."

At about midmorning of the next day, the master was summoned to the telephone.

"This is Maclay," said the voice at the far end.

"Why, hello, Mac!" responded the master, mildly wondering why his old fishing crony, the village's local peace justice, should be calling him up at such an hour. "If you're going to tell me this is a good day for smallmouth bass to bite I'm going to tell you it isn't. It isn't because I'm up to my neck in work. Besides, it's too late for the morning fishing, and too early for the bass to get up their afternoon appetites. So don't try to tempt me into—"

"Hold on!" broke in Maclay. "I'm not calling you up for that. I'm calling up on business; rotten unpleasant business, too."

"What's wrong?" asked the master.

"I'm hoping Titus Romaine is," said the justice. "He's just been here—with his hired man as witness—to make a complaint about your dog, Lad. Yes, and to get a court order to have the old fellow shot, too."

"What!" sputtered the master. "He hasn't actually—"

"That's just what he's done," said Maclay. "He claims Lad killed four of his new sheep night before last, and four more of them this morning or last night. Schwartz swears he caught Lad at the last of the killed sheep both times. It's hard luck, old man, and I feel as bad about it as if it were my own dog. You know how strong I am for Lad. He's the greatest collie I've known, but the law is clear in such—"

"You speak as if you thought Lad was guilty!" flamed the master. "You ought to know better than that. He—"

"Schwartz tells a straight story," answered Maclay, sadly, "and he tells it under oath. He swears he recognized Lad first time. He says he volunteered to watch in the barnyard last night. He had had a hard day's work and he fell asleep while he was on watch. He says he woke up in gray dawn to find the whole flock in a turmoil, and Lad pinning one of the sheep to the ground. He had already killed three. Schwartz drove him away. Three of the sheep were missing. One Lad had just downed was dying. Romaine swears he saw Lad 'running' his sheep last week. It—"

"What did you do about the case?" asked the dazed master.

"I told them to be at the courtroom at three this afternoon with the bodies of the two dead sheep that aren't missing, and that I'd notify you to be there, too."

"Oh, I'll be there!" snapped the master. "Don't worry. And it was decent of you to make them wait. The whole thing is ridiculous! It—"

"Of course," went on Maclay, "either side can easily appeal from any decision I make. That is as regards damages. But, by the township's new sheep laws, I'm sorry to say there isn't any appeal from the local justice's decree that a sheep-killing dog must be shot at once. The law leaves me no option if I consider a dog guilty of sheep killing. I have to order such a dog put to death at once. That's what's making me so blue. I'd rather lose a year's pay than have to order old Lad killed."

"You won't have to," declared the master, stoutly; albeit he was beginning to feel a nasty sinking in the vicinity of his stomach.

"We'll manage to prove him innocent. I'll stake anything you like on that."

"Talk the case over with Dick Colfax or any other good lawyer before three o'clock," suggested Maclay. "There may be a legal loophole out of the muddle. I hope to the Lord there is."

"We're not going to crawl out through any loopholes, Lad and I," returned the master. "We're going to come through, *clean.* See if we don't!"

Leaving the telephone, he went in search of the mistress, and more and more disheartened told her the story.

"The worst of it is," he finished, "Romaine and Schwartz seem to have made Maclay believe their fool yarn."

"That is because they believe it, themselves," said the mistress, "and because, just as soon as even the most sensible man is made a judge, he seems to lose all his common sense and intuition and become nothing but a walking statute book. But you—you think for a moment, do you, that they can persuade Judge Maclay to have Lad shot?"

She spoke with a little quiver in her sweet voice that roused all the master's fighting spirit.

"This place is going to be in a state of siege against the entire law and militia of New Jersey," he announced, "before one bullet goes into Lad. You can put your mind to rest on that. But that isn't enough. I want to *clear* him. In these days of conservation and scarcity, it is a grave offense to destroy any meat animal. And the loss of eight sheep in two days—in a district where there has been such an effort made to revive sheep raising—"

"Didn't you say they claim the second lot of sheep were killed in the night and at dawn, just as they said the first were?" interposed the mistress.

"Why, yes. But—"

"Then," said the mistress, much more comfortably, "we can prove Lad's alibi just as I said yesterday we could. Marie always lets him out in the morning when she comes downstairs to dust these lower rooms. She's never down before six o'clock; and the sun, nowadays, rises long before that. Schwartz says he saw Lad both times in the early dawn. We can prove, by Marie, that Lad was safe here in the house till long after sunrise."

Her worried frown gave way to a smile of positive inspiration. The master's own darkling face cleared.

"Good!" he approved. "I think that cinches it. Marie's been with us for years. Her word is certainly as good as a farmhand's. Even Maclay's 'judicial temperament' will have to admit that. Send her in here, won't you?"

When the maid appeared at the door of the study a minute later, the master opened the examination with the solemn air of a legal veteran.

"You are the first person down here in the mornings, aren't you, Marie?" he began.

"Why, yes, sir," replied the wondering maid. "Yes, always, except when you get up early to go fishing or when—"

"What time do you get down here in the mornings," pursued the master.

"Along about six o'clock, sir, mostly," said the maid, bridling a bit as if scenting a criticism of her work-hours.

"Not earlier than six?" asked the master.

"No, sir," said Marie, uncomfortably. "Of course, if that's not early enough, I suppose I could—"

"It's quite early enough," vouchsafed the master. "There is no complaint about your hours. You always let Lad out as soon as you come into the music room?"

"Yes, sir," she answered, "as soon as I get downstairs. Those were the orders, you remember."

The master breathed a silent sigh of relief. The maid did not get downstairs until six. The dog, then, could not get out of the house

until that hour. If Schwartz had seen any dog in the Romaine
barnyard at daybreak, it assuredly was not Lad. Yet, racking his
brain, the master could not recall any other dog in the vicinity that
bore even the faintest semblance to his giant collie. And he fell to
recalling—from his happy memories of *Bob, Son of Battle*—that
"killers" often travel many miles from home to sate their mania for
sheep slaying.

In any event, it was no concern of his if some distant collie,
drawn to the slaughter by the queer "sixth" collie sense, was killing
Romaine's new flock of sheep. Lad was cleared. The maid's very
evidently true testimony settled that point.

"Yes, sir," rambled on Marie, beginning to take a faint interest in
the examination now that it turned upon Lad whom she loved.
"Yes, sir, Laddie always comes out from under his piano the minute
he hears my step in the hall outside. And he always comes right up
to me and wags that big plume of a tail of his, and falls into step
alongside of me and walks over to the front door, right beside me
all the way. He knows as much as many a human, that dog does,
sir."

Encouraged by the master's approving nod, the maid ventured to
enlarge still further upon the theme.

"It always seems as if he was welcoming me downstairs, like," she
resumed, "and glad to see me. I've really missed him quite bad this
past few mornings." The approving look on the master's face gave
way to a glare of utter blankness.

"This past few mornings?" he repeated, blitheringly. "What do
you mean?"

"Why," she returned, flustered afresh by the quick change in her
interlocutor's manner. "Ever since those French windows are left
open for the night—same as they always are when the hot weather
starts in, you know, sir. Since then, Laddie don't wait for me to let
him out. When he wakes up he just goes out himself. He used to do
that last year, too, sir. He—"

"Thanks," muttered the master, dizzily. "That's all. Thanks."

Left alone, he sat slumped low in his chair, trying to think. He was as calmly convinced as ever of his dog's innocence, but he had staked everything on Marie's court testimony. And, now, that testimony was rendered worse than worthless.

Crankily he cursed his own fresh-air mania which had decreed that the long windows on the ground floor be left open on summer nights. With Lad on duty, the house was as safe from successful burglary in spite of these open windows, as if guarded by a squad of special policemen. And the night air, sweeping through, kept it pleasantly cool against the next day's heat. For this same coolness, a heavy price was now due.

Presently the daze of disappointment passed leaving the master pulsing with a wholesome fighting anger. Rapidly he revised his defense and, with the mistress's far cleverer aid, made ready for the afternoon's ordeal. He scouted Maclay's suggestion of hiring counsel and vowed to handle the defense himself. Carefully he and his wife went over their proposed line of action.

Peace Justice Maclay's court was held daily in a rambling room on an upper floor of the village's Odd Fellows' Hall. The proceedings there were generally marked by shrewd sanity rather than by any effort at formalism. Maclay, himself, sat at a battered little desk at the room's far end; his clerk using a corner of the same desk for the scribbling of his sketchy notes.

In front of the desk was a rather long deal table with kitchen chairs around it. Here, plaintiffs and defendants and prisoners and witnesses and lawyers were wont to sit, with no order of precedent or of other formality. Several other chairs were ranged irregularly along the wall to accommodate any overflow of the table's occupants.

Promptly at three o'clock that afternoon, the mistress and the master entered the courtroom. Close at the mistress's side—though held by no leash—paced Lad. Maclay and Romaine and Schwartz were already on hand. So were the clerk and the constable and one or two idle spectators. At a corner of the room, wrapped in burlap, were huddled the bodies of the two slain sheep.

Lad caught the scent of the victims the instant he set foot in the room, and he sniffed vibrantly once or twice. Titus Romaine, his eyes fixed scowlingly on the dog, noted this, and he nudged Schwartz in the ribs to call the German's attention to it.

Lad turned aside in fastidious disgust from the bumpy burlap bundle. Seeing the judge and recognizing him as an old acquaintance, the collie wagged his plumed tail in gravely friendly greeting and stepped forward for a pat on the head.

"Lad!" called the mistress, softly.

At the word the dog paused midway to the embarrassed Maclay's desk and obediently turned back. The constable was drawing up a chair at the deal table for the mistress. Lad curled down beside her, resting one snowy little forepaw protectingly on her slippered foot. And the hearing began.

Romaine repeated his account of the collie's alleged depredations, starting with Lad's first view of the sheep. Schwartz methodically retold his own story of twice witnessing the killing of sheep by the dog.

The master did not interrupt either narrative, though, on later questioning he forced the sulkily truthful Romaine to admit he had not actually seen Lad chase the sheep flock that morning on Mount Pisgah, but had merely seen the sheep running, and the dog standing at the hill foot looking upward at their scattering flight. Both the mistress and the master swore that the dog on that occasion, had made no move to pursue or otherwise harass the sheep.

Thus did Lad win one point in the case. But, in view of the aftercrimes wherewith he was charged, the point was of decidedly trivial value. Even if he had not attacked the flock on his first view of them he was accused of killing no less than eight of their number on two later encounters. And Schwartz was an eyewitness to this— Schwartz, whose testimony was as clear and as simple as daylight.

With a glance of apology at the mistress, Judge Maclay ordered the sheep carcasses taken from their burlap cerements and laid on the table for court inspection.

While he and Schwartz arranged the grisly exhibits for the judge's view, Titus Romaine expatiated loudly on the value of the murdered sheep and on the brutally useless wastage in their slaying. The master said nothing, but he bent over each of the sheep, carefully studying the throat wounds. At last he straightened himself up from his task and broke in on Romaine's Antonylike funeral oration by saying quietly, "Your honor, these sheep's throats were not cut by a dog. Neither by Lad nor by any 'killer.' Look for yourself. I've seen dog-killed sheep. The wounds were not at all like these."

"Not killed by a dog, hey?" loudly scoffed Romaine. "I s'pose they was chewed by lightnin', then? Or, maybe they was bit by a skeeter? Huh!"

"They were not bitten at all," countered the master. "Still less, were they chewed. Look! Those gashes are ragged enough, but they are as straight as if they were made by a machine. If ever you have seen a dog worry a piece of meat—"

"Rubbish!" grunted Titus. "You talk like a fool! The sheeps' throats is torn. Schwartz seen your cur tear 'em. That's all there is to it. Whether he tore 'em straight or whether he tore 'em crooked don't count in law. He *tore* 'em. An' I got a reli'ble witness to prove it."

"Your Honor," said the master, suddenly. "May I interrogate the witness?"

Maclay nodded. The master turned to Schwartz, who faced him in stolid composure.

"Schwartz," began the master, "you say it was light enough for you to recognize the sheep-killing dog both mornings in Romaine's barnyard. How near to him did you get?"

Schwartz pondered for a second, then made careful answer, "First time, I ran into the barnyard from the house side and your dog cut and ran out of it from the far side when he saw me making for him. That time, I don't think I got within thirty feet of him. But I was near enough to see him plain, and I'd seen him often enough before on the road or in your car; so I knew him all right. The next time—this morning, Judge—I was within five feet of him, or even nearer. For I was near enough to hit him with the stick I'd just picked up and to land a kick on his ribs as he started away. I saw him then as plain as I see you. And nearer than I am to you. And the light was 'most good enough to read by, too."

"Yes?" queried the master. "If I remember rightly you told Judge Maclay that you were on watch last night in the cowshed, just alongside the barnyard where the sheep were; and you fell asleep; and woke just in time to see a dog—"

"To see your dog—" corrected Schwartz.

"To see a dog growling over a squirming and bleating sheep he had pulled down. How far away from you was he when you awoke?"

"Just outside the cowshed door. Not six feet from me. I ups with the stick I had with me and ran out at him and—"

"Were he and the sheep making much noise?"

"Between 'em they was making enough racket to wake a dead man," replied Schwartz. "What with your dog's snarling and growling, and the poor sheep's bl'ats. And all the other sheep—"

"Yet, you say he had killed three sheep while you slept there— had killed them and carried or dragged their bodies away and come back again; and, presumably started a noisy panic in the flock every time. And none of that racket waked you until the fourth sheep was killed?"

"I was dog-tired," declared Schwartz. "I'd been at work in our south-mowing for ten hours the day before, and up since five. Mr. Romaine can tell you I'm a hard man to wake at best. I sleep like the dead."

"That's right!" assented Titus. "Time an' again, I have to bang at his door an' holler myself hoarse, before I can get him to open his eyes. My wife says he's the sleepin'est sleeper—"

"You ran out of the shed with your stick," resumed the master, "and struck the dog before he could get away? And as he turned to run you kicked him?"

"Yes, sir. That's what I did."

"How hard did you hit him?"

"A pretty good lick," answered Schwartz, with reminiscent satisfaction. "Then I—"

"And when you hit him he slunk away like a whipped cur? He made no move to resent it? I mean, he did not try to attack you?"

"Not him!" asserted Schwartz, "I guess he was glad enough to get out of reach. He slunk away so fast, I hardly had a chance to land fair on him, when I kicked."

"Here is my riding-crop," said the master. "Take it, please, and strike Lad with it just as you struck him—or the sheep-killing dog—with your stick. Just as hard. Lad has never been struck except once, unjustly, by me, years ago. He has never needed it. But if he would slink away like a whipped mongrel when a stranger hits him, the sooner he is beaten to death the better. Hit him exactly as you hit him this morning."

Judge Maclay half-opened his lips to protest. He knew the love of the people of the Place for Lad, and he wondered at this invitation to a farmhand to thrash the dog publicly. He glanced at the mistress. Her face was calm, even a little amused. Evidently the master's request did not horrify or surprise her.

Schwartz's stubby fingers gripped the crop the master forced into his hand. He swung the weapon aloft and took a step toward the lazily recumbent collie, striking with all his strength.

Then, with much-increased speed, Schwartz took three steps backward. For, at the menace, Lad had leaped to his feet with the speed of a fighting wolf, eluding the descending crop as it swished past him and launching himself straight for the wielder's throat. He did not growl; he did not pause. He merely sprang for his assailant with a deadly ferocity that brought a cry from Maclay.

The master caught the huge dog midway in his throatward flight.

"Down, Lad!" he ordered, gently.

The collie, obedient to the word, stretched himself on the floor at the mistress's feet. But he kept a watchful and right unloving eye on the man who had struck at him.

"It's a bit odd, isn't it," suggested the master, "that he went for you, like that, just now; when, this morning, he slunk away from your blow, in cringing fear?"

"Why wouldn't he?" growled Schwartz, his stolid nerve shaken by the unexpected onslaught. "His folks are here to back him up, and everything. Why wouldn't he go for me! He was slinky enough when I whaled him, this morning."

"H'm!" mused the master. "You hit a strong blow, Schwartz. I'll say that, for you. You missed Lad, with my crop. But you've split the crop. And you scored a visible mark on the wooden floor with it. Did you hit as hard as that when you struck the sheep killer, this morning?"

"A sight harder," responded Schwartz. "My mad was up. I—"

"A dog's skin is softer than a pine floor," said the master. "Your Honor, such a blow would have raised a weal on Lad's flesh, an inch high. Would your Honor mind passing your hand over his body and trying to locate such a weal?"

"This is all outside the p'int!" raged the annoyed Titus Romaine. "You're a-dodgin' the issue, I tell ye. I—"

"If Your Honor please!" insisted the master.

The judge left his desk and whistled Lad across to him. The dog looked at his master, doubtfully. The master nodded. The collie arose and walked in leisurely fashion over to the waiting judge. Maclay ran an exploring hand through the magnificent tawny coat, from head to haunch; then along the dog's furry sides. Lad hated to be handled by anyone but the mistress or the master. But at a soft word from the mistress, he stood stock still and submitted to the inspection.

"I find no weal or any other mark on him," presently reported the judge.

The mistress smiled happily. The whole investigation, up to this point, and further, was along eccentric lines she herself had thought out and had suggested to her husband. Lines suggested by her knowledge of Lad.

"Schwartz," went on the master, interrupting another fuming outbreak from Romaine, "I'm afraid you didn't hit quite as hard as you thought you did, this morning; or else some other dog is carrying around a big welt on his flesh, today. Now for the kick you say you gave the collie. I—"

"I won't copy *that,* on your bloodthirsty dog!" vociferated Schwartz. "Not even if the judge jails me for contempt, I won't. He'd likely kill me!"

"And yet he ran from you, this morning," the master reminded him. "Well, I won't insist on your kicking Lad. But you say it was a light kick; because he was running away when it landed. I am curious to know just how hard a kick it was. In fact, I'm so curious about it that I am going to offer myself as a substitute for Lad. My riding boot is a good surface. Will you kindly kick me there, Schwartz; as nearly as possible with the same force (no more, no less) than you kicked the dog?"

"I protest!" shouted Romaine. "This measly tomfoolishness is—"

"If Your Honor please!" appealed the master sharply; turning from the bewildered Schwartz to the no less dismayed judge.

Maclay was on his feet to overrule so strange a request. But there was keen supplication in the master's eye that made the judge pause. Maclay glanced again at the mistress. In spite of the prospect of seeing her husband kicked, her face wore a most pleased smile. The judge noted, though, that she was stroking Lad's head and that she was unobtrusively turning that head so that the dog faced Schwartz.

"Now, then!" adjured the master. "Whenever you're ready, Schwartz! A German doesn't get a chance, like this, every day, to kick an American. And I'll promise not to go for your throat, as Laddie tried to. Kick away!"

Awkwardly, shamblingly, Schwartz stepped forward. Urged on by veneration for the law—and perhaps not sorry to assail the man whose dog had tried to throttle him—he drew back his broganed left foot and kicked out in the general direction of the calf of the master's thick riding boot.

The kick did not land. Not that the master dodged or blocked it. He stood moveless, and grinning expectantly.

But the courtroom shook with a wild-beast yell—a yell of insane fury. And Schwartz drew back his half-extended left foot in sudden terror; as a great furry shape came whizzing through the air at him.

The sight of the half-delivered kick, at his worshipped master, had had precisely the effect on Lad that the mistress had foreseen when she planned the maneuver. Almost any good dog will attack a man who seeks to strike its owner. And Lad seemed to comprehend that a kick is a more contemptuous affront than is a blow.

Schwartz's kick at the master had thrown the adoring dog into a maniac rage against this defiler of his idol. The memory of Schwartz's blow at himself was as nothing to it. It aroused in the collie's heart a deathless blood-feud against the man. As the mistress had known it would.

The mistress's sharp command, and the master's hastily outflung arm barely sufficed to deflect Lad's charge. He writhed in their dual grasp, snarling furiously, his eyes red; his every giant muscle strained to get at the cowering Schwartz.

"We've had enough of this!" imperatively ordained Maclay, above the babel of Titus Romaine's protests. "In spite of the informality of hearing, this is a court of law: not a dog kennel. I—"

"I crave Your Honor's pardon," apologized the master. "I was merely trying to show that Lad is not the sort of dog to let a stranger strike and kick him as this man claims to have done with impunity. I think I have shown, from Lad's own regrettable actions, that it was some other dog—if *any*—which cheered Romaine's barnyard, this morning, and yesterday morning."

"It was *your* dog!" cried Schwartz, getting his breath, in a swirl of anger. "Next time I'll be on watch with a shotgun and not a stick. I'll—"

"There ain't going to be no 'next time,'" asserted the equally angry Romaine. "Judge, I call on you to order that sheep killer shot; an' to order his master to indemnify me for th' loss of my eight killed sheep!"

"Your Honor!" suavely protested the master. "May I ask you to listen to a counterproposition? A proposition which I think will be agreeable to Mr. Romaine, as well as to myself?"

"The only prop'sition *I'll* agree to, is the shootin' of that cur and the indemnifyin' of me for my sheep!" persisted Romaine.

Maclay waved his hand for order; then, turning to the master, said, "State your proposition."

"I propose," began the master, "that Lad be paroled, in my custody, for the space of twenty-four hours. I will deposit with the court, here and now, my bond for the sum of one thousand dollars; to be paid, on demand, to Titus Romaine; if one or more of his sheep are killed by any dog, during that space of time."

The crass oddity of the proposal set Titus's leathery mouth ajar. Even the judge gasped aloud at its bizarre terms. Schwartz looked blank, until, little by little, the purport of the words sank into his slow mind. Then he permitted himself the rare luxury of a chuckle.

"Do I und'stand you to say," demanded Titus Romaine, of the master, "that if I'll agree to hold up this case for twenty-four hours you'll give me one thousan' dollars, cash, for any sheep of mine that gets killed by dogs in that time?"

"That is my proposition," returned the master. "To cinch it, I'll let you make out the written arrangement, yourself. And I'll give the court a bond for the money, at once, with instructions that the sum is to be paid to you, if you lose one sheep, through dogs, in the next day. I furthermore agree to shoot Lad, myself, if you lose one or more sheep in that time, and in that way, I'll forfeit another thousand if I fail to keep that part of my contract. How about it?"

"I agree!" exclaimed Titus.

Schwartz's smile, by this time, threatened to split his broad face across. Maclay saw the mistress's cheek whiten a little; but her aspect betrayed no worry over the possible loss of a thousand dollars and the far more painful loss of the dog she loved.

When Romaine and Schwartz had gone, the master tarried a moment in the courtroom.

"I can't make out what you're driving at," Maclay told him. "But you seem to me to have done a mighty foolish thing. To get a thousand dollars Romaine is capable of scouring the whole country for a sheep-killing dog. So is Schwartz—if only to get Lad shot. Did you see the way Schwartz looked at Lad as he went out? He hates him."

"Yes," said the master. "And I saw the way Lad looked at *him*. Lad will never forget that kick at me. He'll attack Schwartz for it, if they come together a year from now. That's why we arranged it. Say, Mac; I want you to do me a big favor. A favor that comes within the square and angle of your work. I want you to go fishing with me, tonight. Better come over to dinner and be prepared to spend the night. The fishing won't start till about twelve o'clock."

"Twelve o'clock!" echoed Maclay. "Why, man, nothing but cat-fish will bite at that hour. And I—"

"You're mistaken," denied the master. "Much bigger fish will bite. *Much* bigger. Take my word for that. My wife and I have it all figured out. I'm not asking you in your official capacity; but as a friend. I'll need you, Mac. It will be a big favor to me. And if I'm not wrong, there'll be sport in it for you, too. I'm risking a thousand dollars and my dog, on this fishing trip. Won't you risk a night's sleep? I ask it as a worthy and distressed—"

"Certainly," assented the wholly perplexed judge, impressed, "but I don't get your idea at all. I—"

"I'll explain it before we start," promised the master. "All I want, now, is for you to commit yourself to the scheme. If it fails, you won't lose anything, except your sleep. Thanks for saying you'll come."

At a little after ten o'clock that night the last light in Titus Romaine's farmhouse went out. A few moments later the master got up from a rock on Mount Pisgah's summit, on which he and Maclay had been sitting for the past hour. Lad, at their feet, rose expectantly with them.

"Come on, old man," said the master. "We'll drop down there, now. It probably means a long wait for us. But it's better to be too soon than too late; when I've got so much staked. If we're seen, you can cut and run. Lad and I will cover your retreat and see you aren't recognized. Steady, there, Lad. Keep at heel."

Stealthily the trio made their way down the hill to the farmstead at its farther base. Silently they crept along the outer fringe of the home lot, until they came opposite the black-gabled bulk of the barn. Presently, their slowly cautious progress brought them to the edge of the barnyard, and to the rail fence which surrounds it. There they halted.

From within the yard, as the huddle of drowsy sheep caught the scent of the dog, came a slight stirring. But, after a moment, the yard was quiet again.

"Get that?" whispered the master, his mouth close to Maclay's ear. "Those sheep are supposed to have been raided by a killer dog, for the past two nights. Yet the smell of a dog doesn't even make them bleat. If they had been attacked by *any* dog, last night, the scent of Lad would throw them into a panic."

"I get something else, too," replied Maclay, in the same all-but-soundless whisper. "And I'm ashamed I didn't think of it before. Romaine said the dog wriggled into the yard through the bars, and out again the same way. Well, if those bars were wide enough apart for an eighty-pound collie, like Lad, to get through, what would there be to prevent all these sheep from escaping, the same way, any time they wanted to? I'll have a look at those bars before I pass judgment on the case. I begin to be glad you and your wife coerced me into this adventure."

"Of course, the sheep could have gotten through the same bars that the dog did," answered the master. "For, didn't Romaine say the dog not only got through, but dragged three dead sheep through, after him, each night, and hid them somewhere, where they couldn't be found? No man would keep sheep in a pen as open as all that. The entire story is full of airholes."

Lad, at a touch from his master, had lain softly down at the men's feet, beside the fence. And so, for another full hour, the three waited there.

The night was heavily overcast; and, except for the low drone of distant treetoads and crickets, it was deathly silent. Heat lightning, once in a while, played dimly along the western horizon.

"Lucky for us that Romaine doesn't keep a dog!" whispered Maclay. "He'd have raised the alarm before we got within a hundred yards of here."

"He told my foreman he gave his mongrel dog away, when he stocked himself with sheep. And he's been reading a lot of rot about dogs being nonutilitarian, too. His dog would have been anything but nonutilitarian, tonight."

A touch on the sleeve from Maclay silenced the rambling whisper. Through the stillness, a house door shut very softly, not far away. An instant later, Lad growled throatily, and got to his feet, tense and fiercely eager.

"He's caught Schwartz's scent!" whispered the master, exultantly. "Now, maybe you understand why I made the man try to kick me? Down, Lad! *Quiet!*"

At the stark command in the master's whisper, Lad dropped to earth again; though he still rumbled deeply in his throat, until a touch from the master's fingers and a repeated *"Quiet"* silenced him.

The hush of the night was disturbed, once more—very faintly. This time, by the muffled padding of a man's bare feet, drawing closer to the barnyard. Lad as he heard it made as if to rise. The master tapped him lightly on the head, and the dog sank to the ground again, quivering with hard-held rage.

The clouds had piled thicker. Only by a dim pulsing of faraway heat lightning could the watchers discern the shadowy outline of a man, moving silently between them and the far side of the yard. By the tiny glow of lightning they saw his silhouette.

By Lad's almost uncontrollable trembling they knew who he must be.

There was another drowsy stirring of the sheep; checked by the reassuring mumble of a voice the animals seemed to know. And, except for the stealthy motion of groping feet, the barnyard seemed as empty of human life as before.

Perhaps a minute later another sulphur-gleam of lightning revealed the intruder to the two men who crouched behind the outer angle of the fence. He had come out of the yard, and was shuffling away. But he was fully a third wider of shoulder now, and he seemed to have two heads, as his silhouette dimly appeared and then vanished.

"See that?" whispered the master. "He has a sheep slung over his back. Probably with a cloth wrapped around its head to keep it quiet. We will give him twenty seconds' start and then—"

"*Good!*" babbled Maclay, in true fever of excitement. "It's worked out, to a charm! But how in the blazes can we track him through this dark? It's as black as the inside of a cow. And if we show the flashlights—"

"Trust Lad to track him," rejoined the master, who had been slipping a leash around the dog's low-growling throat. "That's what the old fellow's here for. He has a kick to punish. He would follow Schwartz through the Sahara desert, if he had to. Come on."

Lad, at a word from the master, sprang to the end of the leash, his mighty head and shoulders straining forward. The master's reiterated "Quiet!" alone kept him from giving tongue. And thus the trio started the pursuit.

Lad went in a geometrically straight line, swerving not an inch; with much difficulty held back to the slow walk on which the master insisted. There was more than one reason for this insistence. Not only did the two men want to keep far enough behind Schwartz to prevent him from hearing their careful steps; but Lad's course was so uncompromisingly straight that it led them over a hundred obstacles and gullies which required all sorts of skill to negotiate.

For at least two miles, the snaillike progress continued; most of the way through woods. At last, with a gasp, the master found himself wallowing knee-deep in a bog. Maclay, a step behind him, also plunged splashingly into the soggy mire.

"What's the matter with the dog?" grumpily demanded the judge. "He's led us into the Pancake Hollow swamp. Schwartz never in the world carried a ninety-pound sheep through here."

"Maybe not," puffed the master. "But he has carried it over one of the half-dozen paths that lead through this marsh. Lad is in too big a hurry to bother about paths. He—"

Fifty feet above them, on a little midswamp knoll, a lantern shone. Apparently, it had just been lighted. For it waxed brighter in a second or so. The men saw it and strode forward at top speed.

The third step caused Maclay to stumble over a hummock and land, noisily, on all fours, in a mud pool. As he fell, he swore—with a loud distinctness that rang through the swampy stillnesses, like a pistol shot.

Instantly, the lantern went out. And there was a crashing in among the bushes of the knoll.

"After him!" yelled Maclay, floundering to his feet. "He'll escape! And we have no real proof who he is or—"

The master, still ankle-high in sticky mud, saw the futility of trying to catch a man who, unimpeded, was running away, along a dry-ground path. There was but one thing left to do. And the master did it.

Loosening the leash from the dog's collar he shouted, "Get him, Laddie! *Get* him!"

There was a sound as of a cavalry regiment galloping through shallow water. That and a queerly ecstatic growl. And the collie was gone.

As fast as possible the two men made for the base of the knoll. They had drawn forth their electric torches; and these now made the progress much swifter and easier.

Nevertheless, before the master had set foot on the first bit of firm ground, all pandemonium burst forth amid the darkness, above and in front of him.

The turmoil's multiple sounds were indescribable, blending into one wild cacophony the yells and stamping of a fear-demented man, the bleats of sheep, the tearing of underbrush—through and above and under all—a hideous subnote as of a rabid beast worrying its prey.

It was this undercurrent of sound which put wings on the tired feet of Maclay and the master, as they dashed up the knoll and into the path leading east from it. It spoke of unpleasant—not to say gruesome—happenings. So did the swift change of the victim's yells from wrath to mortal terror.

"Back Lad!" called the master, pantingly, as he ran. "Back! Let him *alone!*"

And as he cried the command he rounded a turn in the wooded path.

Prone on the ground, writhing like a cut snake and frantically seeking to guard his throat with his slashed forearm, sprawled Schwartz. Crouching above him—right unwillingly obeying the master's belated call—was Lad.

The dog's great coat was abristle. His bared teeth glinted white and blood-flecked in the electric flare. His soft eyes were blazing.

"Back!" repeated the master. "Back here!"

Absolute obedience was the first and foremost of the Place's few simple dog rules. Lad had learned it from earliest puppyhood. The collie, still shaking all over with the effort of repressing his fury, turned slowly and came over to his master. There he stood stonily awaiting further orders.

Maclay was on his knees beside the hysterically moaning German roughly telling him that the dog would do him no more damage, and at the same time making a quick inspection of the injuries wrought by the slashing white fangs in the shielding arm and its shoulder.

"Get up!" he now ordered. "You're not too badly hurt to stand. Another minute and he'd have gotten through to your throat, but your clothes saved you from anything worse than a few ugly flesh cuts. Get up! Stop that yowling and get up!"

Schwartz gradually lessened his dolorous plaints under the stern authority of Maclay's exhortations. Presently he sat up nursing his lacerated forearm and staring about him. At sight of Lad he shuddered. And recognizing Maclay he broke into violent accented speech.

"Take witness, Judge!" he exclaimed. "I watched the barnyard tonight and I saw that schweinhund steal another sheep. I followed him and when he got here he dropped the sheep and went for me. He—"

"Very bad, Schwartz!" disgustedly reproved Maclay. "Very bad, indeed. You should have waited a minute longer and thought up a better one. But since this is the yarn you choose to tell, we'll look about and try to verify it. The sheep, for instance—the one you say Lad carried all the way here and then dropped to attack you. I seem to have heard a sheep bleating a few moments ago. Several sheep in fact. We'll see if we can't find the one Lad stole."

Schwartz jumped nervously to his feet.

"Stay where you are!" Maclay bade him. "We won't bother a tired and injured man to help in our search."

Turning to the master, he added, "I suppose one of us will have to stand guard over him while the other one hunts up the sheep. Shall I—"

"Neither of us need do that," said the master. "Lad!"

The collie started eagerly forward, and Schwartz started still more eagerly backward.

"Watch him!" commanded the Master. *"Watch* him!"

It was an order Lad had learned to follow in the many times when the mistress and the master left him to guard the car or to do sentry duty over some other article of value. He understood. He would have preferred to deal with this enemy according to his own lights. But the master had spoken. So, standing at view, the collie looked longily at Schwartz's throat.

"Keep perfectly still!" the master warned the prisoner, "and perhaps he won't go for you. Move, and he most surely will. *Watch* him, Laddie!"

Maclay and the master left the captive and his guard, and set forth on a flashlight-illumined tour of the knoll. It was a desolate spot, far back in the swamp and more than a mile from any road; a place visited not three times a year, except in the shooting season.

In less than a half-minute the plaintive ba-a-a of a sheep guided the searchers to the left of the knoll where stood a thick birch-and-alder copse. Around this they circled until they reached a narrow opening where the branch ends, several feet above ground, were flecked with hanks of wool.

Squirming through the aperture in single file, the investigators found what they sought.

In the tight-woven copse's center was a small clearing. In this, was a rudely wattled pen some nine feet square; and in the pen were bunched six sheep.

An occasional scared bleat from deeper in the copse told the whereabouts of the sheep Schwartz had taken from the barnyard that night and which he had dropped at Lad's onslaught before he could put it in the pen. On the ground, just outside the enclosure, lay the smashed lantern.

"Sheep on the hoof are worth $12.50 per, at the Paterson Market," mused the master aloud, as Maclay blinked owlishly at the treasure trove. "There are $75 worth of sheep in that pen, and there would have been three more of them before morning if we hadn't butted in on Herr Schwartz's overtime labors. To get three sheep at night, it was well worth his while to switch suspicion to Lad by killing a fourth sheep every time, and mangling its throat with a stripping knife. Only, he mangled it too efficiently. There was too much neatness about the mangling. It wasn't ragged enough. That's what first gave me my idea. That, and the way the missing sheep always vanished into more or less thin air. You see, he probably—"

"But," sputtered Maclay, "why four each night? Why—"

"You saw how long it took him to get one of them here," replied the master. "He didn't dare to start in till the Romaines were asleep, and he had to be back in time to catch Lad at the slaughter before Titus got out of bed. He wouldn't dare hide them any nearer home. Titus has spent most of his time both days in hunting for them. Schwartz was probably waiting to get the pen nice and full. Then he'd take a day off to visit his relatives. And he'd round up this tidy bunch and drive them over to the Ridgewood road, through the woods, and so on to the Paterson Market. It was a pretty little scheme all around."

"But," urged Maclay, as they turned back to where Lad still kept his avid vigil, "I still hold you were taking big chances in gambling one thousand dollars and your dog's life that Schwartz would do the same thing again within twenty-four hours. He might have waited a day or two, till—"

"No," contradicted the master, "that's just what he mightn't do. You see, I wasn't perfectly sure whether it was Schwartz or Romaine—or both—who were mixed up in this. So I set the trap at both ends. If it was Romaine, it was worth one thousand dollars to him to have more sheep killed within twenty-four hours. If it was Schwartz—well, that's why I made him try to hit Lad and why I made him try to kick me. The dog went for him both times, and that was enough to make Schwartz want him killed for his own safety as well as for revenge. So he was certain to arrange another killing within the twenty-four hours if only to force me to shoot Lad. He couldn't steal or kill sheep by daylight. I picked the only hours he could do it in. If he'd gotten Lad killed, he'd probably have invented another sheep-killer dog to help him swipe the rest of the flock, or until Romaine decided to do the watching. We—"

"It was clever of you," cordially admitted Maclay. "Mighty clever, old man! I—"

"It was my wife who worked it out, you know," the master reminded him. "I admit my own cleverness, of course, only it's all in my wife's name. Come on, Lad! You can guard Herr Schwartz just as well by walking behind him. We're going to wind up the evening's fishing trip by tendering a surprise party to dear genial old Mr. Titus Romaine. I hope the flashlights will hold out long enough for me to get a clear look at his face when he sees us."

CHAPTER 11

WOLF

There were but three collies on the Place in those days. There was a long shelf in the master's study whereupon shimmered and glinted a rank of silver cups of varying sizes and shapes. Two of the Place's dogs had won them all.

Above the shelf hung two huge picture frames. In the center of each was the small photograph of a collie. Beneath each likeness was a certified pedigree, abristle with the red-letter names of champions. Surrounding the pictures and pedigrees, the whole remaining space in both frames was filled with blue ribbons—the very meanest bit of silk in either was a semioccasional Reserve Winners—while, strung along the tops of the frames from side to side, ran a line of medals.

Cups, medals, and ribbons alike had been won by the Place's two great collies, Lad and Bruce. (Those were their "kennel names." Their official titles on the AKC registry list were high-sounding and needlessly long.)

Lad was growing old. His reign on the Place was drawing toward a benignant close. His muzzle was almost snow-white and his once graceful lines were beginning to show the oncoming heaviness of age. No longer could he hope to hold his own, in form and carriage, with younger collies at the local dog shows where once he had carried all before him.

Bruce—"Sunnybank Goldsmith"—was six years Lad's junior. He was tawny of coat, kingly of bearing; a dog without a fault of body or of disposition; stately as the boar hounds that the painters of old used to love to depict in their portraits of monarchs.

The Place's third collie was Lad's son, Wolf. But neither cup nor ribbon did Wolf have to show as an excuse for his presence on earth, nor would he have won recognition in the smallest and least exclusive collie show.

For Wolf was a collie only by courtesy. His breeding was as pure as was any champion's, but he was one of those luckless types to be found in nearly every litter—a throwback to some forgotten ancestor whose points were all defective. Not even the glorious pedigree of Lad, his father, could make Wolf look like anything more than he was—a dog without a single physical trait that followed the best collie standards.

In spite of all this he was beautiful. His gold-and-white coat was almost as bright and luxuriant as any prize winner's. He had, in a general way, the collie head and brush. But an expert, at the most casual glance, would have noted a shortness of nose and breadth of jaw and a shape of ear and shoulder that told dead against him.

The collie is supposed to be descended direct from the wolf, and Wolf looked far more like his original ancestors than like a thoroughbred collie. From puppyhood he had been the living image, except in color, of a timber wolf, and it was from this queer throwback trait that he had won his name.

Lad was the mistress's dog. Bruce was the master's. Wolf belonged to the Boy, having been born on the latter's birthday.

For the first six months of his life Wolf lived at the Place on sufferance. Nobody except the Boy took any special interest in him. He was kept only because his better-formed brothers had died in early puppyhood and because the Boy, from the outset, had loved him.

At six months it was discovered that he was a natural watchdog.

Also that he never barked except to give an alarm. A collie is, perhaps, the most excitable of all large dogs. The veriest trifle will set him off into a thunderous paroxysm of barking. But Wolf, the Boy noted, never barked without strong cause.

He had the rare genius for guarding that so few of his breed possess. For not one dog in ten merits the title of watchdog. The duties that should go with that office are far more than the mere clamorous announcement of a stranger's approach, or even the attacking of such a stranger.

The born watchdog patrols his beat once in so often during the night. At all times he must sleep with one ear and one eye alert. By day or by night he must discriminate between the visitor whose presence is permitted and the trespasser whose presence is not. He must know what class of undesirable to scare off with a growl and what class needs stronger measures. He must also know to the inch the boundaries of his own master's land.

Few of these things can be taught; all of them must be instinctive. Wolf had been born with them. Most dogs are not.

His value as a watchdog gave Wolf a settled position of his own on the Place. Lad was growing old and a little deaf. He slept, at night, under the piano in the music room. Bruce was worth too much money to be left at large in the night time for any clever dog-thief to steal. So he slept in the study. Rex, a huge mongrel, was tied up at night, at the lodge, a furlong away. Thus Wolf alone was left on guard at the house. The piazza was his sentry box. From this shelter he was wont to set forth three or four times a night, in all sorts of weather, to make his rounds.

The Place covered twenty-five acres. It ran from the highroad, a furlong above the house, down to the lake that bordered it on two sides. On the third side was the forest. Boating parties, late at night, had a pleasant way of trying to raid the lakeside apple orchard. Tramps now and then strayed down the drive from the main road. Prowlers, crossing the woods, sometimes sought to use the Place's sloping lawn as a short cut to the turnpike below the falls.

For each and all of these intruders Wolf had an ever-ready

welcome. A whirl of madly pattering feet through the dark, a snarling growl far down in the throat, a furry shape catapulting into the air—and the trespasser had his choice between a scurrying retreat or a double set of white fangs in the easiest-reached part of his anatomy.

The Boy was inordinately proud of his pet's watchdog prowess. He was prouder yet of Wolf's almost incredible sharpness of intelligence, his quickness to learn, his knowledge of word meaning, his zest for romping, his perfect obedience, the tricks he had taught himself without human tutelage—in short, all the things that were a sign of the brain he had inherited from Lad.

But none of these talents overcame the sad fact that Wolf was not a show dog and that he looked positively underbred and shabby alongside of his sire or of Bruce. Which rankled at the Boy's heart; even while loyalty to his adored pet would not let him confess to himself or to anyone else that Wolf was not the most flawlessly perfect dog on earth.

Undersized (for a collie), slim, graceful, fierce, affectionate, Wolf was the Boy's darling, and he was Lad's successor as official guardian of the Place. But all his youthful life, thus far, had brought him nothing more than this—while Lad and Bruce had been winning prize after prize at one local dog show after another within a radius of thirty miles.

The Boy was duly enthusiastic over the winning of each trophy; but always, for days thereafter, he was more than usually attentive to Wolf to make up for his pet's dearth of prizes.

Once or twice the Boy had hinted, in a veiled, tentative way, that young Wolf might perhaps win something, too, if he were allowed to go to a show. The master, never suspecting what lay behind the cautious words, would always laugh in good-natured derision, or else he would point in silence to Wolf's head and then to Lad's.

The Boy knew enough about collies to carry the subject no further. For even his eyes of devotion could not fail to mark the difference in aspect between his dog and the two prizewinners.

One July morning both Lad and Bruce went through an hour of anguish. Both of them, one after the other, were plunged into a bathtub full of warm water and naphtha soapsuds and Lux; and were scrubbed right unmercifully, after which they were rubbed and curried and brushed for another hour until their coats shone resplendent. All day, at intervals, the brushing and combing were kept up.

Lad was indignant at such treatment, and he took no pains to hide his indignation. He knew perfectly well, from the undue attention, that a dog show was at hand. But not for a year or more had he himself been made ready for one. His lake baths and his daily casual brushing at the mistress's hands had been, in that time, his only form of grooming. He had thought himself graduated forever from the nuisance of going to shows.

"What's the idea of dolling up old Laddie like that?" asked the Boy, as he came in for luncheon and found the mistress busy with comb and dandy-brush over the unhappy dog.

"For the Fourth of July Red Cross Dog Show at Ridgewood tomorrow," answered his mother, looking up, a little flushed from her exertions.

"But I thought you and Dad said last year he was too old to show any more," ventured the Boy.

"This time is different," said the mistress. "It's a specialty show, you see, and there is a cup offered for 'the best *veteran* dog of any recognized breed.' Isn't that fine? We didn't hear of the Veteran Cup till Dr. Hooper telephoned to us about it this morning. So we're getting Lad ready. There *can't* be any other veteran as splendid as he is."

"No," agreed the Boy, dully, "I suppose not."

He went into the dining room, surreptitiously helped himself to a handful of lump sugar and passed on out to the veranda. Wolf was sprawled half-asleep on the driveway lawn in the sun.

The dog's wolflike brush began to thump against the shaven grass. Then, as the Boy stood on the veranda edge and snapped his fingers, Wolf got up from his soft resting place and started toward him, treading mincingly and with a sort of swagger, his slanting eyes half shut, his mouth agrin.

"You know I've got sugar in my pocket as well as if you saw it," said the Boy. "Stop where you are."

Though the Boy accompanied his order with no gesture nor change of tone, the dog stopped dead short ten feet away.

"Sugar is bad for dogs," went on the Boy. "It does things to their teeth and their digestions. Didn't anybody ever tell you that, Wolfie?"

The young dog's grin grew wider. His slanting eyes closed to mere glittering slits. He fidgeted a little, his tail wagging fast.

"But I guess a dog's got to have *some* kind of consolation purse when he can't go to a show," resumed the Boy. "Catch!"

As he spoke he suddenly drew a lump of sugar from his pocket and, with the same motion, tossed it in the direction of Wolf. Swift as was the Boy's action, Wolf's eye was still quicker. Springing high in air, the dog caught the flung cube of sugar as it flew above him and to one side. A second and a third lump were caught as deftly as the first.

Then the Boy took from his pocket the fourth and last lump. Descending the steps, he put his left hand across Wolf's eyes. With his right he flipped the lump of sugar into a clump of shrubbery.

"Find it!" he commanded, lifting the blindfold from the eyes of his pet.

Wolf darted hither and thither, stopped once or twice to sniff, then began to circle the nearer stretch of lawn, nose to ground. In less than two minutes he emerged from the shrubbery placidly crunching the sugar lump between his mighty jaws.

"And yet they say you aren't fit to be shown!" exclaimed the Boy, fondling the dog's ears. "Gee, but I'd give two years' growth if you could have a cup! You deserve one, all right; if only those judges had sense enough to study a collie's brain as well as the outside of his head!"

Wolf ran his nose into the cupped palm and whined. From the tone underlying the words, he knew the Boy was unhappy, and he wanted to be of help.

The Boy went into the house again to find his parents sitting down to lunch. Gathering his courage in both hands, he asked, "Is there going to be a Novice Class for collies at Ridgewood, Dad?"

"Why, yes," said the master, "I suppose so. There always is."

"Do—do they give cups for the Novice Class?" inquired the Boy, with studied carelessness.

"Of course they don't," said the master, adding reminiscently, "though the first time we showed Lad we put him in the Novice Class and he won the blue ribbon there, so we had to go into the Winners' Class afterward. He got the Winner's Cup, you remember. So, indirectly, the Novice Class won him a cup."

"I see," said the Boy, not at all interested in this bit of ancient history. Then speaking very fast, he went on, "Well, a ribbon's better than nothing! Dad, will you do me a favor? Will you let me enter Wolfie for the Novice Class tomorrow? I'll pay the fee out of my allowance. Will you, Dad?"

The master looked at his son in blank amazement. Then he threw back his head and laughed loudly. The Boy flushed crimson and bit his lips.

"Why, dear!" hurriedly interposed the mistress, noting her son's discomfiture. "You wouldn't want Wolf to go there and be beaten by a lot of dogs that haven't half his brains or prettiness! It wouldn't be fair or kind to Wolf. He's so clever, he'd know in a moment what was happening. He'd know he was beaten. Nearly all dogs do. No, it wouldn't be fair to him."

"There's a mutt class among the specials, Dr. Hooper says," put in the master, jocosely. "You might—"

"Wolf's *not* a mutt!" flashed the Boy, hotly. "He's no more of a mutt than Bruce or Lad, or Grey Mist, or Southport Sample, or any of the best ones. He has as good blood as all of them. Lad's his father, and Squire of Tytton was his grandfather, and Wishaw Clinker was his—"

"I'm sorry, son," interposed the master, catching his wife's eye and dropping his tone of banter. "I apologize to you and Wolf. He's not a mutt. There's no better blood in colliedom than his, on both sides. But Mother is right. You'd only be putting him up to be beaten, and you wouldn't like that. He hasn't a single point that isn't hopelessly bad from a judge's view. We've never taken a loser to a show from the Place. You don't want us to begin now, do you?"

"He has more brains that any dog alive, except Lad!" declared the Boy, sullenly. "That ought to count."

"It ought to," agreed the mistress, soothingly, "and I wish it did. If it did, I know he'd win."

"It makes me sick to see a bushel of cups go to dogs that don't know enough to eat their own dinners," snorted the Boy. "I'm not talking about Lad and Bruce, but the thoroughbreds that are brought up in kennels and that have all their sense sacrificed for points. Why, Wolf's the cleverest —best—and he'll never even have one cup to show for it. He—"

He choked, and began to eat at top speed. The master and the mistress looked at each other and said nothing. They understood their son's chagrin, as only a dog lover could understand it. The mistress reached out and patted the Boy gently on the shoulder.

Next morning, directly after early breakfast, Lad and Bruce were put into the backseat of the car. The mistress and the master and the Boy climbed in, and the twelve-mile journey to Ridgewood began.

Wolf, left to guard the Place, watched the departing showgoers until the car turned out of the gate, a furlong above. Then, with a sigh, he curled up on the porch mat, his nose between his snowy little paws, and prepared for a day of loneliness.

The Red Cross Dog Show, that Fourth of July, was a triumph for the Place.

Bruce won ribbon after ribbon in the collie division, easily taking Winners at the last, and thus adding another gorgeous silver cup to his collection. Then, the supreme event of the day—Best Dog in the Show—was called. And the winners of each breed were led into the ring. The judges scanned and handled the group of sixteen for barely five minutes before awarding to Bruce the dark-blue rosette and the Best Dog Cup.

The crowd around the ring's railing applauded loudly. But they applauded still more loudly a little later, when, after a brief survey of nine aged thoroughbreds, the judge pointed to Lad, who was standing like a mahogany statue at one end of the ring.

These nine dogs of various breeds had all been famed prizewinners in their time. And above all the rest, Lad was adjudged worthy of the Veteran Cup! There was a haze of happy tears in the mistress's eyes as she led him from the ring. It seemed a beautiful climax for his grand old life. She wiped her eyes, unashamed, whispering praise the while to her stately dog.

"Why don't you trundle your car into the ring?" one disgruntled exhibitor demanded of the mistress. "Maybe you'd win a cup with *that*, too. You seem to have gotten one for everything else you brought along."

It was a celebration evening for the two prize dogs, when they got home, but everybody was tired from the day's events, and by ten o'clock the house was dark. Wolf, on his veranda mat, alone of all the Place's denizens, was awake.

Vaguely Wolf knew the other dogs had done some praiseworthy thing. He would have known it, if for no other reason, from the remorseful hug the Boy had given him before going to bed.

Well, some must win honors and petting and the right to sleep indoors, while others must plod along at the only work they were fit for, and must sleep out, in thunderstorm or clear, in heat or freezing cold. That was life. Being only a dog, Wolf was too wise to complain of life. He took things as he found them, making the very best of his share.

He snoozed, now, in the warm darkness. Two hours later he got up, stretched himself lazily fore and aft, collie-fashion, and trotted forth for the night's first patrol of the grounds.

A few minutes afterward he was skirting the lake edge at the foot of the lawn, a hundred yards below the house. The night was pitch dark, except for pulses of heat lightning, now and then, far to westward. Half a mile out on the lake two men in an anchored scow were catfishing.

A small skiff was slipping along very slowly, not fifty feet off shore.

Wolf did not give the skiff a second glance. Boats were no novelty to him, nor did they interest him in the least—except when they showed signs of running ashore somewhere along his beat.

This skiff was not headed for land, but was paralleling the shore. It crept along at a snail-pace and in dead silence. A man, its only occupant, sat at the oars, scarcely moving them as he kept his boat in motion.

A dog is ridiculously nearsighted—more so than almost any other beast. Keen hearing and keener scent are its chief guides. At three hundred yards' distance it cannot, by eye, recognize its master, nor tell him from a stranger. But at close quarters, even in the darkest night, a dog's vision is far more piercing and accurate than man's under like conditions.

Wolf thus saw the skiff and its occupant, while he himself was still invisible. The boat was no concern of his; so he trotted on to the far end of the Place, where the forest joined the orchard.

On his return tour of the lake edge he saw the skiff again. It had shifted its direction and was now barely ten feet off shore—so near to the bank that one of the oars occasionally grated on the pebbly bottom. The oarsman was looking intently toward the house.

Wolf paused, uncertain. The average watchdog, his attention thus attracted, would have barked. But Wolf knew the lake was public property. Boats were often rowed as close to shore as this without intent to trespass. It was not the skiff that caught Wolf's attention as he paused there on the brink, it was the man's furtive scrutiny of the house.

A pale flare of heat lightning turned the world, momentarily, from jet black to a dim sulphur color. The boatman saw Wolf standing, alert and suspicious, among the lakeside grasses, not ten feet away. He started slightly, and a soft, throaty growl from the dog answered him.

The man seemed to take the growl as a challenge, and to accept it. He reached into his pocket and drew something out. When the next faint glow of lightning illumined the shore, the man lifted the thing he had taken from his pocket and hurled it at Wolf.

With all the furtive swiftness bred in his wolf ancestry, the dog shrank to one side, readily dodging the missile, which struck the lawn just behind him. Teeth bared in a ferocious snarl, Wolf dashed forward through the shallow water toward the skiff.

But the man apparently had had enough of the business. He rowed off with long strokes into deep water, and, once there, he kept on rowing until distance and darkness hid him.

Wolf stood, chest deep in water, listening to the far-off oar strokes until they died away. He was not fool enough to swim in pursuit; well knowing that a swimming dog is worse than helpless against a boatman.

Moreover, the intruder had been scared away. That was all which concerned Wolf. He turned back to shore. His vigil was ended for another few hours. It was time to take up his nap where he had left off.

Before he had taken two steps, his sensitive nostrils were full of the scent of raw meat. There, on the lawn ahead of him, lay a chunk of beef as big as a fist. This, then, was what the boatman had thrown at him!

Wolf pricked up his ears in appreciation, and his brush began to vibrate. Trespassers had once or twice tried to stone him, but this was the first time any of them had pelted him with delicious raw beef. Evidently, Lad and Bruce were not the only collies on the Place to receive prizes that day.

Wolf stooped over the meat, sniffed at it, then caught it up between his jaws.

Now, a dog is the easiest animal alive to poison, just as a cat is the hardest, for a dog will usually bolt a mouthful of poisoned meat without pausing to chew or otherwise investigate it. A cat, on the contrary, smells and tastes everything first and chews it scientifically before swallowing it. The slightest unfamiliar scent or flavor warns her to sheer off from the feast.

So the average dog would have gulped this toothsome windfall in a single swallow; but Wolf was not the average dog. No collie is, and Wolf was still more like his eccentric forefathers of the wilderness than are most collies.

He lacked the reasoning powers to make him suspicious of this rich gift from a stranger, but a queer personal trait now served him just as well.

Wolf was an epicure; he always took three times as long to empty his dinner dish as did the other dogs, for instead of gobbling his meal, as they did, he was wont to nibble affectedly at each morsel, gnawing it slowly into nothingness; and all the time showing a fussily dainty relish of it that used to delight the Boy and send guests into peals of laughter.

This odd little trait that had caused so much ridicule now saved Wolf's life.

He carried the lump of beef gingerly up to the veranda, laid it down on his mat, and prepared to revel in his chance banquet after his own deliberate fashion.

Holding the beef between his forepaws, he proceeded to devour it in mincing little squirrel bites. About a quarter of the meat had disappeared when Wolf became aware that his tongue smarted and that his throat was sore; also that the interior of the meatball had a ranky pungent odor, very different from the heavenly fragrance of its outside and not at all appetizing.

He looked down at the chunk, rolled it over with his nose, surveyed it again, then got up and moved away from it in angry disgust.

Presently he forgot his disappointment in the knowledge that he was very, very ill. His tongue and throat no longer burned, but his body and brain seemed full of hot lead that weighed a ton. He felt stupid, and too weak to stir. A great drowsiness gripped him.

With a grunt of discomfort and utter fatigue, he slumped down on the veranda floor to sleep off his sick lassitude. After that, for a time, nothing mattered.

For perhaps an hour Wolf lay sprawling there, dead to his duty, and to everything else. Then faintly, through the fog of dullness that enwrapped his brain, came a sound—a sound he had long ago learned to listen for. The harshly scraping noise of a boat's prow drawn up on the pebbly shore at the foot of the lawn.

Instinct tore through the poison vapors and roused the sick dog. He lifted his head. It was strangely heavy and hard to lift.

The sound was repeated as the prow was pulled farther up on the bank. Then came the crunch of a human foot on the waterside grass.

Heredity and training and lifelong fidelity took control of the lethargic dog, dragging him to his feet and down the veranda steps through no volition of his own.

Every motion tired him. He was dizzy and nauseated. He craved sleep; but as he was just a thoroughbred dog and not a wise human, he did not stop to think up good reasons why he should shirk his duty because he did not feel like performing it.

To the brow of the hill he trotted—slowly, heavily, shakily. His sharp powers of hearing told him the trespasser had left his boat and had taken one or two stealthy steps up the slope of lawn toward the house.

And now a puff of west wind brought Wolf's sense of smell into action. A dog remembers odors as humans remember faces. And the breeze bore to him the scent of the same man who had flung ashore that bit of meat which had caused all his suffering.

He had caught the man's scent an hour earlier, as he had stood sniffing at the boat ten feet away from him. The same scent had been on the meat the man had handled.

And now, having played such a cruel trick on him, the joker was actually daring to intrude on the Place!

A gust of resentful rage pierced the dullness of Wolf's brain and sent a thrill of fierce energy through him. For the moment this carried him out of his sick self and brought back all his former zest as a watchdog.

Down the hill, like a furry whirlwind, flew Wolf, every tooth bared, his back abristle from neck to tail. Now he was well within sight of the intruder. He saw the man pausing to adjust something to one of his hands. Then, before this could be accomplished, Wolf saw him pause and stare through the darkness as the wild onrush of the dog's feet struck upon his hearing.

Another instant and Wolf was near enough to spring. Out of the blackness he launched himself, straight for the trespasser's face. The man saw the dim shape hurtling through the air toward him. He dropped what he was carrying and flung up both hands to guard his neck.

At that, he was none too soon, for just as the thief's palm reached his own throat, Wolf's teeth met in the fleshy part of the hand.

Silent, in agony, the man beat at the dog with his free hand; but an attacking collie is hard to locate in the darkness. A bulldog will secure a grip and will hang on; a collie is everywhere at once.

Wolf's snapping jaws had already deserted the robber's mangled hand and slashed the man's left shoulder to the bone. Then the dog made another furious lunge for the face.

Down crashed the man, losing his balance under the heavy impact, Wolf atop of him. To guard his throat, the man rolled over on his face, kicking madly at the dog, and reaching back for his own hip pocket. Half in the water and half on the bank, the two rolled and thrashed and struggled—the man panting and wheezing in mortal terror; the dog growling in a hideous, snarling fashion as might a wild animal.

The thief's torn left hand found a grip on Wolf's fur-armored throat. He shoved the fiercely writhing dog backward, jammed a pistol against Wolf's head, and pulled the trigger!

The dog relaxed his grip and tumbled in a huddled heap on the brink. The man staggered, gasping, to his feet; bleeding, disheveled, his clothes torn and mud-coated.

The echoes of the shot were still reverberating among the lakeside hills. Several of the house's dark windows leaped into sudden light—then more windows in another room—and in another.

The thief swore roundly. His night's work was ruined. He bent to his skiff and shoved it into the water; then he turned to grope for what he had dropped on the lawn when Wolf's unexpected attack had interfered with his plans.

As he did so, something seized him by the ankle. In panic terror the man screamed aloud and jumped into the water, then, peering back, he saw what had happened.

Wolf, sprawling and unable to stand, had reached forward from where he lay and had driven his teeth for the last time into his foe.

The thief raised his pistol again and fired at the prostrate dog, then he clambered into his boat and rowed off with frantic speed, just as a salvo of barks told that Lad and Bruce had been released from the house; they came charging down the lawn, the master at their heels.

But already the quick oarbeats were growing distant; and the gloom had blotted out any chance of seeing or following the boat.

Wolf lay on his side, half in and half out of the water. He could not rise, as was his custom, to meet the Boy, who came running up, close behind the master and valorously grasping a target rifle; but the dog wagged his tail in feeble greeting, then he looked out over the black lake, and snarled.

The bullet had grazed Wolf's scalp and then had passed along the foreleg; scarring and numbing it. No damage had been done that a week's good nursing would not set right.

The marks in the grass and the poisoned meat on the porch told their own tale; so did the neat kit of burglar tools and a rubber glove found near the foot of the lawn; and then the telephone was put to work.

At dawn, a man in torn and muddy clothes, called at the office of a doctor three miles away to be treated for a half-dozen dog bites received, he said, from a pack of stray curs he had met on the turnpike. By the time his wounds were dressed, the sheriff and two deputies had arrived to take him in charge. In his pockets were a revolver, with two cartridges fired, and the mate of the rubber glove he had left on the Place's lawn.

"You—you wouldn't let Wolfie go to any show and win a cup for himself," half-sobbed the Boy, as the master worked over the injured dog's wound, "but he's saved you from losing all the cups the other dogs ever won!"

Three days later the master came home from a trip to the city. He went directly to the Boy's room. There on a rug lounged the convalescent Wolf, the Boy sitting beside him, stroking the dog's bandaged head.

"Wolf," said the master, solemnly, "I've been talking about you to some people I know. And we all agree—"

"Agree *what?*" asked the Boy, looking up in mild curiosity.

The master cleared his throat and continued, "We agree that the trophy shelf in my study hasn't enough cups on it. So I've decided to add still another to the collection. Want to see it, son?"

From behind his back the master produced a gleaming silver cup —one of the largest and most ornate the Boy had ever seen—larger even than Bruce's Best Dog Cup.

The Boy took it from his father's outstretched hand.

"Who won this?" he asked. "And what for? Didn't we get all the cups that were coming to us at the shows. Is it—"

The Boy's voice trailed away into a gurgle of bewildered rapture. He had caught sight of the lettering on the big cup. And now, his arm around Wolf, he read the inscription aloud, stammering with delight as he blurted out the words:

HERO CUP.
WON BY WOLF, AGAINST ALL COMERS.

CHAPTER 12

IN THE DAY OF BATTLE

Now, this is the true tale of Lad's last great adventure.

For more years than he could remember, Lad had been king. He had ruled at the Place, from boundary-fence to boundary-fence, from highway to lake. He had had, as subjects, many a thorough-bred collie; and many a lesser animal and bird among the Little Folk of the Place. His rule of them all had been lofty and benefi-cent.

The other dogs at the Place recognized Lad's rulership—recog-nized it without demur. It would no more have occurred to any of them, for example, to pass in or out through a doorway ahead of Lad than it would occur to a courtier to shoulder his way into the throneroom ahead of his sovereign. Nor would one of them intrude on the "cave" under the living room piano which for more than a decade had been Lad's favorite resting place.

Great was Lad. And now he was old—very old.

He was thirteen—which is equivalent to the human age of sev-enty. His long, clean lines had become blurred with flesh. He was undeniably stout. When he ran fast, he rolled slightly in his stride. Nor could he run as rapidly or as long as of yore. While he was not wheezy or asthmatic, yet a brisk five-mile walk would make him strangely anxious for an hour's rest.

He would not confess, even to himself, that age was beginning to hamper him so cruelly. And he sought to do all the things he had once done—if the mistress or the master were looking. But when he was alone, or with the other dogs, he spared himself every needless step. And he slept a great deal.

Withal, Lad's was a hale old age. His spirit and his almost uncanny intelligence had not faltered. Save for the silvered muzzle—first outward sign of age in a dog—his face and head were as classically young as ever. So were the absurdly small forepaws—his one gross vanity—on which he spent hours of care each day, to keep them clean and snowy.

He would still dash out of the house as of old—with the wild trumpeting bark which he reserved as greeting to his two deities alone—when the mistress or the master returned home after an absence. He would still frisk excitedly around either of them at hint of a romp. But the exertion *was* an exertion. And despite Lad's valiant efforts at youthfulness, everyone could see it was.

No longer did he lead the other dogs in their headlong rushes through the forest in quest of rabbits. Since he could not now keep the pace, he let the others go on these breath-and-strength-taking excursions without him; and he contented himself with an occasional lone and stately walk through the woods where once he had led the run—strolling along in leisurely fashion, with the benign dignity of some plump and ruddy old squire inspecting his estate.

There had been many dogs at the Place during the thirteen years of Lad's reign—dogs of all sorts and conditions, including Lad's worshiped collie mate, the dainty gold-and-white Lady. But in this later day there were but three dogs beside himself.

One of them was Wolf, the only surviving son of Lad and Lady— a slender, powerful young collie, with some of his sire's brain and much of his mother's appealing grace—an ideal playdog. Between Lad and Wolf there had always been a bond of warmest affection. Lad had trained this son of his and had taught him all he knew. He unbent from his lofty dignity, with Wolf, as with none of the others.

The second of the remaining dogs was Bruce ("Sunnybank Goldsmith"), tawny as Lad himself, descendant of eleven international champions and winner of many a ribbon and medal and cup. Bruce was—and is—flawless in physical perfection and in obedience and intelligence.

The third was Rex—a giant, a freak, a dog oddly out of place among a group of thoroughbreds. On his father's side Rex was pure collie; on his mother's, pure bull terrier. That is an accidental blending of two breeds which cannot blend. He looked more like a fawn-colored Great Dane than anything else. He was short-haired, full two inches taller and ten pounds heavier than Lad, and had the bunch-muscled jaws of a killer.

There was not an outlander dog for two miles in either direction that Rex had not at one time or another met and vanquished. The bull terrier strain, which blended so ill with collie blood, made its possessor a terrific fighter. He was swift as a deer, strong as a puma.

In many ways he was a lovable and affectionate pet; slavishly devoted to the master and grievously jealous of the latter's love for Lad. Rex was five years old—in his fullest prime—and, like the rest, he had ever taken Lad's rulership for granted.

I have written at perhaps prosy length, introducing these characters of my war story. The rest is action.

March, that last year, was a month of drearily recurrent snows. In the forests beyond the Place, the snow lay light and fluffy at a depth of sixteen inches.

On a snowy, blowy, bitter cold Sunday—one of those days nobody wants—Rex and Wolf elected to go rabbit hunting.

Bruce was not in the hunt, sensibly preferring to lie in front of the living-room fire on so vile a day rather than to flounder through dust-fine drifts in search of game that was not worth chasing under such conditions. Wolf, too, was monstrous comfortable on the old fur rug by the fire, at the mistress's feet.

But Rex, who had waxed oddly restless of late, was bored by the indoor afternoon. The mistress was reading; the master was asleep. There seemed no chance that either would go for a walk or otherwise amuse their four-footed friends. The winter forests were calling. The powerful crossbred dog would find the snow a scant obstacle to his hunting. And the warmly quivering body of a new-caught rabbit was a tremendous lure.

Rex got to his feet, slouched across the living room to Bruce and touched his nose. The drowsing collie paid no heed. Next Rex moved over to where Wolf lay. The two dogs' noses touched.

Now, this is no Mowgli tale, but a true narrative. I do not pretend to say whether or not dogs have a language of their own. (Personally, I think they have, and a very comprehensive one, too. But I cannot prove it.) No dog student, however, will deny that two dogs communicate their wishes to each other in some way by (or during) the swift contact of noses.

By that touch Wolf understood Rex's hint to join in the foray. Wolf was not yet four years old—at an age when excitement still outweighs lazy comfort. Moreover, he admired and aped Rex, as much as ever the school's littlest boy models himself on the class bully. He was up at once and ready to start.

A maid was bringing in an armful of wood from the veranda. The two dogs slipped out through the half-open door. As they went, Wolf cast a sidelong glance at Lad, who was snoozing under the piano. Lad noted the careless invitation. He also noted that Wolf did not hesitate when his father refused to join the outing but trotted gaily off in Rex's wake.

Perhaps this defection hurt Lad's abnormally sensitive feelings. For of old he had always led such forest runnings. Perhaps the two dogs' departure merely woke in him the memory of the chase's joys and stirred a longing for the snow-clogged woods.

For a minute or two the big living room was quiet, except for the scratch of dry snow against the panes, the slow breathing of Bruce and the turning of a page in the book the mistress was reading. Then Lad got up heavily and walked forth from his piano-cave.

He stretched himself and crossed to the mistress's chair. There he sat down on the rug very close beside her and laid one of his ridiculously tiny white forepaws in her lap. Absent-mindedly, still absorbed in her book, she put out a hand and patted the soft fur of his ruff and ears.

Often, Lad came to her or to the master for some such caress; and, receiving it, would return to his resting place. But today he was seeking to attract her notice for something much more important. It had occurred to him that it would be jolly to go with her for a tramp in the snow. And his mere presence failing to convey the hint, he began to "talk."

To the mistress and the master alone did Lad condescend to "talk"—and then only in moments of stress or appeal. No one, hearing him, at such a time, could doubt the dog was trying to frame human speech. His vocal efforts ran the gamut of the entire scale. Wordless, but decidedly eloquent, this "talking" would continue sometimes for several minutes without ceasing; its tones carried whatever emotion the old dog sought to convey—whether of joy, of grief, of request or of complaint.

Today there was merely playful entreaty in the speechless speech. The mistress looked up.

"What is it, Laddie?" she asked. "What do you want?"

For answer Lad glanced at the door, then at the mistress; then he solemnly went out into the hall—whence presently he returned with one of her fur gloves in his mouth.

"No, no," she laughed. "Not today, Lad. Not in this storm. We'll take a good, long walk tomorrow."

The dog sighed and returned sadly to his lair beneath the piano. But the vision of the forests was evidently hard to erase from his mind. And a little later, when the front door was opened again by one of the servants, he stalked out.

The snow was driving hard, and there was a sting in it. The thermometer was little above zero; but the snow had been a familiar bedfellow, for centuries, to Lad's Scottish forefathers; and the cold was harmless against the woven thickness of his tawny coat. Picking his way in stately fashion along the ill-broken track of the driveway, he strolled toward the woods. To humans there was nothing in the outdoor day but snow and chill and bluster and bitter loneliness. To the trained eye and the miraculous scent-power of a collie it contained a million things of dramatic interest.

Here a rabbit had crossed the trail—not with leisurely bounds or mincing hops, but stomach to earth, in flight for very life. Here, close at the terrified bunny's heels, had darted a red fox. Yonder, where the piling snow covered a swirl of tracks, the chase had ended.

The little ridge of snow-heaped furrow, to the right, held a basketful of cowering quail—who heard Lad's slow step and did not reckon on his flawless gift of smell. On the hemlock tree just ahead a hawk had lately torn a bluejay asunder. A fluff of gray feathers still stuck to a bough, and the scent of blood had not been blown out of the air. Underneath, a fieldmouse was plowing its way into the frozen earth, its tiny paw-scrapes wholly audible to the ears of the dog above it.

Here, through the stark and drifted undergrowth, Rex and Wolf had recently swept along in pursuit of a half-grown rabbit. Even a human eye could not have missed their partly covered tracks; but Lad knew whose track was whose and which dog had been in the lead.

Yes, to humans, the forest would have seemed a deserted white waste. Lad knew it was thick-populated with the Little People of the woodland, and that all day and all night the seemingly empty and placid groves were a blend of battlefield, slaughterhouse and restaurant. Here, as much as in the cities or in the trenches, abode strenuous life, violent death, struggle, greed and terror.

A partridge rocketed upward through a clump of evergreen, while a weasel, jaws aquiver, glared after it, baffled. A shaggy owl crouched at a treelimb hole and blinked sulkily about in search of prey and in hope of dusk. A crow, its black feet red with a slain snowbird's blood, flapped clumsily overhead. A poet would have vowed that the still and white-shrouded wilderness was a shrine sacred to solitude and severe peace. Lad could have told him better. Nature (beneath the surface) is never solitary and never at peace.

When a dog is very old and very heavy and a little unwieldy, it is hard to walk through sixteen-inch snow, even if one moves slowly and sedately. Hence Lad was well pleased to come upon a narrow woodland track; made by a laborer who had passed and repassed through that same strip of forest during the last few hours. To follow in that trampled rut made walking much easier; it was a rut barely wide enough for one wayfarer.

More and more like an elderly squire patrolling his acres, Lad rambled along, and presently his ears and his nose told him that his two loving friends Rex and Wolf were coming toward him on their home-bound way. His plumy tail wagged expectantly. He was growing a bit lonely on this Sunday afternoon walk of his, and a little tired. It would be a pleasure to have company—especially Wolf's.

Rex and Wolf had fared ill on their hunt. They had put up two rabbits. One had doubled and completely escaped them; and in the chase Rex had cut his foot nastily on a strip of unseen barbed wire. The sandlike snow had gotten into the jagged cut in a most irritating way.

The second rabbit had dived under a log. Rex had thrust his head fiercely through a snowbank in quest of the vanished prey; and a long briar thorn, hidden there, had plunged its needle point deep into the inside of his left nostril. The inner nostril is a hundredfold the most agonizingly sensitive part of a dog's body, and the pain wrung a yell of rage and hurt from the big dog.

With a nostril and a foot both hurt, there was no more fun in hunting, and—angry, cross, savagely in pain—Rex loped homeward, Wolf pattering along behind him. Like Lad, they came upon the laborer's trampled path and took advantage of the easier going.

Thus it was, at a turn in the track, that they came face to face with Lad. Wolf had already smelled him, and his brush began to quiver in welcome. Rex, his nose in anguish, could smell nothing; not until that turn did he know of Lad's presence. He halted, sulky, and ill-tempered. The queer restlessness, the prespringtime savagery that had obsessed him of late, had been brought to a head by his hurts. He was not himself. His mind was sick.

There was not room for two large dogs to pass each other in that narrow trail. One or the other must flounder out into the deep snow to the side. Ordinarily, there would be no question about any other dog on the Place turning out for Lad. It would have been a matter of course, and so, today, Lad expected it to be. Onward he moved, at that same dignified walk, until he was not a yard away from Rex.

The latter, his brain fevered and his hurts torturing him, suddenly flamed into rebellion. Even as a younger buck sooner or later assails for mastery the leader of the herd, so the brain-sick Rex went back, all at once, to primal instincts, a maniac rage mastered him—the rage of the angry underlying, the primitive lust for mastery.

With not so much as a growl or warning, he launched himself upon Lad. Straight at the tired old dog's throat he flew. Lad, all unprepared for such unheard-of mutiny, was caught clean off his guard. He had not even time enough to lower his head to protect his throat or to rear and meet his erstwhile subject's attack halfway. At one moment he had been plodding gravely toward his two supposedly loyal friends; the next, Rex's ninety pounds of whalebone muscle had smitten him violently to earth, and Rex's fearsome jaws —capable of cracking a beef bone as a man cracks a filbert—had found a vise grip in the soft fur of his throat.

Down amid a flurry of high-tossed snow, crashed Lad, his snarling enemy upon him, pinning him to the ground, the huge jaws tearing and rending at his ruff—the silken ruff that the mistress daily combed with such loving care to keep it fluffy and beautiful.

It was a grip and a leverage that would have made the average opponent helpless. With a shorthaired dog it would have meant the end, but the providence that gave collies a mattress of fur—to stave off the cold, in their herding work amid the snowy moors—has made that fur thickest about the lower neck.

Rex had struck in crazy rage and had not gauged his mark as truly as though he had been cooler. He had missed the jugular and found himself grinding at an enormous mouthful of matted hair—

and at very little else; and Lad belonged to the breed that is never to be taken wholly by surprise and that acts by the swiftest instinct or reason known to dogdom. Even as he fell, he instinctively threw his body sideways to avoid the full jar of Rex's impact—and gathered his feet under him.

With a heave that wrenched his every unaccustomed muscle, Lad shook off the living weight and scrambled upright. To prevent this, Rex threw his entire body forward to reinforce his throat grip. As a result, a double handful of ruff hair and a patch of skin came away in his jaws. And Lad was free.

He was free—to turn tail and run for his life from the unequal combat—and that his hero heart would not let him do. He was free, also, to stand his ground and fight there in the snowbound forest until he should be slain by his younger and larger and stronger foe, and this folly his almost-human intelligence would not permit.

There was one chance and only one—one compromise alone between sanity and honor. And this chance Lad took.

He *would* not run. He *could* not save his life by fighting where he stood. His only hope was to keep his face to his enemy, battling as best he could, and all the time keep backing toward home. If he could last until he came within sight or sound of the folk at the house, he knew he would be saved. Home was a full half-mile away and the snow was almost chest deep. Yet, on the instant, he laid out his plain of campaign and put it into action.

Rex cleared his mouth of the impeding hair and flew at Lad once more—before the old dog had fairly gotten to his feet, but not before the line of defense had been thought out. Lad half wheeled, dodging the snapping jaws by an inch and taking the impact of the charge on his left shoulder, at the same time burying his teeth in the right side of Rex's face.

At the same time Lad gave ground, moving backward three or four yards, helped along by the impetus of his opponent. Home was a half-mile behind him, in an oblique line, and he could not turn to gauge his direction. Yet he moved in precisely the correct angle.

(Indeed, a passerby who witnessed the fight, and the master, who went carefully over the ground afterward, proved that at no point in the battle did Lad swerve or mistake his exact direction. Yet not once could he have been able to look around to judge it, and his footprints showed that not once had he turned his back on the foe.)

The hold Lad secured on Rex's cheek was good, but it was not good enough. At thirteen, a dog's biting teeth are worn short and dull, and his yellowed fangs are blunted; nor is the jaw by any means as powerful as once it was. Rex writhed and pitched in the fierce grip, and presently tore free from it and to the attack again, seeking now to lunge over the top of Lad's lowered head to the vital spot at the nape of the neck, where sharp teeth may pierce through to the spinal cord.

Thrice Rex lunged, and thrice Lad reared on his hind legs, meeting the shock with his deep, shaggy breast, snapping and slashing at his enemy and every time receding a few steps between charges. They had left the path now, and were plowing a course through deep snow. The snow was scant barrier to Rex's full strength, but it terribly impeded the steadily backing Lad. Lad's extra flesh, too, was a bad handicap; his wind was not at all what it should have been, and the unwonted exertion began to tell sharply on him.

Under the lead-hued skies and the drive of the snow the fight swirled and eddied. The great dogs reared, clashed, tore, battered against treetrunks, lost footing and rolled, staggered up again and renewed the onslaught. Ever Lad maneuvered his way backward, waging a desperate "rear-guard action." In the battle's wage was an irregular but mathematically straight line of trampled and blood-spattered snow.

Oh, but it was slow going, this ever-fighting retreat of Lad's, through the deep drifts, with his mightier foe pressing him and rending at his throat and shoulders at every backward step! The old dog's wind was gone; his once-superb strength was going, but he fought on with blazing fury—the fury of a dying king who *will* not be deposed.

In sheer skill and brainwork and generalship, Lad was wholly Rex's superior, but these served him ill in a death grapple. With dogs, as with human pugilists, mere science and strategy avail little against superior size and strength and youth. Again and again Lad found or made an opening. Again and again his weakening jaws secured the right grip only to be shaken off with more and more ease by the younger combatant.

Again and again Lad slashed as do his wolf cousins and as does almost no civilized dog but the collie. But the slashes had lost their one-time lightning speed and prowess. And the blunt rending fangs scored only superficial furrows in Rex's fawn-colored hide.

There was meager hope of reaching home alive. Lad must have known that. His strength was gone. It was his heart and his glorious ancestry now that were doing his fighting—not his fat and age-depleted body. From Lad's mental vocabulary the word *quit* had ever been absent. Wherefore—dizzy, gasping, feebler every minute —he battled fearlessly on in the dying day; never losing his sense of direction, never turning tail, never dreaming of surrender, taking dire wounds, inflicting light ones.

There are many forms of dogfight. Two strange dogs, meeting, will fly at each other because their wild forbears used to do so. Jealous dogs will battle even more fiercely. But the deadliest of all canine conflicts is the murder-fight. This is a struggle wherein one or both contestants have decided to give no quarter, where the victor will fight on until his antagonist is dead and will then tear his body to pieces. It is a recognized form of canine mania.

And it was a murder-fight that Rex was waging, for he had gone quite insane. (This is wholly different, by the way, from going mad.)

Down went Lad, for perhaps the tenth time, and once more— though now with an effort that was all but too much for him—he writhed to his feet, gaining three yards of ground by the move. Rex was upon him with one leap, the frothing and bloody jaws striking for his mangled throat. Lad reared to block the attack. Then suddenly, overbalanced, he crashed backward into the snowdrift.

Rex had not reached him, but young Wolf had.

Wolf had watched the battle with a growing excitement that at last had broken all bounds. The instinct, which makes a fluff-headed college boy mix into a scrimmage that is no concern of his, had suddenly possessed Lad's dearly loved son.

Now, if this were a fiction yarn, it would be edifying to tell how Wolf sprang to the aid of his grand old sire and how he thereby saved Lad's life. But the shameful truth is that Wolf did nothing of the sort. Rex was his model, the bully he had so long and so enthusiastically imitated. And now Rex was fighting a most entertaining bout, fighting it with a maniac fury that infected his young disciple and made him yearn to share in the glory.

Wherefore, as Lad reared to meet Rex's lunge, Wolf hurled himself like a furry whirlwind upon the old dog's flank, burying his white teeth in the muscles of the lower leg.

The flank attack bowled Lad completely over. There was no chance now for such a fall as would enable him to spring up again unscathed. He was thrown heavily upon his back, and both his murderers plunged at his unguarded throat and lower body.

But a collie thrown is not a collie beaten, as perhaps I have said once before. For thirty seconds or more the three thrashed about in the snow in a growling, snarling, right unloving embrace. Then, by some miracle, Lad was on his feet again.

His throat had a new and deep wound, perilously close to the jugular. His stomach and left side were slashed as with razorblades. But he was up. And even in that moment of dire stress—with both dogs flinging themselves upon him afresh—he gained another yard or two in his line of retreat.

He might have gained still more ground. For his assailants, leaping at the same instant, collided and impeded each other's charge. But, for the first time the wise old brain clouded, and the hero heart went sick; as Lad saw his own loved and spoiled son ranged against him in the murder-fray. He could not understand. Loyalty was as much a part of himself as were his sorrowful brown eyes or his tiny white forepaws. And Wolf's amazing treachery seemed to numb the old warrior, body and mind.

But the second of dumbfounded wonder passed quickly—too quickly for either of the other dogs to take advantage of it. In its place surged a righteous wrath that brought back youth and strength to the aged fighter.

With a yell that echoed far through the forest's sinister silence, Lad whizzed forward at the advancing Rex. Wolf, who was nearer, struck for his father's throat—missed and rolled in the snow from the force of his own momentum. Lad did not heed him. Straight for Rex he leaped. Rex, bounding at him, was already in midair. The two met, and under the berserk onset Rex fell back into the snow.

Lad was upon him at once. The worn-down teeth found their goal above the jugular. Deep and raggedly they drove, impelled by the brief flash of power that upbore their owner.

Almost did that grip end the fight and leave Rex gasping out his life in the drift. But the access of false strength faded. Rex, roaring like a hurt tiger, twisted and tore himself free. Lad realizing his own bolt was shot, gave ground, backing away from two assailants instead of one.

It was easier now to retreat. For Wolf, unskilled in practical warfare, at first hindered Rex almost as much as he helped him, again and again getting in the bigger dog's way and marring a rush. Had Wolf understood teamwork, Lad must have been pulled down and slaughtered in less than a minute.

But soon Wolf grasped the fact that he could do worse damage by keeping out of his ally's way and attacking from a different quarter, and thereafter he fought to more deadly purpose. His favorite ruse was to dive for Lad's forelegs and attempt to break one of them. That is a collie maneuver inherited direct from Wolf's namesake ancestors.

Several times his jaws reached the slender white forelegs, cutting and slashing them and throwing Lad off his balance. Once he found a hold on the left haunch and held it until his victim shook loose by rolling.

Lad defended himself from this new foe as well as he might, by dodging or by brushing him to one side, but never once did he attack Wolf, or so much as snap at him. (Rex after the encounter, was plentifully scarred. Wolf had not so much as a scratch.)

Backward, with ever-increasing difficulty, the old dog fought his way, often borne down to earth and always staggering up more feebly than before. But ever he was warring with the same fierce courage; despite an ache and bewilderment in his honest heart at his son's treason.

The forest lay behind the fighters. The deserted highroad was passed. Under Lad's clawing and reeling feet was the dear ground of the Place—the Place where for thirteen happy years he had reigned as king, where he had benevolently ruled his kind and had given worshipful service to his gods.

But the house was still nearly a furlong off, and Lad was well-nigh dead. His body was one mass of wounds. His strength was turned to water. His breath was gone. His bloodshot eyes were dim. His brain was dizzy and refused its office. Loss of blood had weakened him full as much as had the tremendous exertion of the battle.

Yet—uselessly now—he continued to fight. It was a grotesquely futile resistance. The other dogs were all over him—tearing, slashing, gripping, at will—unhindered by his puny effort to fend them off. The slaughter time had come. Drunk with blood and fury, the assailants plunged at him for the last time.

Down went Lad, helpless beneath the murderous avalanche that overwhelmed him. And this time his body flatly refused to obey the grim command of his will. The fight was over—the good, *good* fight of a white-souled Paladin against hopeless odds.

The living-room fire crackled cheerily. The snow hissed and slithered against the glass. A sheet of frost on every pane shut out the stormy twilit world. The screech of the wind was music to the comfortable shut-ins.

The mistress drowsed over her book by the fire. Bruce snored snugly in front of the blaze. The master had awakened from his nap and was in the adjoining study, sorting fishing tackle and scouring a rusted hunting knife.

Then came a second's lull in the gale, and all at once Bruce was wide awake. Growling, he ran to the front door and scratched imperatively at the panel. This is not the way a well-bred dog makes known his desire to leave the house. And Bruce was decidedly a well-bred dog.

The mistress, thinking some guest might be arriving whose scent or tread displeased the collie, called to the master to shut Bruce in the study, lest he insult the supposed visitor by barking. Reluctantly —very reluctantly—Bruce obeyed the order. The master shut the study door behind him and came into the living room, still carrying the half-cleaned knife.

As no summons at bell or knocker followed Bruce's announcement, the mistress opened the front door and looked out. The dusk was falling, but it was not too dark for her to have seen the approach of anyone, nor was it too dark for the mistress to see two dogs tearing at something that lay hidden from her view in the deep snow a hundred yards away. She recognized Rex and Wolf at once and amusedly wondered with what they were playing.

Then from the depth of snow beneath them she saw a feeble head rear itself—a glorious head, though torn and bleeding—a head that waveringly lunged toward Rex's throat.

"They're—they're killing—*Lad!*" she cried in stark, unbelieving horror. Forgetful of thin dress and thinner slippers, she ran toward the trio. Halfway to the battlefield the master passed by her, running and lurching through the knee-high snow at something like record speed.

She heard his shout. And at sound of it she saw Wolf slink away from the slaughter like a scared schoolboy. But Rex was too far gone in murder-lust to heed the shout. The master seized him by the studded collar and tossed him ten feet or more to one side. Rage-blind, Rex came flying back to the kill. The master stood astride his prey, and in his blind mania the crossbreed sprang at the man.

The master's hunting knife caught him squarely behind the left foreleg. And with a grunt like the sound of an exhausted soda siphon, the huge dog passed out of this story and out of life as well.

There would be ample time, later, for the master to mourn his enforced slaying of the pet dog that had loved and served him so long. At present he had eyes only for the torn and senseless body of Lad lying huddled in the red-blotched snow.

In his arms he lifted Lad and carried him tenderly into the house. There the mistress's light fingers dressed his hideous injuries. Not less than thirty-six deep wounds scored the worn-out old body. Several of these were past the skill of home treatment.

A grumbling veterinarian was summoned on the telephone and was lured by pledge of a triple fee to chug through ten miles of storm in a balky car to the rescue.

Lad was lying with his head in the mistress's lap. The vet looked the unconscious dog over and then said tersely, "I wish I'd stayed at home. He's as good as dead."

"He's a million times better than dead," denied the master. "I know Lad. You don't. He's got into the habit of living, and he's not going to break that habit, not if the best nursing and surgery in the state can keep him from doing it. Get busy!"

"There's nothing to keep me here," objected the vet. "He's—"

"There's everything to keep you here," gently contradicted the master. "You'll stay here till Lad's out of danger—if I have to steal your trousers and your car. You're going to cure him. And if you do, you can write your bill on a Liberty Bond."

Two hours later Lad opened his eyes. He was swathed in smelly bandages and he was soaked in liniments. Patches of hair had been shaved away from his worst wounds. Digitalis was reinforcing his faint heart action.

He looked up at the mistress with his only available eye. By a herculean struggle he wagged his tail—just once. And he essayed the trumpeting bark wherewith he always welcomed her return after an absence. The bark was a total failure.

After which Lad tried to tell the mistress the story of the battle. Very weakly, but very persistently he "talked." His tones dropped now and then to the shadow of a ferocious growl as he related his exploits and then scaled again to a puppylike whimper.

He had done a grand day's work, had Lad, and he wanted applause. He had suffered much and he was still in racking pain, and he wanted sympathy and petting. Presently he fell asleep.

* * *

It was two weeks before Lad could stand upright, and two more before he could go out of doors unhelped. Then on a warm, early spring morning, the vet declared him out of all danger.

Very thin was the invalid, very shaky, snow-white of muzzle and with the air of an old, old man whose too-fragile body is sustained only by a regal dignity. But he was *alive*.

Slowly he marched from his piano cave toward the open front door. Wolf—in black disgrace for the past month—chanced to be crossing the living room toward the veranda at the same time. The two dogs reached the doorway simultaneously.

Very respectfully, almost cringingly, Wolf stood aside for Lad to pass out.

His sire walked by with never a look. But his step was all at once stronger and springier, and he held his splendid head high.

For Lad knew he was still king!

AFTERWORD

The stories of Lad, in various magazines, found unexpectedly kind welcome. Letters came to me from soldiers and sailors in Europe, from hosts of children, from men and women everywhere.

Few of the letter writers bothered to praise the stories, themselves. But all of them praised Lad, which pleased me far better. And more than a hundred of them wanted to know if he were a real dog, and if the tales of his exploits were true.

Perhaps those of you who have followed Lad's adventures, through these pages, may also be a little interested to know more about him.

Yes, Lad was a real dog—the greatest dog, by far, I have known or shall know. And the chief happenings in nearly all of my Lad stories are absolutely true. This accounts for such measure of success as the stories may have won.

After his "Day of Battle," Lad lived for more than two years—still gallant of spirit, loyally mighty of heart, uncanny of wisdom—still the undisputed king of the Place's Little People.

Then, on a warm September morning in 1918, he stretched himself to sleep in the coolest and shadiest corner of the veranda. And, while he slept, his great heart very quietly stopped beating.

He had no pain, no illness, none of the distressing features of extreme age. He had lived out a full span of sixteen years—years rich in life and happiness and love.

Surely, there was nothing in such a death to warrant the silly grief that was ours, nor the heartsick gloom that overhung the Place! It was wholly illogical, not to say maudlin. I admit that without argument. The cleric author of "The Mansion Yard" must have known the same miserable sense of loss, I think, when he wrote:

> Stretched on the hearthrug in a deep content,
>   Fond of the fire as I.
> Oh, there was something with the old dog went
>   I had not thought could die!

We buried Lad in a sunlit nook that had been his favorite lounging place, close to the house he had guarded so long and so gallantly. With him we buried his honorary Red Cross and Blue Cross—awards for money raised in his name. Above his head we set a low granite block, with a carven line or two thereon.

The mistress wanted the block inscribed: "The Dearest Dog!" I suggested: "The Dog God Made." But we decided against both epitaphs. We did not care to risk making our dear old friend's memory ridiculous by words at which saner folk might one day sneer. So on the granite is engraved:

LAD

THOROUGHBRED IN BODY AND SOUL

Some people are wise enough to know that a dog has no soul. These will find ample theme for mirth in our foolish inscription. But no one, who knew Lad, will laugh at it.

ALBERT PAYSON TERHUNE

Sunnybank
Pompton Lakes, New Jersey